BROKEN
PROMISES

BROKEN PROMISES

NICK NICHOLS

BROKEN PROMISES
Copyright © 2016 by James "Nick" Nichols

Regalia Publishing, LLC

Media & publisher inquiries:
STRATEGIES Public Relations
P.O. Box 178122
San Diego, CA 92177

Cover and Book design by GKS Creative, Nashville
www.gkscreative.com

FIRST EDITION

Printed in the United States of America

ISBN: 978-0-9905434-3-5 (trade paperback)

ISBN: 978-0-9905434-4-2 (ePub)

ISBN: 978-0-9905434-5-9 (mobi)

For Emma,
the love of my life.

"Up until 2002, not a single state had a law that explicitly prohibited attorneys from sleeping with their clients."

RICHARD KOMAIKO

What follows is a cautionary tale.

1

THIRTY-FOUR FLOORS ABOVE ATLANTA, Jack Adams was about to change his client's life forever. He'd tried to prepare her, but how did you prepare a woman to watch her world crumble around her?

In previous meetings, he had counseled her on her rights and the legal process. He had answered her many questions, and he had started the arduous path of guiding her through the turmoil she faced with her divorce. She seemed to have taken it in stride.

Monica Henderson now sat next to him in the wood paneled conference room. Rows of chairs lined the long, marble table and an 85-inch ultra HD monitor dominated one of the walls.

He reached for the remote that would start the surveillance video. Monica flinched.

"Monica, are you sure I can't get you something to drink?"

"No, thank you." Her posture stayed straight in the padded wingback chair. Every strand of her mahogany hair was gathered up and in place. A black Louboutin pump, angling from her tossed leg, tapped the open air.

They both knew the surveillance video contained an act of betrayal that would seal the fate of her marriage. He wished there were some way to spare her the pain, but even if she hadn't insisted on seeing the video, he would have had gotten her to do so. It was critical that she have all the facts to deal with the upcoming legal battle. What had only been suspicion of her husband's infidelity was now her horrible reality.

He clicked on the remote.

Surveillance could be wildly hit-or-miss. Hours of watching and thousands invested could yield nothing. This time had been different.

Monica squinted and began to sob quietly. Jack wondered which reaction might come next. In his previous meetings with her, she'd struck him as both reasonable and rational. She had maintained poise so far. This would test her.

The video showed George Henderson's black Range Rover Sport SVR in the parking lot of Atlanta's Peachtree-DeKalb Airport, eleven miles north of downtown. A few other super luxury vehicles dotted the private airport's parking lot. This vehicle was parked away from the other vehicles. Its lone occupant was a man, anxiously looking around.

The man's gaze soon fixed upon an approaching car. The sports car glided across the lot, stopping next to his. A young woman with flowing blonde hair in a short, black, fitted dress emerged from the car and looked at the other driver with knowing familiarity. She was wearing sunglasses and made her way around to the passenger side of the SUV, her face scanning the parking lot as she hopped inside.

There was a cautiousness about her. Even with the high-powered long-range lens, the woman's specific facial features escaped the camera's view, as though the woman instinctively was able to avoid detection. She moved with ease.

Jack noticed her slim form as she slid into the SUV, and immediately knew he shouldn't be homing in on that. Thoughts and details that mattered were strewn throughout the scene; her taut figure shouldn't be among them. *Focus.*

The man and woman on screen immediately kissed. The man looked over his left shoulder as if to check on something, looking directly back into the camera that was watching him.

Jack couldn't help but appreciate this irony. Mr. Henderson had looked right at their investigator taking the video. Jack liked that the husband had given a perfect profile while trying to be careful.

The man in the SUV brought his face and his attention back to the woman who leaned into him. He kissed her fully on the mouth, and they struggled to get their arms into an embrace within the close confines of the front seat. His left hand went into her hair, grasping it as they kissed passionately.

Monica's voice then trembled.

"I want him to suffer for ruining my life."

Her hands twisted into fists.

Another facet of this normally cool, collected woman? Jack stirred in his chair now, hoping his previous impression of his client's stability hadn't been erroneous. This case was crucial to his bid for partnership. Huge assets at stake; bad conduct, some custody issues, and now he had this damning video.

3

His gut tightened with his now-hostile client. The anger must have been festering inside her. Ugliness endangered the whole case.

His mind couldn't suppress how critical this was. After years in college and law school, a clerkship for a judge, and then six years as an associate, he finally had the chance to make partner. An equity stake in the firm. But, a volatile client—in a prime case—risked it all.

Maybe enough was enough. He paused the video.

"You don't have to watch anymore of this. We can—"

"No. I have to see it." Her tone had settled to quiet desperation.

He felt her outrage and torment. No matter how many times he'd been through it with clients, there was always a sense of sharing their pain. His mentor had called him on it a couple of times, but caring was just part of his nature.

Regardless of his feelings, though, he needed the insight into how she'd react. Later in the case, she would need to endure more. A grueling cross-examination was possible.

He clicked the remote back on.

The woman soon shifted her position so that she was facing him, her right hand sliding down and out of view below the dashboard. After a few seconds, the woman brought her arm back around to the back of the man's head, and in a quick, athletic move, straddled her companion's lap. Taking her time, the woman lifted her hands to her head and ran them through her hair, pausing a moment with her hands still in her hair as she stared at the man.

The man seemed to slide a little lower in the seat as the woman's hands again went out of view. The woman brought her face back to his, forcefully kissing his mouth again. She seemed to start nodding at him, but in fact was rocking back and forth on top of him.

The woman's hands reached up to hold the seat just behind the man's head, and her frame bucked forward. The woman threw her head back and away from him. The man's head tilted backward, bumping repeatedly against the headrest.

Monica Henderson leapt up and cried out. "Oh!"

"Okay, that's it!" She grabbed her purse from the conference room table. "Prepare the papers."

"I will." Jack turned off the monitor and stood. "I'll call you when they're ready for you to sign, so they can be filed."

She nodded back to him and stepped towards the door as if in a daze. "I'll never get past this."

"Eventually, you will, Monica. Please believe that."

The facts reeled through Jack's mind. Seventeen years of marriage. Two sons, ages eleven and thirteen. Plans and dreams of a once bright future with a man she'd grown up with.

Monica's case also raised huge financial stakes. George Henderson ran a highly successful commercial construction business. He and Monica had started the business from nothing. Nothing that is, except an inheritance Monica had received from her grandmother. Now, Jack and the firm wanted Monica's interests protected. Protected at all costs.

She turned to him. Her eyes burned with intensity through her tears. Her hands fidgeted holding her purse in front of her.

"Make him pay for this. I'm serious. I want him to suffer. Can you do that?"

Jack stiffened and nodded vigorously. "Absolutely. Nothing matters more. We'll have his ass."

She shook her head. "No, I mean it." She leveled a glare.

"Whatever it takes, he doesn't get away with this."

Her intensity stirred his own. "Monica, listen, I get what this means. Seventeen years ago you were twenty-five. You had your degree from Emory, a comfortable trust fund, and a career ahead of you. He was starting with nothing and learning the construction industry. You gave him two sons, his seed money, and all those years of your life."

She leaned towards him eagerly as he continued.

"If he thinks he's going to take his eight-figure earnings and business and walk out the door, he's very much mistaken. He has no idea the hell he's unleashed. *But...he will.*"

Whatever comfort she took from his words dissipated quickly. "How could he do this me?"

"Monica, it's critical you maintain your composure with this. It really is. If he can provoke you to lose your temper or lash out, he'll use that against you. You have to remember that."

Monica finally exhaled. She unclenched her fists.

Deep under the surface of it all, Jack shared something in common with Monica. He would never discuss it aloud, but family had forsaken him, too. For Jack, it was a father who openly had doubted him. Doubted his ability even to become a lawyer, and doubted that Jack had what it took at all.

Jack carried this around with him. Rather than have it weaken him, though, it drove him. Pushed him to work harder. He was determined he wouldn't succumb to the same weakness that led his father to the endless drinking and gambling that doomed him. Jack felt himself different. He would work harder and stay focused.

But his focus was lacking at times. Moments like the video caused him to think about the adventure, the excitement that was going on out there. He figured there were all sorts of this kind of wildness, and yet he had never experienced anything like this. Night and day, he worked on his cases. He wondered if he'd ever know the kind of adventure others seemed to relish. He wanted to know that thrill.

Jack pushed the thought aside. He was charged with Monica's protection. He had a case to win.

"Monica, you're going to be fine. You'll get through this. Remember that."

She gazed back at him but didn't react. Jack couldn't believe he had such an unpredictable client in such an important case. Finally, she blinked and nodded; a deep breath appeared to steel her in check.

Jack turned to open the door for Monica. His hand grasped the doorknob when he heard her blurt out for him to stop.

"Wait!" Her eyes opened wide. "There's something I need to tell you."

Uh oh.

❧

The silence in the conference room now felt ominous. Monica paced away from him several steps. Her head tilted down and she stared at the floor. She was shaken. He didn't doubt it.

Jack braced for what was to come. His mind raced. She had a secret. The question was, how bad was it? He could fix a lot of things, but not everything. Usually when a client had a secret to tell him, it meant trouble.

She shook her head in frustration. She turned back to him and wrapped her arms around herself. Her eyes were fiery.

"That bastard. I cannot believe him." Her slender frame shook.

"Monica, the important thing is that you tell me. Listen, as long as you let me know what it is, I can prepare accordingly and deal with it."

She looked to the side and frowned.

Jack continued, his tone firm. "When clients don't tell me something—that's when it becomes a problem. When I'm standing in court and hear something horrible for the first time, I'm at a terrible disadvantage. That's when we get hurt. It's critical that I know everything."

Monica nodded slightly. Maybe he was getting through to her. She pulled tighter to herself, though. The modest, beige blouse had looked so neat when she first stepped into his office earlier, but now it crumpled from her hold.

"Jack, I need you to fight for me. That man is capable of anything. He really is."

"Absolutely, I will fight for you. No one will fight harder. At the same time, you have to give me what I need to win the fight."

He would wait. They were not going further until this issue was addressed. It must be serious.

He saw her exhale hard enough to sound like a snort. Only moments ago, she seemed so demure.

Her tone became exasperated. "I did. I gave him my *best* years. Now, I am used up."

Jack piped up. "Monica, you're going to get past this. I know you will."

She feigned a smile at Jack and her eyes had a gloss of tears. "My life is ruined. You don't understand. Now, now...he'll destroy me. He really will."

"It's unlikely it's as bad as you think," Jack lowered his voice slightly. "It seldom is. I need to have all of the information. The good and the bad. I need to know."

She closed most of the distance between them and leaned forward. Her voice cracked.

"He's a bastard, Jack. Everything is all about *him*. It really is. I see that now. I see how evil he is and it sends chills through me. It really does."

Jack stayed still. He widened his eyes. He would wait her out.

She shook her head side to side, and propped her hands on her hips. They didn't settle there for long, as she quickly yanked them to her face. Her outstretched fingers poised over her mouth as though she was guarding herself. Her eyes squinted and watered. He couldn't believe how instantaneously she went from anger to pain. "Are you alright?"

"Jack," her tone sharpened, "he made me do something. I'm so very...ashamed." Tears welled up in her eyes.

Jack didn't react outwardly, but his gut clenched.

"Can you stop him?" Her eyes looked at him pleadingly. "He's going to make this look very bad. He is. Can you stop him?"

Jack had to remind himself she was upset. She was going through an ordeal in her life. *Don't snap at her. This is a good case.*

"We can deal with it, but I have to know more."

She again paced away from him, and as she did, her right hand went into her hair and her left hand rested on her hip. She walked towards the far wall that had the only window in the room. She looked out over the city. After a moment staring away, her torso lifted and lowered with a deep breath she drew to push forward.

Her arms fell to her sides and she turned back to him. She gazed right at Jack, as she stepped back over to face him. She stopped only a few feet in front of him, looking distinctly unlike the frail, shaken woman with whom he had just watched the video. Her words were measured but muted as she spoke to him.

"A couple of years ago, George told me he was really bored. We had been married fifteen years at that point. We had this family—this life—and I wanted him to be happy, you know?"

Jack nodded slowly.

"Anyway, he stressed to me how attractive I was, told me he was so very lucky and all." She scowled and blinked slowly. "But at the same time, he said we needed more excitement."

Jack stayed still.

"Also, he had this client; he was always harping on just how competitive and cutthroat the construction business is. He wanted us to meet, have dinner with this guy. He made it very clear to me that this client was *very important*. George said he was very important to *us*."

Dinner with a client wasn't something she would be ashamed of. This was about to take a turn. She didn't even want to explain this in a private conference.

"So, you met them for dinner?"

"We met them for dinner. They were nice. The man was professional. His wife was very attractive and personable. We went to their place for drinks afterwards. Everyone drank a lot that night."

Monica paused, but her eyes didn't leave Jack's. He sensed she was measuring him, seeing how he was handling her story. She spoke softer as she finished.

"George went with the wife to go see their basement. I toured the house with the husband. I felt wretched. It wasn't something I was up for at all and I regret it very much. If I hadn't been drinking as I was, I could never have done it. Not at all."

He saw her gulp and he wasted no time. His voice was strong. "Hey, this was *his* idea. *He* found this couple. *He* was the one who wanted this to happen. We can deal with this. We'll handle it."

She kept staring at him.

Jack immediately thought of how shocking this request must have been to Monica at the time, and he also thought of how scandalous it would be to some of the Atlanta judges who might hear her case. Jack refrained from showing his concern.

"*That*," Jack leaned towards her, "was totally different from what we saw on that video. Totally. What's on that video is betrayal. And...if he tries to equate it...he'll regret it. It will be him attempting to add insult to your injury."

Monica flinched. Her eyes batted as she took in the argument Jack made to her. He thought he could see her relax somewhat as she absorbed his take on her secret.

"Okay." Her head moved gradually up and down. "Alright."

"Stop worrying. Let me handle it."

They started leaving the room. Her words came with renewed tension.

"But, you have to make him pay, Jack. He's got to suffer for how he's ruined our family."

Jack certainly knew he was in for a fight, and it was coming at a great time, too. This case presented a perfect fit for Jack, because he knew how to prepare it and how to leverage the evidence for Monica's best interests. The timing couldn't have been better.

Yet, on a gut level, he knew he needed to keep an eye on

Monica. The soft, fragile woman he first met had morphed. Monica had another side to her, lurking just beneath the surface. A vicious side.

Jack needed to stay alert.

ᴄᴶᴾ

Jack engaged on a mission now. Angst and energy propelled him. He hurried back to his office, as he needed to prepare and file Monica's case right away. If he could file first, they would have distinct strategic advantages.

Monica's case was huge. This case promised to boost his previous effective results. An aggressive case, an outstanding outcome, and the solid block of billed hours would make his chance for partnership that much stronger. He had never felt so invigorated.

Now, he just needed his time and focus. *Gotta have some time and space.* He would strictly protect his world with the help of his assistant, Fran. Bless her. She would buffer him at this critical time.

As he reached his office, Fran stood directly in front of him. She bore an unmistakably serious look on her face. When people of the firm displayed such, it typically meant one of the two name partners at Hatcher & Sneed were involved. The partners had fostered such a reaction and it was now evident in her expression. Jack motioned for her to come ahead with him to his office.

"What now?" He snapped the words as a declaration not needing response.

He had to get Monica's case ready for filing. Jack tried settling behind his desk, and he wasn't even seated before Fran was forthcoming.

Fran folded her arms over her chest. Her words almost squealed.

"Hatcher's looking for you," she warned.

"Hatcher" as in "Gene Hatcher." As in the senior name partner. The senior partner who Jack worked for and the senior partner who impressed all with his drive and intensity. Gene Hatcher was the no-nonsense and intense litigator who had fought in court for many years and who had survived and prevailed.

"Well, now's a bad time," Jack growled in response as he glanced through his emails. Before he could finish, he sensed an eerie quiet in his office.

It dawned on him that Fran had abruptly left and someone else was there. The atmosphere had palpably changed. Air had been sucked from the room.

As he looked up, Hatcher stood directly in front of him. The older man's chest jutted forward, and his posture held perfectly straight. Hatcher smiled broadly, and Jack felt unsure how to respond initially. Hatcher's right hand clutched a file and his left hand rested on his hip, standing tall and with his head tilted a little back, as if proud. Jack became aware of how slumped he was behind his desk. Jack was now losing his own oxygen from Gene's presence.

As Jack opened his mouth to speak, Hatcher flipped the hand with the file in Jack's direction. The slender file folder managed somehow to hit the top of Jack's desk and then slid towards Jack, with Jack having to half-catch the folder as some pages slipped out.

13

Jack imagined the fluid motion of half-standing and shoving the file back to the older guy with a quickness that would catch Hatcher square in the face with the file. Instead, Jack just listened to the one word Hatcher spoke: "Turner."

Turner, as in Bob Turner. As in Robert Turner, wealthy and successful real estate developer. As in big client at the firm. Big matters, big cases, and big bills. Very important client to the firm.

Jack felt his heart find a higher gear. This case, too, could make Jack's career. Special. *Another career case*. After Monica's meeting and now the chance of this assignment, Jack reached a level of giddiness.

Jack gathered the file into his hands with a reverence. He didn't have to be told what an opportunity this case represented. The label referenced the matter of Andrea Turner versus James Hadley. This assignment meant Gene Hatcher was entrusting Jack with a gem of a career opportunity.

Gene Hatcher gave instructions quickly. "Review this and then let's talk tomorrow. Eight a.m."

"Absolutely."

Gene turned to his right and walked the few steps to the wall there. "How did it go with Monica?"

"Intense. She's a handful."

Gene tossed his head back and laughed. "I figured so. Has she screamed at you yet?"

"As a matter of fact, yeah, she has." Jack's eyes darted to the left, thinking back. "When the video showed George getting off with his lover in his Range Rover at Peachtree-DeKalb, she lost it."

Gene pivoted to him and his face stretched wide. "Wait a

minute. What? He got off in his Range Rover? At Peachtree-DeKalb?" He nervously chuckled. "And we've got that on video?" Jack laughed with him. "Yep. It's unreal. She's hot, too. Whoever she is. So Monica exploded at that. She wants his balls."

"Well, let's go get them. You know who George is, right?" Jack swallowed hard. He hated that he really didn't and didn't want to admit that. He shrugged before he caught himself, and Gene continued on.

"This guy's supposed to be something else. 'Master of the universe' type but with construction. He was a partier when he was younger. Supposed to have done everything and done it at least twice, you know? But the word is that everything changed for him when his father died. His father blew out his heart making money and never got to see George get his shit together."

All Jack could do was nod.

"The old man leaves George some money, enough to really work with, and George goes ape shit, a hundred and eighty degrees in the other direction. He goes from impossible hedonist to raging capitalist, like that." Gene snapped his fingers.

Jack stared at Gene, absorbing the history.

Gene's brow lifted and he continued. "Since then, he's turned into this mega-developer, this construction god. Supposed to be as ruthless as you can imagine. His mother's probably not safe from being sold out by him."

"Well, he pimped Monica out, that's for sure."

Gene blurted. "What?"

"Yeah, I was going to get to that. She wanted me to go after his balls and then it hit her that she might have a little soft spot.

She didn't want to say it out loud at first. She's really ashamed. Guess they went out a couple of years ago with some client of George's. George evidently pushed her to sleep with the guy."

"Have sex with him? Really?"

Jack shrugged. "That's what she said."

Gene mustered a supposed concern on his face. "How dare he. George *made* her screw another guy, huh? *That's* her story?"

"Well, she's pretty adamant about that actually. And you know—I believed her when she said it, too."

Gene cocked his head and gestured his hands palms up. "Who knows? I don't put it past this guy. Not a bit."

"Wow."

"Hey, listen." Gene went from propped by the wall over to one of the two high back chairs facing Jack's desk. He plopped down into the chair and Jack leaned forward, sensing Gene needed to impart something vital.

Gene took his time and spoke carefully. Jack noticed, and admired, the precision Gene used.

"George Henderson is a mega real estate and construction player. A big deal. Monica is his wife and comes to see us, because she gets it—I mean, gets it in her heart and in every fiber of her being—she's gotta fight George and doing that puts her at absolute risk, you know? I mean, she's crossing her husband, but she's betraying *George fucking Henderson*. Now, she didn't come see us just because we do divorces. Okay?"

Jack half-closed his eyes, tensed his brow, and muttered. "Okay."

Gene kept a patient pace explaining this to Jack. Jack got that it was important he understand this. Part of him wanted to take notes, but he worried that would look goofier than he already felt. Plus, he didn't want to miss a thing.

Gene lifted his eyes cueing Jack to appreciate this fact. "Monica Henderson didn't just come to us because we do divorces. She came to us because of Bob Turner."

"Huh?"

"Bob Turner is also a huge developer and real estate guy, and he's likely the only other human being in George Henderson's stratosphere, understand? And, by the way, Bob Turner is my buddy and this firm has represented him and his companies for, like, a million years."

"Uh, yes." Jack was already well aware.

Gene wasn't finished. "Hey, they're not just competitors, Jack. They're rivals. You gotta understand. They *hate* each other."

Jack gulped. "Wow."

"'Wow' is right."

"So...when Monica comes to us..."

"Monica comes to us, because we're the one firm she can be certain isn't going to be influenced by George Henderson. But let me tell you something else," Gene shook his head with a bit of disbelief, "Monica coming to us is probably the loudest 'fuck you' statement she could make to George. It's about like going to Bob Turner for help to fight George. And...well, let's just say George is *not* going to like that."

Jack swirled those thoughts about as Gene pressed his hands to his knees and bolted himself from the chair. Gene turned and took several steps towards the door. Jack offered his humble take on what he had learned.

"I knew we were in for a fight, but this..."

Gene spun back to Jack with a huge grin and pointed to the file Gene had tossed to Jack just earlier.

"Just to spice it up—Bob's daughter is coming to see us, too. Guess there must be something in the air. His daughter is Andrea and she's getting divorced, too. We have to be very careful with this one. Andrea is...let's just say she's one of a kind." Jack wasn't quite sure what to make of Gene's mischievous smile.

Gene left him wondering. "See you at eight tomorrow."

Throughout the rest of his day and into the evening, Jack's mind buzzed. Over and over again, he thought about Monica's case and the challenges that came with it. Alimony was in play. They had strong evidence of George Henderson's adultery. The construction business George built would need to be analyzed and valued.

Now, the prospect of also getting Bob Turner's daughter's divorce magnified his thrill.

Getting home, Jack bounded inside the older house through the side door that led from the garage into the den. As reliable as clockwork, he expected to find his girlfriend, Carla Knight, in the high-ceilinged family room, and there she sat.

It amazed him that he had been so methodical about his love life. There had been a few different girlfriends. He usually liked to move them in. And he rationalized to himself that every one of them knew the rule when they came in. His practice meant everything to him. He didn't really care if they always thought they could change him. That was their calculation, not his.

Jack liked reaching the warmth of the house in the cold

evening darkness. Fresh from his workout, he had his gym bag slung over his shoulder, and he felt the same slowing of his pace he typically did at this point. His work day was finished, his exercise was done, and he was home for rest. It was a solid routine for him. He would just need some space and time. He brought the Andrea Turner file to look over before his meeting with Gene and his expected initial consultation with her.

Carla looked up from her trance with the television. "Hi."

Her lithe, five foot six inch frame curled in a ball on their long sofa. Like most days it seemed, her ginger-brown hair was piled up, and her green eyes looked sleepy. It didn't necessarily mean she was sleepy, he knew; they just always showed a half-closed air.

She shot him the same cute smile he normally got from her. "How's it going?"

Her hand reached over for the glass of chardonnay that was perched beside her. He got a hankering for a beer but then let it pass. He'd just savor the post work out buzz he had.

"Going great. Busy day. Lots going on. And you?"

Carla shrugged. "Same old things. Placed a couple of good people, so that worked well."

Carla's work in executive placement and recruitment meant she handled substantial volumes of telephone calls and emails, but the upside was that she worked from home. About once a month, she packed a bag and flew to a job fair or career day most anywhere in the south or east.

"Cool." Jack went by her and kissed her quickly as he did. "I'm headed up. Gonna get relaxed."

"I'll be up soon," Carla replied.

Jack climbed the stairs to the bedroom, and he actually

looked forward to the silence that awaited him. The bustle from the day was still with him, as it often was. He looked forward to reading the Turner file notes.

He had managed to undress down to his boxers and make his way to his side of the bed, when Carla appeared. She brought a plate with half a sandwich.

"Here you go. I'm betting you didn't eat." She handed him the food, let a glance drift from his bare chest over his abdomen, and started readying for bed herself.

"Hey, thanks." Jack didn't hesitate to delve into the sandwich. His protein smoothie at the gym had been good, but this was better. The ham was succulent.

"Sounds like things went well today." Carla stood at the closet and pulled on a nightshirt.

"Yeah, it did. Saw a surveillance video and got a new case today. Maybe two. So, it was pretty busy."

"Mmmmm. Surveillance video. Now that sounds fun."

"Yeah, it was. My client didn't think so. It was sad for her really. I mean, she suspected he'd been cheating. Still, nothing like seeing it actually play out in front of you to bring it home."

"Ouch. I bet." Carla shook her head and slipped into bed with him. Jack had finished the half sandwich quickly and laid back.

"It's great evidence though. The husband is in the cab of this Range Rover and the lover gets in. They're in the parking lot at PDK, and they must've been pressed for time or something."

"Yeah? Peachtree-DeKalb? Where the private jets fly?" Carla raised her eyebrows. She drew close and propped her head onto her hand.

"Yeah. They get at it right there in this parking lot. Broad daylight. Making out. She climbs onto him. It's great."

"Wow." Carla slowly smiled, considering the scene.

"The client could barely watch it though. She didn't even want to finish it really."

"Oh, I'm sorry. That's got to be tough." Carla shifted on her side of the bed. The arm she had propped herself up with now flattened and she laid her head against it. Still looking to him, she dangled a hand over his chest.

"Yep."

"Hey," Carla sounded like she was switching gears in her mind, "so what's it like for you?" She traced her fingers about the skin of his pecs.

"What?"

"I mean, you're sitting there, and you got him now, right?"

Jack nodded slightly. "Yeah, true. As her lawyer, I'm ecstatic, sure. I try to be empathetic as well though. I knew it was tough on her." He thumbed into the pages of the Turner file.

"Sure." Carla's mind seemed to spin a little more. She licked her lips. "You know, it's also kind of wild when you think about it."

Jack's eyes stayed on his notes. "What's that?"

"I mean, you're sitting there. You and this woman, there alone. Watching a sex video. In one sense, it's a bit...I don't know. Erotic, maybe?" Carla's voice trailed.

"No," Jack didn't hesitate. "It wasn't that."

Carla scrutinized him, he could tell without even looking. He really needed to review these notes for tomorrow.

He spoke matter-of-factly. "Really, it wasn't. Wasn't that kind of vibe at all." He made his words certain.

"Okay." Carla didn't sound very convinced.

Jack half-turned to her and tried to explain.

"It's something that should never happen. Those kinds of

feelings or situations with clients. Never. You can't even think that way. I mean, you're in a professional relationship where they're trusting you, you know? There's something fundamentally wrong with that. So, you don't even let it go there."

Jack worried he may be coming off a little righteous, and he added another aspect to the mix.

"And besides, you do something like that, and you're suddenly vulnerable to them. You're supposed to be able to exercise this 'detached, professional' judgment for them, and it's hard to say you were detached and professional when you've had sex with them, right? An upset client with some bombshell like that can seriously hurt you, you know?"

Carla now nodded to him. She appeared disappointed, like Jack had spoiled something about it. "I get it."

She put her hand into Jack's thick hair. "Well, you're not at work right now..."

Jack sank further into the sheets with her, and he brought his face to hers. Gently, he brought his lips to hers, and for the first time in weeks it seemed they were really relaxing together.

She kissed back and he felt his pulse quicken. When she pulled just back from him, he took it as a sign for him to move closer. His torso lifted and he started to position over her and her hand traced from his chest over to his hip.

Her eyes half-closed in a way he'd always loved before.

As he moved in bed, the papers spread from the file onto the sheet beside him. The case was right there with him. Other times, he would have put aside the matter.

This time he couldn't quite push the day's events out of his mind.

The video. The filings. Now, a new case, too. In the morning.

"Wait." His eyebrows wrinkled.

"What? What's the matter?"

"Um...give me a few." He caressed her cheek with his hand but continued to withdraw. "I gotta look over these notes. Won't take but a couple of minutes."

Without another word, Jack pulled back. He hoped he hadn't perplexed her too much by the mixed signals. He would make it up to her. He gathered his notes back in front of him. As he picked back up reading, he was distinctly aware that she lay frozen beside him. If he looked her way, he wasn't sure what he'd find, but he knew he needed to have this information firmly in mind for his meeting. The prenup was twenty-something pages long itself.

Halfway into the agreement from the file, he heard her turn over. A brief thought of resuming their moment passed, but he had to have this down. He forged ahead.

His review took a little more than forty-five minutes, but he got it done.

Feeling a deep relief, he turned off the light and edged over to Carla. His hand went to her shoulder and rubbed from her neck over onto her back. Rather than pull towards him, she sunk lower away from him.

He paused and brought his hand back. With a sigh, he turned back over onto his back. He would just get on to sleep.

He had a big day tomorrow.

2

SOMETHING WAS WRONG.

When Jack had an appointment to see Gene, he would usually go to Gene's office and walk right in. It was just that way.

Jack always acknowledged Gene's matronly assistant, Liz. That's what you did. Liz was the gatekeeper. She relished her place of guarding Gene. Jack showed her respect each time because he certainly did respect her.

Jack arrived at Gene's office at ten minutes before eight that morning for his eight a.m. conference with Gene. Gene's door was closed, and the look Liz shared with him as he walked up shook him. She clipped her 'good morning' and stared.

"He'll be right with you." She was trying to sound as considerate as she could.

The moment was so out of the norm that Jack couldn't even think of a response or small talk. He just eked out an 'okay.'

As he waited, he considered the matter about to be discussed. He reminded himself of the significance of this. Yesterday, he cleared the hurdle with Monica's case and now this case loomed.

"Turner files." Matters or cases involving Bob Turner, Bob Turner's family, Bob Turner's friends, Bob Turner's businesses, Bob Turner's families' businesses, Bob Turner's friends' businesses. On and on and on, Jack thought.

Bob Turner had been a client since right around the time the firm had started, Jack realized. This was more than eighteen years ago. Hatcher was eighteen years younger then, as was Turner. Jack wondered about the messes, deals, or other legal business that Hatcher and Turner had weathered in that time. Substantial. Turner built an empire as a developer, buying up land, building commercial centers, and gobbling up businesses, both big and small.

There had to have been fights. Wars with competitors, battles with regulators. Gene Hatcher fought the battles alongside Turner, and William Sneed guided Turner's quest through all the complex transactions and regulatory compliance required to reach a fortune in eight figures. Hatcher and Sneed didn't do too badly either as they rode the journey with Turner.

Eight figures. Jack marveled at that kind of vantage point. He craved the kind of freedom and independence that meant. Jack had long yearned for legal success, but lately he found himself seduced by what financial success could mean.

Jack shook his head to break his dreaming and orient himself for his meeting with Gene. Before any financial success at all, he had better get results at Hatcher and Sneed. He must get the Andrea Turner case, win both Monica's and Andrea's cases, and then graciously accept the partnership offer that would surely come.

Yeah, right. That's the plan, anyway.

Suddenly, Gene's office door slung open.

"Come on in."

Gene's jaw set tightly. He proceeded to lead Jack into his office and both sat quickly. Jack didn't like this stern look from Gene. Where was the broad, proud smile of yesterday?

"I've been on the phone with Bob." Gene said it and stared off to the side like he might still be in deep thought.

Jack simply nodded.

"Andrea Turner's case is important to me." Gene's words were direct and now his look bore into Jack.

Jack wanted to say it was likewise important to him, but he thought better of it.

"I absolutely understand, Gene."

"Bob is a dear friend to me. And listen, Andrea's stunningly beautiful and all, but ... she's complicated." Gene finished his thought shaking his head and with a furrowed brow.

Jack quietly nodded. There was nothing he could say to that.

"The point is he's going to be concerned. I'm going to be concerned. And we all want this working out, and coming out the way it should."

Jack's gut churned. Gene sounded like he was leading up to breaking the news that Gene would just handle the case himself. Jack couldn't have that. He spoke up.

"I completely get how very important this case is, Gene. I really do. I'm all over it. I have already been getting ready, and we have pleadings started. I did prenup work on three cases in the last couple of years. I want this win more than anyone." He

let the words hang in the air and then added. "I absolutely do."
Gene looked at his desk top still in contemplation. A moment
passed in complete silence. Jack started to add something else,
then thought it better to keep his thoughts to himself.

Gene brought his arms to rest on his desk. His hands angled
up and his fingers stretched out, tapping back and forth.

"Remember how I was talking about how heated the rivalry
is between George Henderson and Bob?"

Jack suppressed a smirk. "How they hate each other?"

"Yes, how they hate each other." Gene's look convinced Jack
it would have been better if he hadn't smirked.

Gene continued. "With Andrea going through with her
divorce, there's another layer you should know."

"There is?"

"There's this kind of 'open secret' in the big time real estate
world and some circles. You know 'Palisades'?"

"Yeah, the huge place on the Northside. Office towers, luxury
apartments, shops, some good restaurants. Cool pedestrian
kind of place."

"Yep, exactly. Well, George started that whole development."

"He did?"

Gene nodded. "Back before the real estate bust. I mean, he
dreamed up this monument he was going to leave as a legacy.
Something to be around forever, right?"

"Okay. But?"

"The real estate market hit its bust. George said that he
didn't want to keep sinking money in it. Claimed he wanted
someone else to finish it. Well, what really happened was that
Bob had this phantom entity that had helped provide some
bridge financing. The other lenders were ready to cut slack to

Henderson during the bust. But not Bob."

"Uh oh."

"Uh oh is right. Bob swept in with his phantom entity and took it over. He took Henderson's dream project, finished it, and made it his own. The most successful commercial project in town and Bob's legacy. Not Henderson's."

"Holy shit."

"Yeah, holy shit."

Jack tried to picture just how pissed off Henderson could be. Gene helped. "Henderson has wanted blood ever since, Jack. Okay? And now, Monica comes to see us. The man's gonna want blood."

Jack slowly nodded.

Gene straightened up in his chair and held his hands apart. "Bob's not stupid. He sees Monica come to us, and now he's got Andrea getting divorced. He's not sure how, but he worries a problem could come up with Andrea."

Jack thought quickly. *Ah, so that explains the trepidation here. Bob's called Gene back and Bob's tight about Andrea's case going wrong. Two big battles at once.*

Jack piped up. He wanted this case right now. "Listen Gene, Bob doesn't have to worry. We've got a tight prenup here. We go in, hit hard to enforce it fast, and close the damn case down."

Finally, a faint smile teased at Gene's lips.

Jack didn't let up. "I read the prenup last night. It's good. It's fair." *In other words, Gene, I've already started on the case.*

Gene inhaled deeply and opened the file on his desk. "Here's a copy of the trust agreement for her divorce file."

Jack started to take a look as Gene continued. "The short story is that she gets $10,000.00 a month right now, and then that increases to $25,000.00 a month at age thirty. Also at age thirty, she gets a lump sum of $3,000,000.00."

"Interesting," Jack added. "Sounds low for Turner."

"Yes, it is, huh?" Gene tensed a bit. "Bob wants her comfortable, but he wants her to try to be sensible, too. He'd call it teaching her appreciation and she calls it maniacal control."

Jack chuckled. "Hey listen, they've gone at it. Publicly, too. She swears he tries to control her. Micromanage her."

Jack shifted in his chair, still not sure he had the case. "I saw where Jim Hadley is due for a payout. Three million after five years of marriage?"

"I think that was Bob thinking that made the prenup sound reasonable. Plus look, Bob knows Hadley is a slacker. If Bob could entice Hadley to leave, then he was fine with doing that."

"But now Andrea wants out after all. And it's only year three."

"Andrea has had enough. She wants out alright..." Gene blinked a couple of times and looked off as though an image distracted him. "Something you should know about Andrea. And... I really can't overemphasize this. She's got it all. A gorgeous young woman, smart, savvy, comes from a wealthy family. But all that doesn't come close..."

Gene paused again and Jack couldn't wait. "Doesn't come close? Doesn't come close to what?"

Gene's eyes gradually made their way back to Jack and fixed on his. "There is nothing else like how ambitious Andrea is. I've met a lot of people in my life. But, I've known her for years and let me tell you—you absolutely cannot underestimate her."

Jack flinched. Gene had to be wrong about this. "Andrea Turner?"

Gene bobbed his head like he realized Jack didn't believe him. "Andrea Turner."

Jack couldn't make himself believe Gene. "Um, I guess. But... her dad is Bob Turner."

"Let's just say, dad holds the dollars tight."

Gene moved forward with their meeting.

Gene raised his hands, palms up. "Best part for last."

"Yeah? What's that?"

Damn it. Here it comes. I'm toast. Will I at least get to second-chair it? Gene, at least let me be co-counsel.

Gene chose his words carefully. "I'm too close to this thing. Bob and all. Have known Andrea forever, too. I can keep up with it. Keep a hand in it. Advise. But I can't go lead."

Perfect. Fine by me. Just go ahead and hand it over then. I'll go lead. But why do I sense you're not going to, Gene.

Jack found the most reassuring tone he could. "Gene, I get how huge this is. I really do. With me on it, you'll know everything and know it every step of the way. It's covered."

Gene set his chin. "Hadley retained Richard Bourne. It rattled Bob a little."

Geez. What's Hadley doing getting Bourne?

Jack hated himself for revering Bourne but there was no getting around it. The pro athlete and celebrity clients. Great results. The poignant talks at conferences. The insightful articles on cutting issues. He admired and loathed Richard Bourne.

Jack spoke up with defiance. "Good."

Gene blurted out a laugh. "Good?"

Jack grinned. "Yes sir, good. This will make enforcing this prenup even better."

"Really?"

"Gene, I've got something Bourne doesn't have."

Gene hung on Jack's words.

Jack leaned to him. "I'm hungry. Hungrier than he's ever been. In his life."

Gene studied Jack closely. Neither man moved a second. Stillness. Absolute silence.

Jack held his breath.

Finally, Gene smiled. "Alright."

Gene patted the desk and started moving his chair back.

"Okay," Hatcher was bringing their meeting to a close, "Prep her financial affidavit and disclosures. The other side is entitled to at least that. Get theirs. Bring her along gently. She may need some reassurance. Keep up with her. She needs to stay away from him. Get a motion started to enforce the prenup. Press Bourne. Let him know that if fees are run up on this thing, that Hadley's fucking paying for them."

With that, Hatcher was on his feet. He slid some documents into a folder, came around his desk, and was out the door, with Jack trailing behind.

Evidently, he'd cleared Gene's hurdles. He was on the Andrea Turner case after all.

He grinned as he walked past Liz.

She seemed happy to return the favor.

Liz almost seemed to purr. "Ms. Turner will be here at ten."

Andrea Turner appreciated her reflection in the mirror as she often did.

Even early in the morning, she saw radiance. Bright blue

eyes. Smooth, clear skin. She permitted herself a contained smile, and moved on. There was much to do, and she felt ready to get started. Plus, she needed to navigate around Jim Hadley, her husband.

The young, petite woman walked from the bedroom she used for yoga, and headed across her spacious home to the kitchen. Her blonde hair was full and tossed about. She moved slowly but gracefully, luxuriating in the effects of having pushed herself with her early morning workout. Her soft complexion was as yet without make-up, but her features had a natural attractiveness to them. She kept her posture straight and her breathing was smooth.

Andrea liked that she had made herself feel exactly like she wanted. She picked out some grapes to nibble and eased into a chair at her breakfast table. Seated across from her was the slender frame of her husband.

Even after four years of dating and then three years of marriage, Andrea could still command Jim Hadley's attention early in the morning, and she took considerable satisfaction as she did that again. She looked to him with some acknowledgment but didn't speak. She picked up her phone and read her affirmations a couple of moments.

"You're already looking lovely." His voice was playful.

"Yeah?" She glimpsed him, grinned, but looked back to her phone. Any mention of her looks caused her to think the same thing. *You love my looks, and yet you're sure I'm stupid. Always.*

"You still have your meeting?" His voice subtly shifted to a more serious tone. They both knew why.

Andrea hummed a 'yes,' but didn't look up.

Jim sat there, surely expecting more, but it wasn't coming.

She knew his brooding look well. *Go ahead and brood, Jim. Been outside yet to get high?* She had no respect for his 'habits.' There was simply too much to get done in life for that. She had made that clear to him. Once a couple of quiet moments had passed, he got up leaving the table. She shot her eyes quickly to him and back, and as she expected he only wore thin, white boxers. He sauntered just past her, and when he passed by her, his hand traced her shoulder and brushed in parting. She still said nothing.

Andrea listened as he climbed the stairs and contemplated his question and tone. She didn't feel it necessary to say to him yet again what they had already discussed repeatedly. She still had her appointment with her lawyer. This showed how well he paid attention to her. Today she had an early acting class first. Afterwards, she'd see her divorce lawyer.

It wasn't some surprise or secret. They had talked about it again the evening before. She decided he was just toying with her. They both knew the day had come. Perhaps he was trying to prompt some response. She was glad she gave him none.

She gently shook her head from side to side. A slight frown formed. She prided herself on her usual self-control, especially with her expressions, but this thought moved her. She would go see her divorce lawyer this morning, after having awakened in bed with her husband.

Not that their relationship remained passionate. She wondered just how unusual this was. *Am I the only one reduced to just being roommates with their spouse?*

At twenty-five, she had never heard anyone talk of their marriage actually getting to that point. Sure, she suspected. But no one admitted it. Now, she cared about Jim, loved their history, but they had long ceased being lovers.

Andrea expected that Jim was probably putting on some clothes to go start his day, and instead of going upstairs herself, she detoured. There was a small sitting room at the front of the house. She went straight to it. She closed the door behind her. She drew drapes closed, darkening the confined space. She found the large, plump pillow always where it was on the floor and moved to center it in front of her.

She lowered lightly onto the cushioned pillow and found her familiar pose. Her back was straight, and she tilted her pelvis forward. Her eyes rested shut. Her arms dangled down and her hands rested on her thighs. She concentrated on her breathing and slowed her mind. As she had practiced many times, she meditated herself to a place where she let the thoughts drift up and away. For several long moments, she found a quiet and a peace. For her, such a peace meant clarity. She had cleared her mind. Even as she completed her meditation and rose to leave the room, she held this clarity for herself.

On this particular day, she knew this clarity was especially meaningful. Andrea reminded herself she must stay on track. She knew for certain that she would. She also recapped something essential. She knew there were really only two questions. One was 'what do you want?.' The other was 'how are you going to get it?'. It was now about an hour before she needed to leave.

There was enough time for one last thing, she decided. She let herself have twenty minutes with a script she was reading before getting ready to go. She was invigorated with the anticipation of her upcoming acting class getting underway. There was nothing more exciting for her. She felt more alive and engaged while acting than she did with anything else in her life.

Once she squeezed all the time she could from the morning before having to leave, she got in her Porsche. Now, she figured, she was fully prepared. It was time for her to go to her acting class. Then, she'd meet with her divorce lawyer.

She was on track to breaking free.

✦

The time had come. Jack had checked his watch over and over since his meeting with Gene. In fact, the idea of meeting Andrea had stayed in Jack's mind ever since Gene brought up her case. Remember—she's a young woman getting a divorce. This is about Andrea Turner, and it's not about Bob Turner or anyone else.

From his experience, he knew what needed to be done. Establish control with this interview, get the facts and information, and address her concerns. He would also assess her as his client. See who he really had. He would have to orient and manage her as he needed. He wanted her confident. And, on top of it all, this was Andrea Turner. He'd heard enough to be deeply intrigued.

He did as he always did, and he ventured to the lobby to bring her back to his office. His steps had some pop and his posture set straight. He had waited for this.

He rounded the turn into the well-appointed reception area, and he immediately saw her. The blonde hair was lush and tied back to try to hold it, but appeared it might be too thick to stay. Her smooth, clear skin looked delicate. But when her face peered up to see him, he saw only her eyes—bright blue eyes that smiled openly.

"I'm Jack Adams."

"Andrea Turner. Nice to meet you."

He led her back and they settled into place easily. One of the dark auburn wingback chairs cuddled her. She sat comfortably from the start with her hands folded in her lap.

"What we'll do is start with basic and background information, and then we'll move into history and the facts. It's important I get the context and the relevant information. I can address any questions you have and talk to you about the process. Then, I'll also have what I need to prepare the necessary documents."

She nodded and then smiled.

She sat and paid attention. Like a lot of clients in an initial consultation, her face held a blank stare at first. He figured she was taking everything in and orienting herself. It seemed she had been in professional meetings a lot already. She just had that kind of bearing. No idle, nervous chatter.

The opening questions about education, work, and background served their intended purpose. He learned about her college education, her grades that could have been better, and her exciting travels that he didn't let himself envy.

A couple of times she wanted to learn the same things of Jack, but he politely dodged, keeping the focus on her. He was flattered that she showed an interest but he wouldn't indulge. He was careful not to turn it into a conversation. This was his interview.

Whatever ordinariness there may have been at the start soon disappeared. Jack needed to know of any past difficulties in case they were thrown at him later. It was just part of the preparation, he explained.

She nonchalantly replied that there was mostly nothing remarkable. But she did bring up a drinking and driving incident in Florida. There had been a 'fender bender' involved, too. Of course, no one died or anything. She wasn't sure what exactly the injuries had been, but certainly she had checked on the other driver's surgeries and recovery. It had all worked out fine.

Jack followed up, and she assured him that by "all worked out fine" she had meant the drinking and driving charge had been dismissed as well. Her father, Bob, had a good lawyer in Destin that had picked up on the mishandling of the intoxication evaluation. Andrea ended that anecdote with admitting she had been lucky it had worked out as well as it had.

"Oh," she added, "there's something else."

"Maybe you should know there was this other thing, this minor thing." Her hand hooked some hair behind her ear. "It was just a small possession kind of thing. One time Jim and I were at the beach, and Jim had saved some pot. He left it in my car. Well, the bag rolled onto a back floorboard. A cop came by and saw it one day at the beach. Crazy thing, really. Thankfully, Dad and I straightened that all out."

They smiled at each other. He jotted more notes and asked if there was anything else. When he didn't hear a reply, he looked up from his pad to her. She was blushing. She kept her head a little lower and with a grimace she had to add one more thing.

"I feel horrible about this. Geez, I sound like such a dreg." She shook her head quickly a couple of times. "There is this one other time."

"Okay."

"I was like odd one out at this big dinner party. At Bones in Buckhead. About ten of us. Great food, expensive bottles of wine. I was last to leave the table.

"The check had been passed around just like several others were making payments. But it got to me and no one had paid anything. Nothing, Jack. It was like twenty-two hundred dollars!

"I was NOT getting stuck with that, not the whole damn thing. No way. It wasn't right. So I left, too."

For a short moment she looked to the side, obviously embarrassed. She looked back to him and finished. Unpleasant but necessary. At least she said it matter of factly.

"Anyway, with my luck, I'm the one the police come to. I explained it all. Dad understood. And thank goodness, he did help."

Jack finished more notes and then reassured her.

"Hey, don't worry. All that's manageable. It really is."

She sighed heavily.

"Let me ask you this. Of these three things, how many involved Jim?"

At first, she just stared blankly at him. Then, in a slow awakening of her own, she admitted aloud Jim had been involved in all of them.

"Hey, listen though." Her words were soft. Careful. "I don't want it to be like that. He's not necessarily the bad guy here. He's not a monster. Really, he's not. I mean, he can be monster-like, sure. But he's not all to blame. He's just not."

"I understand." More notes and then a gentle pivot. "Speaking of you and Jim, any issues of abuse?"

Her eyes darted fast away and then back. Her words came carefully again.

"He has never hit me. I have never hit him. Now, I gotta tell you. We both would say that we torment one another."

Jack chuckled. She joined in but continued.

"I mean we really can get into some serious mental warfare. It's crazy. Insane." She looked past him a second in contemplation and then back to him.

"And it's got to stop."

After a long silence, Jack felt his office walls close in. It was a clean, well-organized office. But right then it was small.

"Part of the issue in the case is separation. I have to ask about the physical side of your relationship. First, I understand you're still living in the marital residence?"

"Yeah, but that's weird. It really needs to change. It does."

"Well, that brings me to your physical relationship with him. There's something I always explain to clients. Once we file, if the two of you have sexual relations, then the case can be dismissed. Thrown out."

"I understand." She shrugged and tried to act unaffected by the topic.

"I also have to ask when you last had sexual relations."

Her eyes froze onto his. She didn't move for a few seconds. He expected at least some immediate reaction. But nothing immediately came.

With this, he noticed something. Yes, he felt sure of it. In a short clip of a moment, he captured her calculating. It was over in an instant, but he was absolutely certain it happened. She stared right at him, and in a flash she looked like she weighed her perception and decided something important. It felt like a rare glimpse under the surface of her.

Just as quickly, the charming affectation of self-consciousness was back. She grinned, looked down and around. And then, her brow tensed and loosened, all in a smooth flow.

"Um, it's kind of weird really. In college, we were crazy wild. He was one of the most passionate men I'd ever met, and I've met several." Her comment hung in the air a second before she continued.

"He also gave me some of my own most passionate times as well. Brought out sides of me I never would have known."

She stopped a moment. Her head tilted down as she reflected and acknowledged something to herself before saying it out loud. When her face lifted partially up to face Jack again, her eyes were sad and her voice lower.

"That was all some time ago. We are close still. Always will be. But, um, you know, now it's more like we're brother and sister. It really is. As fucked up as that might sound, that does sum us up."

Jack twinged inside with hearing her get graphic, but he didn't let on. It was a little bit of a surprise, but it was also raw. It had an appeal to it he savored. He pushed himself on.

"Hey, I understand. And it's not uncommon, if that helps." He moved on to the business side of things. "Luckily, you have a good prenup. We'll..."

Jack heard three loud bangs on his office door and the door swung open. An older man's lined, weathered face peered in. Bushy, white hair topped off the man's head.

The man entered and spoke in a loud voice. "How's it going?"

Jack stood and his hands shot to his hips. Who the hell is interrupting my conference?

Gene Hatcher appeared in the doorway right behind the older man, tilting his head to one side, seeming to signal regret for the interruption.

Gene spoke up. "Hey, Bob dropped by." And with that Gene

proceeded into Jack's office right behind Bob Turner. The office seemed to shrink for Jack, as first Bob's intense, formidable presence faced him, and then Gene's stature centered there.

Jack circled his desk promptly. He switched to courtesy. "Good morning," Jack offered his hand and he and Bob shook. Bob and Jack had met in passing previously but hadn't worked directly with each other.

"Good morning, Jack," Bob Turner's voice boomed a bit in return and the men were facing each other. Bob was about the same height as Jack, but where Jack was trim and showed a tennis background of past agility and speed, Bob stood solid and barrel chested, no doubt having played football at some point in his past. He still appeared to have a strength and ruggedness. His white, full hair and bright blue eyes capped off an extraordinary and impressive bearing.

"Please have a seat," Jack gestured towards a chair facing his desk, and Jack circled back around to sit, but Bob didn't accept.

"I really don't have long. I just wanted to drop by and say hello." When Bob continued standing, Jack didn't sit either, leaving him just standing behind his desk. All three of the men stood around the desk.

Andrea had flinched with the knocks and now she rolled her eyes.

Bob's eyes went from Jack to see Andrea sitting to the side. "Hey darling."

Andrea blinked several times quickly, glanced to Jack and then looked back to Bob.

"Hey, Dad." Her words came slow. She looked like she braced as he closed the space between them.

Bob bent and kissed her cheek and she forced a smile.

When Bob raised back up, he looked back to Jack.

"Gene told me you and Andrea were meeting. I didn't want to interrupt, but I wanted to say hello."

Jack nodded. "Yes, we have been. She's very nice, and I've enjoyed meeting her. I look forward to working with her."

Bob looked over knowingly to Gene who stood beside him. He glanced down at Andrea before grinning back to Jack again.

"Yeah, she can be nice alright, but she can be a damn handful, too." Bob said it while keeping a good-natured grin, and Jack smiled back. "Watch yourself with her. She'll drive you crazy."

An awkward silence slipped by as it seemed the men waited on Andrea to play along with Bob's tease. She didn't. An icy glare was all Bob got.

Finally, Jack thought he should break the moment.

"Oh, I understand, but I don't expect any trouble. I'm eager to get her prenup enforced."

"Good." Bob nodded quickly. "I'm sure this thing will work out fine."

"Yes," Jack started. He figured Bob could be expected to keep up with Andrea's case with him. "It's a solid prenup, and there've been no substantial changes to contend with. Looks very positive." Jack was about to describe what risks also existed but was cut right off.

"Alright, great then. It is a short marriage after all." Bob regarded Gene a moment and then again returned his attention to Jack. "Listen," the older man tilted his head emphatically towards Jack, "the sooner she's away from this son of a bitch Hadley the better, you know?" Bob's eyes were serious.

Andrea cringed and groaned at Bob. "Dad..."

"Well. I understand." Jack pursed his lips.

Bob pivoted towards the door, ready to move on. His purpose of saying hello to Jack and setting a tone was complete. "Hey, you keep me up to date. If you need anything, let me know."

"Yes sir, I will." Jack moved towards the door to follow them out. Bob led and was facing out, when Gene looked back at Jack and nodded approvingly.

To Jack's left, Andrea got up from her seat.

"Bye, Dad." Andrea stopped Bob and hugged him, leaving him with a peck on his cheek.

As Bob and Gene left his office, Jack felt a pang of concern. Different things could also go wrong. Was that still understood? The brief interchange had gone well, but the understanding was clear. Bob Turner thought he controlled this case, and he conveyed a determination to get the outcome he wanted: Andrea extricated from Jim Hadley.

Swiftly, Bob and Gene were gone, leaving Jack and Andrea in his office alone. He shook his head. That had gone too quickly and too superficially. Bob had made the case sound too easy. How could he fix that now?

As he got back behind his desk, he saw Andrea shut her eyes and take a breath. Her face lifted just up and then leveled again. A slow exhale left her lips.

Her words came deliberately. "Where were we?"

Jack wondered. Andrea struck him as having been thrown off by her father's interruption, and then became flustered with him present. Now, she projected a calm once more. Collected.

"Um," Jack answered, "we will prepare the pleadings to be filed to start your case. We'll push to have the Court enforce your prenuptial agreement at the earliest opportunity."

She smiled and her eyes held his. Her hand rose from her lap and played with her necklace. The diamond pendant fell to her skin right where her blouse first buttoned.

"Yeah? You think it looks good?"

Jack cleared his throat. "Yes, I do. But at the same time we take nothing for granted. Anything can happen. So, we take care of it. "

"Great." Her smile broadened and her eyes stayed fixed on Jack's. He let himself admire her stare, then caught himself.

"Okay," he straightened his notes and rose to his feet to show her out. "I'll get the initial pleadings prepared. You'll need to come back in and sign them."

She stood and he watched her smoothly turn away from him and towards the door, showing the well-fitted backside of her skirt. Her measured strides to the door were captivating as she cooed her reply.

"Just let me know what you want me to do."

Jack's attention delighted Andrea. She had not known what to expect before, but she was now certainly impressed. She wondered how he perceived her.

Andrea saw it as a good sign that he was walking closely behind her from his office. She found herself thinking of ways to learn him, take a temperature on him and gauge his level of interest. She set a goal. If she couldn't prompt his hand on her by the time she got into the elevator, then she was not where she should be with him. She was certain of that.

They quickly moved down the hall from his office. Andrea

noticed a low steady hum of office culture, yet inexplicably no one was visible to them. Jack was talking of how it had been a pleasure meeting her and how he looked forward to working with her. She replied in kind and knew she sounded sincere because she was.

They passed into the reception area, and just like before, the pert, attractive receptionist exchanged pleasantries with Andrea. Andrea couldn't help but think that the receptionist likely appreciated Jack walking past again. Andrea was already learning what his presence was capable of.

How did he manage the appearance of a man who spent many leisurely hours in the sun yet pulled off this suit in a law office so well? He certainly did wear that suit well. Did he play tennis? Baseball? Basketball? He damn sure worked out.

He was probably as disciplined and focused on his work as he was his health. Was she just another client? Had she moved him at all?

These thoughts inspired her. The two were now crossing the threshold of where the office opened into a lobby and a bank of elevators. Andrea abruptly pirouetted to inquire of Jack if she had said too much earlier. It was a graceful spin she landed with confidence.

Jack ran right into her. Their chests meshed and Jack eased back. Andrea loved catching him glimpse at her cleavage jostle from the impact. He had to be affected.

"I'm ... uh so sorry. "

"That's okay. My mistake." Andrea waved a hand and took a step toward the elevator. Her wave dismissed any notion that their bump was his fault. The bump had accomplished... exactly what she intended.

About to board the elevator, she suddenly looked concerned and searched his eyes.

"I don't know about all this. I'm very worried. But I really like you. I believe you can help me fix this."

As she spoke, his demeanor softened and his body drew a little closer to her. She had seen men take this tack many times before. With Jack, she knew it was genuine.

"You're going to be fine Andrea. You really are. We're going to take care of this."

He closed their distance so that he stood at her side. He put his right hand first to her arm and then to her lower back.

"Everything's going to work out." His words sounded true.

She got onto the elevator and looked back at him beaming. They held each other's glance until the doors had closed. Andrea had silently let Jack know that he had reassured her. Everything is going to work out beautifully.

ЯР

After a long day, Jack needed a good workout. His mind raced, and the gym served as the best cure. He savored his routine.

The stair climber did its job, as he grinded away. Lines of gleaming machines stood in the gym, waiting to serve members like Jack ready to sweat. The wide-open room had a wall of televisions to distract the members on one end, and a floor to ceiling glass wall on another to give an even more expansive effect. Music pulsed in the background.

Something about the physical exertion and music from the smartphone created the respite he needed from the day. After a long day of talking, reading, and analyzing, the physical exertion gave him the break he needed. Layers of stress could just melt away.

This was the border for him. That break from the world of being the divorce lawyer to going back to normal that his workout facilitated. He'd gotten used to this and now he depended on it.

The stair climber churned over and over at its constant rate. He glimpsed, but didn't really follow the readings illuminated on the display. It may show his pace, the floors climbed, and the time elapsed, but the specifics didn't matter. Instead, the legs climbing higher counted. A towel draped the handle, ready if needed.

He soaked up the driving music from his headset, and kept trying to follow it rather than think. The Bose headset secluded him just as he intended, even though other members labored nearby. His feet worked methodically and his hands gripped the handles at his sides.

Tonight, he cursed that his mind returned to her. He remembered the sight of Andrea's blonde hair as she walked in front of him towards the elevators that day. His mind flashed to her alluring smile, to her blue eyes that fixed on him, the smooth skin that had disappeared into her blouse earlier.

This must stop, he told himself. This was trouble. He shook his head.

As if on cue, the music faded. He looked to the phone where instinctively he expected to see an incoming call to break his trance. The phone didn't fail him and showed "Monica Henderson."

He hit the pause button for the stair climber. He took a couple more steps to ride out the delay for the machine. He grabbed the phone and climbed down to the floor, angry that she was interrupting him.

As soon as he was down from the machine, his fingers clicked the phone to start the call. The display rebuffed him. Monica's call had already diverted to voicemail.

Frustration bit at him. Hadn't he reacted quickly enough? Now, he was off the machine. He just knew he had gotten down fast enough. His fingers worked the phone to play back the message.

The recording crackled. "Hey, it's Monica. Just checking in. Remembered the names of three more entities George uses I wanted to tell you about. Also, will email you more about Brandon and William. Plus, wondered if you'd heard anything. Let me know if there's any progress. Do we know who George's sleeping with? I have to know who's doing this to my family. Have to know what's going on. It's brutal not knowing. Thanks."

He closed his eyes a moment. Surely, she remembered him telling her that it would take time. She needed to be patient. He was working on it. He sent himself a reminder for the next day to check the status and call her back.

A guy nearby left his machine, and it reminded Jack to get back with it. He was running out of time. There was more exercising to be done.

He mentally pushed himself, and he lumbered back onto the steps. He clicked the phone to get back to his music. He started back on his routine.

The music didn't last long and faded once again.

Jack jerked his face back to the display. "Andrea Turner."

This time he clicked the phone and then descended the machine. He was still breathing hard as he answered her call.

"Hey."

"Hmmm, you sound like you're in the middle of something. Out of breath?" There was a playfulness in her voice.

Jack noted her flirtatiousness and tried to disregard it. "Yeah. Was on a stair climber. How are you doing?"

"Mmmm, not as good as you, it sounds. I like hearing you out of breath. Getting a good workout, huh?"

His instant reaction was to like her tease, but he shifted at once. Stay in your role. "Yeah. It's essential for me. You doing okay?"

"Let's see, I'm soaking in a hot bath and there are candles flickering. But, I'm on the phone with my divorce lawyer. At least he's hot." She giggled.

Her candor and flattery struck him hard as he caught his breath and bearings. He hated that it made him smile. His pause let her continue without his response.

"Just wanted to check in. Is there anything I should be doing?"

"Well, we need a bit more financial information. I sent an email earlier."

"Okay. Great then. Enjoy your workout."

The phone clicked and she was gone.

He stood there a moment and stared at the phone. He had not been able to gently prod her back from flirting with him and it unsettled him. He couldn't let their rapport be that casual.

He squinted his eyes with his next thought though. He knew better.

She flirts perfectly.

⁂

Andrea loved performing.

Still downstairs, she hung up from her call with Jack and sprawled on her sofa. The early evening rays of the setting sun streamed into the house, making for the only light. Chopin's *Prelude in E Minor* sounded slow and haunting in the background.

Her thin, white, silk V-neck top, without a bra, delicately touched her skin and her thin, red silk panties left her mostly bared. It had been just the relaxed feel she wanted when she made her call to him, and as usual, her plan worked flawlessly.

She rose from the sofa with smartphone in hand and strode the length of her large living room. The floor-to-ceiling glass windows that formed the complete back wall of her living room hid nothing, and she could not care less. Whether it was the immodest top and panties or her delightful prance across the floor, she didn't care who saw what.

She ascended the stairs evenly, more attuned to the strands she heard from Chopin than the inevitable remarks soon to come from Jim. She didn't fret handling him, but she knew the piece would soon end, and then it would just be their voices.

Once up the stairs and at her bedroom door, she paused at its entry and waited for him to look at her. She tilted her head just up and she set her chin. *Let him see that I know it went well.*

"You've been downstairs a long time."

So much for answering his questions with simply a pose. I married a fool.

She shook her head and crossed the room, answering him over her shoulder.

"The call went fine." Her tone was gentle. She made it across the expansive master bedroom and put her smartphone on the night stand. "Remember, I do have to call him at times. He's my lawyer. And... you and I have talked about how I need to manage this guy. He's got a lot of clients. He's not easy to keep focused. You gonna keep understanding?"

He spoke aloud firmly. "Of course I understand. You really don't have to worry about that."

He sat up in bed on his computer. She was certain he had spent part of the night surfing online and reading, while the other part of the time he had been thinking of his situation with her. His frown showed he still fought angst.

She climbed onto the bed, and she propped herself to raise up on two knees. In case that wasn't silly enough to break his darkness, she ran her hands through her hair and then left her hands in her hair atop her head. Her pose at least brought his face to survey her body, lingering at the two points on her chest in the thin, white silk.

Her voice purred at him. "Are you okay? I don't want you worrying."

He cocked his head and broke into a grin. "Me worry? You've filed for divorce, darling. Why should I worry?"

They both chuckled but only for a second. She lowered onto the bed to where she could sit near him, but still have space. Her smooth legs and bare feet stretched out and then tucked to the bottom of her. She propped on her elbow and faced up at him.

"Jim, you know how important this is. We're talking millions and getting out from under my father's grip. This will work, but it will take us both."

He shut off his laptop and began putting it away. He unplugged the Radiohead feed he had set earlier. His eyes said he was drained from the day. "I'm with you." His words were muted.

He moved to get under the covers.

Her voice softened. She took a great deal of time pulling the covers open and slipping herself between them. There was ample time to watch her. She whispered to him. "I'm sorry. I shouldn't have doubted you."

She turned towards him in the bed and didn't pull the sheet to cover her torso. Her tone sounded remorseful. "I mean, just because I was talking to another man. At night. I know that isn't any worry to you." She took a long look over at him.

Somehow he managed to grin. It was a goofy grin, sure, but it came naturally. He probably didn't care if she was toying with him.

Before he could give back something clever, she continued on.

"You should have heard his voice, Jim. He liked hearing from me." She pulled even closer to him and she wondered if he detected the light, fresh vanilla scent that never failed to amaze him. Her bright eyes danced at his.

She then lowered her face a bit, confessing more, "You know me. I mean, the chance to tease a young lawyer... well I couldn't pass that up."

Her hooded gaze peered up at him, and Jim slowly shook his head.

Her hand deftly went to his chest. "You would have liked my effect. He was putty, Jim." She smirked. Her eyes stayed half-opened.

"Yeah? I bet he was." Jim's voice had ratcheted down a couple of levels. Both of them knew what this meant. Jim was now won over by her. She was sure he hated it, but there was no getting around it. Andrea had taken him to where she wanted. In that moment, it didn't matter.

Suddenly, she paused. "I am so glad you understand. You see, I have to keep him in line, right?"

Jim was done talking but answered her anyway. "Sure you do. It's necessary."

Andrea embraced him, slowly and delicately. "You know, I can make this up to you."

Her approach wasn't really fair. They had long ago stopped such things together. He would avoid her overture somehow; she knew it. Still, she hoped it reassured him.

The workout always calmed Jack. Rarely did it disappoint. This night had been no different, even with the client calls interrupting. There was something satisfying about being very aware of his body as he made the short drive home that night from the gym. He savored the feeling.

For him, his trips to the gym served as a kind of break from his professional day. A decompression of sorts, he went and became physical for an hour or so after having been cerebral all day long. He shed tremendous amounts of stress this way. Plus, of course, it was supposed to be healthy for him. He just knew it was his habit.

He pulled the car into the garage, and he couldn't help but frown as he turned off the car. The frown immediately felt wrong, but it came anyway. Carla was good to him. He knew that. She truly cared about him.

At the same time, there was no doubt about her routine either. He was practically certain she would be inside and on either her first or second glass of chardonnay. Maybe he could get through the evening without any grief.

Earlier on in their relationship, he hadn't thought much of it. They both worked hard. They both had a good bit of stress. But over a few months of living together, she had slowly lost interest in trying to keep up a workout routine. Eventually, her routine had gravitated to simply dinner and then a drink, as she mostly worked from home while he was at the office.

"Hi," he called out as he entered the den from the garage.

"Hi Sweetheart." Her tone was warm as she shot him a smile over some papers spread in front of her on their couch.

"How's it going?" He flipped through some mail on the table by the door and then swung by where she was sitting and kissed her briefly.

"Good. Busy. Got three new openings today, so just taking a look at these." She relished being a conscientious recruiter who worked to stay caught up with matching resumes and candidates to job openings.

"Cool," he commented without conviction as he pulled a bottle of water from the fridge. "It's good to be with such a smart woman." He hoped flattery would help somehow.

"If I'm so smart, then how did I wind up with you?" She chuckled and immediately added, "Just kidding, Sweetie."

Jack felt the sting and knew the tension. He also knew he didn't even want to poke back. *When did it get to this?*

He stood in the kitchen a minute and let it pass. The water

bottle opened easily and up it went. Perfectly chilled, he pulled long gulps before he turned back to Carla.

She gathered her papers and powered down her laptop. She put her papers and laptop on the dining room table and sipped from her wine.

He remembered the last time she had cut at him like that. It had been his reaction to having children and being a parent. She often daydreamed about it, and he said that was how he felt about trying cases. It wasn't the smartest thing he'd done lately, but it was honest.

To him, she would never get just how long of a road it had been to go to law school and pass the bar. He came from modest circumstances and had been introverted. Nothing looked likely, especially a successful legal career. It seemed every day he worried he could lose his focus and fail.

"Good workout?" she asked as they both made their way to the stairs.

"Yeah, great workout actually." He started to say more, but he didn't. They were each on their own evening tracks, he felt. Plus, he was still thinking back to his interesting conversation with Andrea. A little more reflection on it might be fun, he figured.

"Have a good day?" She asked up to him, as he led them up the stairs.

"Busy but good, yeah. Couple of intense cases right now."

"That's a good thing, right?"

"Yeah," he nodded as they entered the bedroom. "Yeah, it is."

"Everything alright?" Her voice sounded tight. They both readied for bed.

"Yeah, just going to read some. That's all."

He looked over as she went into the bathroom, and his eyes

caught the glass of chardonnay on her night stand.

He tried to scold himself. *What's wrong with you? When did you become so harsh?*

As she brushed her teeth, and he changed clothes, the notion lingered that it wasn't so much the wine he found a problem but her change. He didn't understand why she changed.

She passed by him as he went to brush his teeth. A light blue t-shirt served as her nightshirt and it wasn't clear what was underneath. She called over to him as he brushed.

"I got some great news today." She sipped from her glass.

He looked to her. "Yeah?"

"I heard from Cathy." She beamed when she spoke of her sister. "She's pregnant. She's due in September."

He froze in place. "That's great." *Uh oh.*

She stared at him. She looked doubtful.

"Carla, that's great news."

She seemed to force a smile. "Thanks, Jack." Another sip before she put the glass back on the nightstand. "She's very excited. I'm excited for her."

He came around the bed and slipped inside the covers.

"Yeah, me too. That's great for them."

Immediately, Jack wanted the words 'for them' back. It said too much. The silence in the room hung there.

He didn't take his paperwork from his nightstand and he turned out the light.

Her voice was quick in the darkness. "I thought you were going to read some."

"Nah, changed my mind. I'm beat."

There was a click and a sudden glow came from over his shoulder where Carla was. He could assume she was going to read some herself or he could expect one more in a line of discussions about getting married and having children. He braced.

As he perched on his side facing away from her, his mind returned to Andrea's case. He needed something, some idea, to accelerate the case. Get leverage over Hadley and Bourne to where they had to react to Jack. He would file a motion to enforce the prenuptial agreement, and he would do it at once. But they would have thirty days to answer that motion. Then, the Court would later have a hearing, and then there would likely be time that would pass before a ruling. No, he needed something else.

He listened out for something from Carla. Nothing came.

With a deep breath, his mind turned to the vision of Andrea herself. He pictured her bright blue eyes. The way her smile could widen slowly.

Carla shifted in bed next to him and he waited. He wondered how Carla would approach him about the children issue. What was next? A couple of seconds passed and then a few more. The lamp clicked off, but there were no words. *Maybe that's it for the night.*

His mind drifted back to Andrea. There was a slight wince as he thought of how her circumstances were changing all about her. The stress of divorce could be challenging.

The sight of her walking away from him in the office floated to him in his pre-sleep daze. She moved so gracefully.

He felt a pang of guilt letting himself think about a client this way, but he indulged himself anyway. Keep it very limited, he told himself. Always remember she's a client, he chided self-consciously. Then his mind went back to her voice and the unexpectedness of her asking about him.

Did she really say 'hot'?

3

THE NEXT MORNING CAME QUICKLY FOR JACK. He was up and out of the house fast, as he thought of the overwhelming press of his cases and upcoming hearings. The partnership decisions were less than five months out. *I can see the finish line.*

He navigated the roads easily in the pre-dawn blackness. He loved how there was so little traffic. There was also this hint of a feeling that he was ahead of most everyone else.

His smartphone sounded and he looked to it. "David Cell." He snatched it up. "Hi."

"How's it going?" His brother had been up a while too it seemed.

"Heading in. Ready to get started. What city are you in today?" It always intrigued Jack how his brother got to travel most every week. Jack would love to do that. He was unsure whether he'd be any good at being a regional sales manager like his brother, but it had to be adventuresome going about the country.

"New Orleans."

"Wow." Jack thought of the French Quarter.

"Yeah. No doubt."

"How are Patty and the kids?" Jack at least had to ask, since he saw his sister-in-law and nieces and nephew quarterly, at best.

"Great, great. Katie's doing well in her honors program. What's it like with you."

Jack turned into the homestretch of his route to work and resolved he'd be succinct. "All's good. Well," he paused and felt compelled to clarify, "all's good with work anyway. I'm slammed. New, good cases. Plenty to do. I've got my shot, buddy."

"Excellent. Anything really interesting?"

"Hatcher gave me a great case with a prenup. Client is attractive, loaded. But I got this real prince of darkness on the other side."

"Yeah?"

"Richard Bourne. Supposed to be Atlanta's best divorce lawyer. He represents the husband."

"*You're* Atlanta's best divorce lawyer."

Jack grinned. "Thanks, brother."

"Fuck this guy, Jack. Go after him. The best defense is a good offense, right? You want this more than him. You'll work harder than him. May God help him, because he's up against Jack Adams."

Jack chuckled. "Yeah, right..."

"Just remember, *pay attention.*"

Jack immediately got his brother's short-hand with him. He and David had this running theory. They believed the rest of the world spread itself thin watching email, texts, and entertainment. Instead, there was an advantage to concentrating on the one thing in front of you. They had mused that when you did this you literally paid or spent your time and attention, but that this was like an investment that would inevitably pay off. They worried it might sound trite to others, but they swore by it.

"Thanks, buddy."

"Hey," David's voice tightened, "you're pacing yourself, right?"

"Yeah, of course. Don't worry about me. All's good."

"I know you. I know you'll go full out. It's just..."

When Jack heard David's voice trail, he flinched. He didn't need this right now.

"David, stop worrying."

"Just keep some balance. Gotta stay charged. And... don't be trying to lug all Dad's shit around with you."

As much as he appreciated David's concern, he didn't need any nagging right now. Not when it was all coming together.

"I hear you, David. Listen, I'm here. I have to get to it."

David paused. Then, he came around. "Give 'em hell, man. Make Bourne hate to see you coming."

Jack chuckled. "Alright."

He was ready for the fight.

⟡

SATURDAY, FEBRUARY 19, 2011

Jack's bright idea came out of nowhere.

In the quiet morning hours after his arrival at seven, Jack stirred with concern. No one else roamed the law office but Jack, and even being there on a Saturday didn't make him feel any better about the challenges he faced. He needed ideas.

Prepare, prepare, prepare.

He loved that there would be no calls and interruptions. Savored the solitude. He must work on preparing Monica's case for the battle that would soon be raging. He relished how important his next step was.

The next step in Monica's case was a temporary hearing. Georgia law provided that parties in a divorce case could have a temporary hearing and obtain a temporary order. Such an order would address issues, such as temporary custody and support. This order worked to stabilize everything until a more permanent resolution could be attained by a settlement or trial.

Jack wanted to position Monica and her children in the very best circumstances he could early on. Jack knew from experience how a spouse who earned much, much more could use the earnings and the control that came with those earnings to pressure and manipulate the other spouse during the pendency of the case. A good temporary order guarded against that. Going up against someone like George Henderson meant Jack needed to get any advantage he could, and as early as he could.

As he drafted documents to get his temporary order and gain this advantage in Monica's case, it hit him. Temporary hearings came early in a case to establish stability in a case. They represented strategic benefits so they were favored.

Why not use this in Andrea's case?

There wouldn't typically be a temporary hearing in a case without children. Usually temporary hearings provided stability for cases involving children. But, Andrea's case involved some potentially risky financial issues. And, the only *other* reason to do something on a temporary basis in a case like Andrea's would be if there was a prospect of violence. Jack was not going to make such an allegation. But... Jack could insist the hearing was necessary. He knew inferences might be drawn as to why. Plus, he knew *any* divorce situation had a risk for violence. Emotions often ran high.

Jack got up and paced. First in his own office. Then, he went into the quiet, dim halls of the law firm. Moving about felt good. His blood rushed. The concept unsettled him. Maybe the push for partner had finally affected him. *No, this is the fight. It's all on the line. This is what's needed.*

Jack passed by Hatcher's office. *Yeah, let's air this out.* The solution was to pitch it to Hatcher. Jack would present his idea to Hatcher. Hatcher wouldn't hold back. That was for sure.

Jack held up his phone and punched the keys. Might as well text Hatcher. Jack would give Hatcher a heads up he had an idea. And it wouldn't hurt Gene would see him hard at it on the weekend.

"Have an idea for Andrea's case. Will update with more."

Jack figured it might be a while before any response, or if there even would be a Saturday response from Gene. Gene had talked before about his usual Saturday raquetball match. He had a group of guys he played with regularly at his athletic club. Odds were Gene was there.

As Jack ventured back to his office, his phone pinged.

Gene was right back to him. "How good of an idea?"

Jack drew a breath and then typed. "May be onto something."

"Any lunch plans?"

Jack grinned at the prospect of meeting up with Gene for lunch. "Nope."

"Come on out to CAC. 11:30."

Jack got right back with him. "See you then." CAC meant Capital Athletic Club. Jack had been right that Gene was at his club.

The plans left Jack just enough time to prepare the documents for Monica's case to seek her temporary hearing, and then to start drafts of similar papers for Andrea's case. Jack noted the time entries so they would be billed later and left for CAC.

Clear blue skies welcomed Jack back into the living world as he emerged from the office. His SUV hurried from the parking deck and worked to one of the highways to head north of town. Jack made good time while pounding alternative rock sounded from his speakers. He savored the energy.

That same energy stuck with Jack as he found the athletic club, got past the reception desk and jacketed hosts, and made his way over to the club's restaurant. A maître d' escorted Jack through the tables in the cozy dining room. A couple of glass doors were at the wall to the left, and the pleasant hostess ushered Jack through them.

The doors led back outside, but now they were on a patio. The patio perched above a large swimming pool, no doubt heated given the swimmers that managed to do laps in the cool February air. Jack shook a chill that ran through him as he appreciated being where he was instead of down in the water where the swimmers would have to eventually leave.

Gene's table perched at the most advantageous spot, where Gene could look out onto the pool in front of them, over to tennis courts to his right, or back over to the city skyline silhouetted out over on his left. Jack liked the view.

Gene smiled to him and they said their hellos.

"What's up?"

Jack quickly launched his idea. "I was thinking about a way to get some leverage in Andrea Turner's case. Push it along."

Gene just looked right at him.

A server appeared. Gene ordered the steak salad. The sound of strips of hot ribeye steak laid over romaine lettuce, red wine vinaigrette, and Gorgonzola crumbles all piqued Jack's appetite. Jack ordered the same.

Gene appeared to absorb Jack's enthusiasm. "So, something good for Andrea's case?"

"Get a temporary hearing. Get sole temporary use and possession of the house." Jack saw Gene's eyebrows arch, and took that as a positive sign. "Andrea's talked to me about how Hadley won't leave her alone at times. It's like he can be in denial about this divorce even happening. She's worried about how he'll be the longer this goes on if they're under the same roof."

Gene slowly turned in his chair and surveyed the swimmers frolicking below. He nodded almost imperceptibly. He seemed to like it. Jack sensed momentum and finished his rationale.

"The house was deeded to her before the marriage, albeit not long beforehand, and she feels at risk with them both there. The trial Court may just go along, play it safe. If so, then the Court has taken a step towards enforcing the prenup."

Gene pondered it. His eyes darted about, now along the skyline.

Gene's eyes came back to Jack and he spoke directly. "I like it. The Court may wonder where Hadley goes. Even temporarily." Jack was ready. "He's got relatives in town. He'll be fine." "As does she." Gene still liked the idea, Jack knew, but Gene was evaluating the argument. "And, with Andrea's family, doesn't Andrea have more of an ability to relocate? Realistically speaking."

Gene paused and tested once more. "What if we don't get sole use and possession? Doesn't the leverage go the other way?"

Jack was caught off guard. He didn't think there would be much to counterbalance the fact that Andrea had the house prior to the marriage, but now hearing Gene frame the issue, he didn't feel so sure. "So, you don't think it's a good idea?"

"It'd come up in about four weeks? Rather than months?"

"Yes."

Gene stared straight at him evenly a while longer and then smiled broadly. "Hell yeah, I like it. It's aggressive." The steaks arrived. Gene's steak had red stripes lined in the middle. "Let's do it."

Jack swallowed hard and readied his fork for his own salad. He had raised the stakes in the case alright. As well as for himself.

Anything could happen.

4

FRAN, JACK'S ASSISTANT, APPEARED IN HIS DOORWAY. "Andrea Turner is here."

"I'll be right up."

He didn't hesitate. Jack was up and around his desk. *Let's knock this out.* He would explain what she needed to know about the next day's hearing, reassure her, and then be gone.

As he headed to the reception area, he checked his watch. 5:25. He grimaced. He didn't like later afternoon appointments in the first place, but Andrea was also late.

Take your time. Take your time. Jack knew his own typical routine the night before a hearing. Don't stay at the office late. Get to the gym and burn stress with a workout. Get to bed early. Still, he needed to spend time with Andrea and calm her. After all, this was her life they were dealing with. Where and with whom she would be living for several months.

At the end of tomorrow's hearing, he would go home like he wanted and like he always did. For Andrea, she would live with whatever court ruling *Jack* obtained. He always made it a point to remember this. And he always took this duty seriously.

Some staff people walked out the doors as he entered the reception area. Andrea's blonde hair stood out immediately, pulled back and perfect. Her bright eyes lifted to him at once, and it struck him just how compelling she was. Even her simple white blouse and designer jeans appeared exceptional.

"Hey Andrea," Jack smiled to her.

Andrea rose from her chair and beamed back. "How are you doing?"

"Good thanks," he replied, "come on back."

They walked to his office, and once she had come inside, he closed the door behind them.

"Tomorrow's a big day," he started.

"Yeah, and I'm nervous."

"Well, nothing to be too nervous about, really." Jack couldn't help but notice how thin her blouse now appeared. His eyes couldn't resist noticing her bare skin at her arms, shoulders and upper chest where the first buttons of her blouse were open. There was a sexiness to her look that surprised him for their appointment. He resisted thinking she had intended to be this alluring.

She sat forward. "But, the hearing is about my house, right?" Her eyebrows arched, but her mouth still grinned.

"Yes, you're right. It is. And there's no question it's serious. I just don't want you anxious about being involved directly tomorrow. I do not expect you or Jim to testify tomorrow. It's always possible, should the Court want to question you. But it's unlikely since you have both testified through affidavits. The attorneys agreed to that. The Court will probably go by those for this hearing, and it will be a matter of the lawyers arguing."

She shrugged. "Okay."

"If you have any questions during the hearing, just jot notes to me."

"Alright."

She played with her hands as he described how the Court would proceed with the hearing and how the lawyers would present their arguments. When he summarized the arguments he himself would make, her shoulders raised and she seemed to withdraw into a ball in her seat.

"Hey, hey. Relax. It'll be fine." He smiled.

She nodded.

He stood up, and she gathered her purse and got to her feet.

As he rounded his desk, he saw her bring a hand to her face, covering her eyes. He stepped to her and put a hand on her shoulder.

"Andrea, please stop worrying. Let me worry."

"Okay." She looked up to him and then surprised him. She closed their distance and then put her arms around him. She stayed close to him a second before he could react. His hands went to her arms and started pulling her back, when she looked to his face again.

He started to speak and saw she was leaning in to kiss his cheek.

"Andrea..." He shook his head slowly.

She got to his face and in an instant turned her face from his cheek to his lips. Her lips softly pecked his and remained a moment. As quickly as their lips had touched, their lips parted when she eased her face backward. Her gesture happened in a flash.

He stood still a second, stunned.

She smiled briefly at him and then turned to the door. She waited, and he got that she was waiting on him to open the door. He quickly obliged and she walked outside.

They went without a word out to the reception area, and his mind raced with what to say to her. When they reached where the reception area opened into the hall, she spun to him and hugged him. Before he could react, she parted and backed from him.

"See you tomorrow." Her voice was low.

When she turned and stepped on over to the elevators, he stood in place, frozen. He was still processing the moment, when the elevator doors opened. She hopped inside and then turned to see him still looking to her.

Her eyes lifted and her mouth parted as if in surprise. It hit him. She looked like she was catching him. She acted as if she had caught him watching her leave to ogle her. She was chuckling at him as the elevator doors closed.

He stood just another moment more, shaking his head.

What? What have I gotten myself into?

He replayed the kiss in his mind.

A chill swept over him. His stomach felt queasy. A line had been crossed. He knew that. She had shown she had feelings for him. And right at that moment, it hit him that he cared for her more than he should. *I should get out. Get out of this case.*

The facts spun around. Huge case. Big hearing tomorrow—it would need to be canceled if he left the case. Partnership in the balance.

I'm not stupid. I have to go forward. I'll just have to handle it. Control it. That's all.

⁂

Andrea worried about Jim; he acted too restless. Dinner had been quiet. The takeout Chinese unremarkable. They both anticipated tomorrow's hearing.

"Let's go upstairs." Her voice was even and low-key. She loved the quiet stillness of her big, expansive home. The high ceilings, her favorite original paintings. The soothing way she could set whatever music matched her mood. And the peacefulness when she wanted nothing to disturb her.

Upstairs, Jim undressed and jumped into bed before Andrea could finish removing her makeup and taking out her contacts. She hummed to herself as she listened to him already tossing and turning in the bedroom. *What is with him?*

When she emerged from the bathroom, she moved languidly. She took small steps from the bathroom. Her simple white tee hid little from her braless chest. The string bikini panties made her feel edgy, in a good way.

She made her way over to the bed and stood beside it, facing towards Jim. She checked her phone one last time and then set it on the nightstand. She glanced to Jim lying there. Yes, he was waiting, and yes, he was watching her.

She liked how focused he was on her and she appreciated how utterly predictable he was. Even now, years into their relationship and past the times of passionate sex. He still paid attention. She smiled and saw his eyes pin to the points sticking to the thin, thin fabric of her tee. The dark circles under her top were the last thing he glimpsed before she hit the light.

She positioned herself in the bed as she spoke to him in half whispers. She nudged closer to him and let him feel her hips touch his as she snuggled. He rose to his elbow onto his side. She knew he faced her even though it was dark.

"You should relax."

His hand brushed through his hair. His hand then went onto her stomach. It strummed lightly.

She continued. "We have nothing to worry about. Remember our plan. It's simple. I want you out of the house."

He groaned a bit.

"That's right. You don't want to go. Just let it play out. Stop with this 'what about this' and 'what about that.'"

She heard nothing from him in response, but still he perched there at her side. She wondered if he might ask her something, something that showed he doubted her.

She purred a question. "Will you do something for me?"

Silence still.

"Go do whatever you need to do to take care of yourself."

His voice went sharp. "What?"

She sighed. "Jim, go do *something*. We both need to be alert tomorrow. Rested. So, get some sleep. Don't keep me up."

The thick stress of anticipation for the hearing had required her simple suggestion. He huffed aloud and then flipped over.

For a brief moment, the thought of trying to be sweet to him, and maybe even physical, flitted through her mind. When a chill swept over her, she realized it was out of the question. She hoped he would act on what she recommended, but the sleepier she got, the less she really cared.

In the darkness, one last time she tried to listen for any movement on his side of the bed. Nothing. She turned on her side facing away from him. They had a long day tomorrow.

⁓

Jack trudged from his SUV, through the garage, and to the side door of the house, and he couldn't wait to get inside. Of all nights, the night before the Andrea Turner case was the night he needed some peace and quiet. His workout bag weighed down his shoulder.

Tomorrow is big.

At the door, he paused. He drew a deep breath and then slowly let it go. *Home at last.*

As he stepped inside, he smiled. The air was thick with the scent of fresh warm bread. He could also detect some spices. Carla grinned from the kitchen.

He blinked a couple of quick times, processing the fact she wasn't sitting in the living room with paperwork strewn or the TV on. In fact, there was no television or music at all. Just glasses clinking when she gathered them and took them into the dining room.

A few slow steps into the den took him closer to the kitchen, and he could see into the dining room just on the other side of the kitchen. She had lowered the lights in the dining room and it gave a cozy feel to the settings she had laid out.

In the kitchen, dishes had already been rinsed and put in the dishwasher, but the mix of cheese, garlic, and beef he smelled clued him in to the lasagna that awaited.

"Wow, Carla."

She stood next to a chair on the other side of the table. Her chin was up and her grin still there. Usually, she didn't stand with her chest swelled forward but she did tonight.

Carla's voice rang cheerful as she sat. "Bon appetit."

Jack's cell chimed. It was Gene. Jack's shoulders slumped. Carla's eyes went downward.

Jack circled around the table towards the kitchen. "Let me get a glass of water."

He winced inside. They both knew he had to take the call. She eased into her chair quietly, and he clicked for the call as he retreated to the kitchen.

He appreciated that she had set out a cold beer for him, but he didn't drink the night before a hearing, and for that matter, he didn't want any arguments the night before a hearing. Especially this hearing. He'd slip away, get the water, take care of the call, and pick back up with dinner with her.

"Hi Gene."

"Jack, just wanted to give you a heads-up. I just saw an email. Late this afternoon, Bourne filed a motion. Says that the prenup should be set aside."

"What?" Jack took the bottle from the fridge and then froze.

"Yeah. They make this elaborate argument about a bunch of money Bob evidently funneled to Andrea prior to the wedding. Well, she and Jim had a ton of bills, and they needed it. Of course, they don't say anything about that."

Jack turned from the kitchen and made it to the doorway right before sitting back down in the dining room. Carla's fingers toyed at her wine glass. Her eyes didn't look to Jack and he tried to motion to her to go ahead and start eating. She turned her head to look out the large window into the night sky.

Gene continued. "So, Bourne is arguing that the money amounted to income."

"Ah."

"And, Georgia law requires full financial disclosure by each party for a prenup to be valid. So they say Andrea should have made a written disclosure of Bob's payments but she didn't."

"Therefore they want the prenup thrown out."

"They want the prenup thrown out and they brought it up to the Court right before our hearing."

"Damn it." Jack clipped the words as he watched Carla fold her arms over her chest.

"It's bullshit, but we gotta deal with it."

"Yep."

"Anyway, I emailed you the motion they filed. I've also sent over some research to take a look at. Maybe in the morning before the hearing, we can talk it over if you need to."

"Sounds good."

"Talk to you tomorrow."

Jack hurried back in. "Sorry about that."

Carla nodded and forced a smile.

He returned to the table and sat across from her. "Wow, great spread. Thanks for preparing all this."

Next to his plate was the hot lasagna, a favorite of his. He also loved Caesar salad, and a nice bowl of it awaited. Carla had arranged the table perfectly, from the food and drinks to the silverware and napkins.

They started their salads and Carla stirred in her chair.

"Ready for tomorrow?" She asked.

How do you think I feel the night before the hearing?

"Yeah. Of course. Ready to go."

As good as the salad was, Jack moved on to the lasagna. He sliced into the layers of soft buttery pasta and he wasn't disappointed. She had managed to combine the juicy tomato flavor well with the beef. He tilted his head back as he savored the perfect mix of some ricotta cheese, hot mozzarella cheese, and a crunchy Parmesan cheese crust.

I have to get her to do this more often.

"It's a shame it didn't work out for them." Her words trailed off.

"Huh?" Jack stuck his fork deeper into the heap of lasagna and pulled a large lump of it to his mouth.

"Jim and Andrea. I mean, they're divorcing, right?"

"Well, they're not divorcing tomorrow. It's a hearing about use of the house while the case is pending." *Let's just eat.*

"They've been together, like, since college. That's what you said once before. I just think it's a shame they can't make it work. That's all."

Jack worried where this was heading.

Carla sipped her wine and then held her glass aloft as she studied Jack. "Seeing all that has got to have an effect on you."

He glimpsed her a couple of times between bites of the lasagna. *Is it the ricotta that makes this so damn good? How much did she put in?*

"No. Listen." He tried to talk without also chewing, but he really wanted to eat. "I just know that sometimes things don't work out. When they don't, I'm there to help solve the problem so they can move on. It does not make me cynical. It *doesn't.*"

He worried for a second that there was an edge to his words, but he refocused on the beefy portion of the remaining portion on his plate. Then, there was the rest of his garlic bread.

Carla watched her fork and took slow, careful bites.

Jack tried to slow down and set his knife on the table. "How are you doing?"

Her eyes peered up at him, and for a second they just looked at each other.

Her words came soft and gradually. "I'm fine. Work was busy."

Jack nodded. "Everything okay?"

She batted her eyes as she nibbled some of her salad. She put her fork down and sipped her wine. She kept her words measured.

"I've been thinking a lot about stuff."

"Stuff?"

"About us."

This dinner wasn't the first time they had discussed their relationship recently. Jack knew the state of their relationship had been a simmering issue for Carla. But this felt different. Why did she have to do this the night before one of his biggest hearings?

Here the entrée wasn't even finished, and she had placed the relationship issue front and center. His mind kept returning to the motion that was in his email, too. *Bourne's such a bastard. He wants the judge to be disinclined to rule for Andrea tomorrow.*

"I just don't understand your thinking. At all, Jack." It seemed she couldn't contain herself any longer. She pulled a deep breath. "I don't know what we're doing. It's been two years. Two years now." She put her napkin on the table.

"Hey, things have been good." He tried to ignore the last couple of weeks she had been brooding about this very issue. "We're living together. We're both busy. Life is good." He emphasized 'good.'

"Jack, you are thirty-five. I am twenty-nine. Yes, life is good, but life is also about growing. It's about creating the right life, you know?" She struck a plaintive tone.

"Carla, I know you're anxious, but why rush? We're living together. We love each other. Why can't we have it that way and enjoy that, and then give things more time?"

Jack tensed for anger, but instead her eyes cast down to the table and her shoulders sagged.

She half-whispered. "More time. Yeah, we're living together. We've lived together for a year, Jack. A *year*."

She looked up and peered deeply into his eyes. "I want a family. I want kids." She took another breath. "I love you, and I believe you love me."

"Listen, I'm in a challenging place right now. I need my focus. I have to. I've worked my whole life for this. You have to understand that." He moved his knife and fork onto his plate, angling from the lower-right up to left. "You know I have the Turner hearing tomorrow. Of all nights for you to bring this up..."

Carla's bottom lip quivered. "I had to bring this up tonight."

Across the table, Jack stiffened. He set his jaw and his lips pressed. He wouldn't give way on this. He also needed to get upstairs and get on his laptop to see that motion.

"We are good, Carla. There is still plenty of time. But, now is not a good time. They will evaluate me for partner this year. I just got these two new cases. I'm sorry. I just can't take on more right now."

She nodded and lifted her glass. The last of the wine went very slowly before she spoke again.

"You're really a great guy, Jack. You're compassionate. Sweet. We're just in different places. That's all...I'm sorry."

His eyes went from her to his plate and back to her. He

hadn't expected her to understand after all. Jack spoke softly but clearly. "I'm sorry, too."

She brought her fingers to her eyes and dabbed them. She blinked hard a couple of times.

He despised how this had made her feel. He tried to fix it. "Hey, let's do something for your sister. Let's take her and Robert out to dinner."

She closed her eyes a second and then opened them to look back at him. She leaned slightly in when she answered him. "Let's just wait on all of that for now."

His brow wrinkled. "Huh?"

She sat back in her chair and her hands clutched her napkin. Her eyes moistened. "Let's just not even get into all of that. You've got court tomorrow. That's all."

He studied her a moment more. A strange notion started inside him. "We're talking about dinner plans with your sister... Before, you said you had to bring this up tonight. What's going on?"

A tear escaped the corner of her eye. She squinted. "Cathy's garage apartment has become available. It won't be for long. In fact, there's someone else who was interested in it."

His stomach clenched. "Are you leaving me?"

"Jack, I love you."

"You love me...'but,' right?"

"Jack, please let's not go there now. Not tonight. You were right. I should not have even brought this up. I just...if...if I didn't tell you tonight then I didn't think I would ever be able to tell you."

"Carla, I love you, too. I hope you know that."

She nodded vigorously and wiped at her eyes.

He stayed gentle. "And, I get it. It takes more than that."

She started to nod again, but her head just bowed. Her shoulders shook and she hopped from her chair. Her hand went to her mouth as she walked from the table and left the room.

He swallowed hard and gazed out the window into the black night. He sat there, staring for some time. When his eyes came back to the room, he glimpsed the table, the plates, and the unfinished food.

Upstairs, he could hear Carla going down the stairs from the master bedroom to the front door, and then back. She made the same trip three times. Then, she called out from the front.

"I'll be back Saturday for my things."

"Alright."

The door closed and she was gone.

He forced himself up to find his computer bag. He still needed to read some research. It was something he could do before sleeping alone for the first time in two years.

5

How could she?

JACK AWOKE BEFORE HIS ALARM EVER SOUNDED at five a.m., and he was shaved, showered, ready, and out the door by six. Something about the dark pre-dawn comforted him on mornings like this. He felt ahead of the game.

He caught himself sitting stiffly behind the wheel as he drove down the interstate to the courthouse. Now and then, he slowly shook his head. He told himself it wasn't so much the break-up itself as it was that she had done it. He choked a laugh in disbelief.

Twice he caught himself driving too fast. His thoughts wanted to ricochet from Carla to Andrea's case to Richard Bourne and the expected arguments.

Halfway to downtown, his stomach settled and his mind cleared. He had always had his practice and that was all he had ever let himself really depend on, and things weren't different now. They absolutely were not.

He called Gene, and they spent several minutes talking about how Jack could deal with Bourne's new argument. They talked about the research Gene sent the previous night. Gene reassured Jack. Reminded Jack that he was ready.

He exited at the downtown cloverleaf and angled to get to the parking deck. He left the night's surprise behind him. He had a battle ahead. Once he got out of the SUV, there would be no more thoughts of Carla and the break-up. None.

All that matters is this fight this morning. Only this.

✑

Courtrooms have pews like churches.

Jack noticed this every time. The pews, the portraits of past judges looking down from the wall, stern and dignified, the way the judge's bench always perched higher and formidably. Even the air itself felt thicker.

And every time he made sure to get to court early. The hearing didn't start until nine a.m., and Jack had arrived, parked, passed through security, and found a spot in the attorney's conference room by seven-fifteen. Out came the file and notes and Jack got back to preparing. He followed each argument outlined in his notes, and then tried to think further about the opposing arguments Bourne would make.

He had to make himself not think of Bourne and his record of wins. It served no purpose. He did relish that Bourne wasn't sitting in the attorney's conference room preparing. *Do what you need to do.*

Jack paid attention to his watch and phone. He had arranged to meet Andrea outside the courtroom at eight-thirty. He wanted to get there first. He didn't want Andrea finding herself sitting alone either around Jim or, even worse, around Jim and his lawyer, without her own lawyer there. Jack wouldn't let that happen.

At eight-thirty, several people congregated outside the courtroom, but Jack was the only one in his case. No Andrea. No Hadley. No Bourne.

He busied again with his notes and followed his watch closely. At eight-fifty, he fretted. No one else? Was he in the wrong place? He exchanged texts with Andrea, and she said she was getting parked. He told her he was going on inside the courtroom and to meet him there.

Jack pushed through the initial doors of the courtroom, passed through a foyer-like space before a second set of doors, and then a looming presence emerged as he opened the second set of doors into the courtroom. Jack held the doors for whomever was behind him and he half-turned to see the person.

At eye-level, the calm, dark eyes of Richard Bourne pierced his own. No smile or words came. Jack wasn't sure he hadn't flinched, but he deeply hoped he hadn't. They both went on into the courtroom, with Jack venturing to the right side of the gallery and Bourne peeling off to the left.

Jack took a seat on the first row, and when he glanced over to his left, Bourne had settled into the first row as well. On his side, Bourne let a tall, lanky younger guy into the row to sit beside him. The young man had a tight, dirty-blonde ponytail and a very expensive suit with no tie. Bourne shook the younger man's hand and they started talking. *That must be Hadley.* Jack would confirm this with Andrea, but she wasn't there. At once, Jack felt chagrin at the obvious higher quality of Hadley's suit. *What the hell is that made of, anyway?*

At nine a.m., a bailiff loudly proclaimed, "ALL RISE, the Honorable Robert Speer presiding."

Everyone in the courtroom stood and a moment passed before the Judge let everyone be seated. Jack looked over his shoulder into the audience. He searched frantically around. No Andrea.

Judge Speer shuffled the papers up on the bench and thin beads of sweat formed on Jack's upper lip. Judge Speer would soon start calling out the names of the cases on the court's docket for the morning. Andrea's would be one of them. Jack would be expected to announce whether he was ready to proceed with the case.

Where the hell is she?

Jack looked to Judge Speer and a metal clanking sound came from the back of the courtroom. It had to be the doors at the back there. Jack saw the Judge's eyes sweep to the back and Jack turned to look there, too. A young woman in a white dress struggled to pry the doors open and then she let them fall back shut with a louder banging than the first.

There stood Andrea. She faced into the courtroom and waited a couple of seconds. All eyes were on her.

In the slightest of gestures, her face lifted with poise. She stood still for a beat and then she ran her tongue over her lips. She glanced around the courtroom and pulled the strap of her purse higher on her shoulder.

Andrea's eyes paused at the front of the courtroom and Jack followed her gaze. Judge Speer returned her look, as yet noncommittal. Jack took his eyes back to Andrea and she was tucking strands of hair behind an ear, and her chin hadn't lowered.

Jack raised himself a bit where he sat, and the move caught Andrea's attention. She smiled to him and started in his direction. As she made her way to him, Jack looked back to the Judge. Judge Speer studied Jack a quick moment but then launched into his call of the cases on the docket.

As names of cases were called out, Andrea slipped into the pew beside him. "Hi," she whispered.

Her white dress appeared plain and conservative from a distance, and up close, it still seemed discreet but clearly was silk-like and high-end. Jack leaned closer and said hello, and there was a vague, but alluring, jasmine scent wafting about.

Andrea's case was called and both attorneys rose to their feet.

"Good morning, Gentlemen."

"Good morning, Your Honor." Bourne and Jack agreed on something for the last time that day.

"After I call the rest of this docket, we'll start with your case." The Judge went back to his listings.

Jack flipped through his notes, Andrea didn't interrupt him, and the Judge stayed true to his word. Before long, the arguments for the case of Turner v. Hadley got underway.

"Your Honor, we are before you today on Ms. Turner's claim for temporary use and possession of the house. This case involves a relatively short marriage. There are no minor children. And, there is a prenuptial agreement."

Jack paused for effect, as Gene had taught him to do previously. The idea was to let the idea or argument resonate with the judge or jury to whom you were arguing. Don't rush things or somehow lessen the impact of the argument by moving on just because you're unimpeded.

He continued. "Significantly, Ms. Turner had acquired and lived in the house before the marriage. It's her house. It's titled in her and her father's name."

Jack saw the Judge shoot a glance over to his opposing counsel and felt relief that this point had registered, as it evidently had.

"In Ms. Turner's affidavit in support of our claim, which is on file," Jack held aloft his copy of the affidavit, "she sets forth her testimony of how she obtained this property prior to the marriage, with the assistance of her father, and the deed is attached as an exhibit to the affidavit. These circumstances cannot be disputed by Mr. Hadley. There is no denying the purchase date, the deed, or the source of the funds that bought this home."

Jack reached to the lectern, and he put down the affidavit and picked up the copy of the prenuptial agreement.

"Judge, the prenuptial agreement is clear as well. Very clear. The house is premarital, and it is owned by Ms. Turner. While the enforceability of this prenuptial may be technically still at issue, it would take substantial evidence—evidence that has not been provided—to overcome or invalidate this prenuptial agreement."

Judge Speer spoke evenly. "Mr. Bourne filed a motion to set aside the prenuptial agreement yesterday. He doesn't agree with your take on the enforceability of this agreement."

"Judge," Jack leaned forward, "their chief argument has to do with disclosure."

"An important factor in our case law."

"Yes, Judge. Disclosure is important. But disclosure usually comes up when a party is arguing that an asset was hidden, or that some income wasn't known by the parties."

"Mr. Adams, isn't that what Mr. Bourne states here, that the money provided by your client's father was income that wasn't disclosed?"

"Yes, Judge, that is the argument." Jack took a deep breath. "However, the parties had been together two years already when that had happened. They had taken trips and spent money about which Mr. Hadley was well aware. All that had to be paid for. Paid for by someone."

Jack saw Judge Speer glimpse over to Hadley, and Jack kept arguing.

"Judge, we expect the evidence will show that Mr. Hadley knew Ms. Turner's father was helping with that. Mr. Turner helped fund these parties, both of them, by paying these bills. Now, Mr. Hadley is trying to use this against Ms. Turner by making it sound like some mysterious source of income. It wasn't mysterious at all."

Judge Speer jutted his chin and stayed silent. Jack took that as a good sign and pressed on.

"We expect the prenuptial agreement will be enforced, and all that we ask today is for temporary relief, that the parties have their distance. Going through this divorce—and the tension that comes with that—is something that better occurs with the parties not spending each day together, right there in the same household."

Judge Speer swayed in place and his face tightened.

Jack tried to strike a reassuring tone. "The courts typically will award sole temporary use of a home..."

Judge Speer interjected. "You know, lawyers ask me all the

time. 'Judge, give us temporary use of the home.' I get it. I understand it. But, you know, Mr. Adams, the other side of that coin is that the other spouse is kicked out of their home. I mean, kicked right out."

The Judge shrugged hard before continuing. "People act like it's akin to handing out a speeding ticket or something. But you know, I'm kicking a person out of their home, Mr. Adams."

Jack nodded, but didn't miss a beat. "I appreciate that, Your Honor. It's serious and something that shouldn't be done lightly. Absolutely. At the same time, the law recognizes the stress and... volatility that can come in divorces." Jack waited till Judge Speer's eyes met his own and then spoke directly. "Mr. Hadley doesn't want this divorce. There is real antagonism here. That's an atmosphere that is fraught with risk."

Jack paused and his words hung in the silence of the courtroom. He waited on a counter from the Judge that he would address, but none came and he kept moving.

"Judge, we've detailed in our motion and affidavit on file with the Court the various relatives and ability Mr. Hadley has available to him for temporary residence. In this case, the temporary relief can be managed."

Jack shifted his weight forward to the balls of his feet. He decided to return to the arguments he had prepared and handle whatever other comments the Judge brought up.

"We respectfully submit that the existence and pendency of this written agreement between the parties is yet another factor that should weigh heavily in favor of Ms. Turner having sole temporary use and possession of this home... her home."

"Finally, Your Honor," Jack took a deep breath to bring his argument to a close, "Ms. Turner sets forth in her affidavit, both candidly and clearly, just how vulnerable and very concerned she is. She describes how Mr. Hadley has acted determinedly to try to dissuade her from proceeding with this divorce. He's gone so far as to push her for sex, no doubt knowing, full well, that if such were to occur it would be grounds to dismiss these proceedings altogether."

Jack paused for effect. Bourne had to stay silent and the courtroom was dead quiet. "This isn't healthy. This isn't safe. And most of all it isn't fair, Your Honor. Ms. Turner should have her peace and she should have distance from this man as she goes through this ordeal."

Jack was moving towards his chair when he heard the Judge call to him. "Mr. Adams."

"Yes, Your Honor."

"What do you say to Mr. Hadley's point that he has no place to live *and* that he's not working? He doesn't have the resources of Ms. Turner, he says. He argues that the validity of the prenuptial agreement remains undecided, of course."

From the Judge's face, Jack couldn't quite discern how seriously the Court was taking their argument, but he wasn't going to underestimate it either.

"Judge, the case has been pending forty-five days. Mr. Hadley is able-bodied and healthy. He *should* be working. Plus, he has a sister and a brother who live in town. He can make other arrangements, and he already should have made them. Mr. Hadley's reference to Ms. Turner's 'resources' is really just a reference to Mr. Turner. Bob Turner. And, candidly, Bob Turner has been the resource for these parties for long enough."

Jack waited for just a moment, but then he continued on to his seat. The silence in the courtroom was deafening to him.

He was never quite sure how these hearings went immediately. He was just too caught up in it.

Behind him, Jack heard the Judge's voice growl at the approaching Bourne.

"Mr. Bourne, what about it? Why hasn't Mr. Hadley made other arrangements?"

A joyous chill swept Jack when he heard the Judge's remark.

Bourne's voice boomed back full. "Your Honor, this has been Mr. Hadley's home for some three years now. There are serious questions about this so-called prenuptial agreement, and as Mr. Adams admits, the validity of it remains to be seen. It's neither fair nor reasonable for Mr. Adams to assume that it will be. That remains to be determined."

Bourne seemed to bore into the Judge's gaze as he intoned. "Mr. Hadley has been devastated by all this. He left a promising and lucrative opportunity to stay in this city and get married, putting everything he has into this. Now, Ms. Turner is done with him? She wants a divorce and him on the street without regard for the fact he is unemployed and quite vulnerable himself."

"She owned the house before the marriage, Mr. Bourne." The Court was unequivocal. Jack's pulse raced.

"Judge, it was acquired before the marriage alright. But, it was just two months before the marriage. They both moved in there together. They've maintained and improved it together. There is no disputing that whatsoever."

Bourne lifted his head and spoke carefully, imploringly. "Your Honor, the fair thing to do is wait to see what comes from the prenuptial issues. These parties should remain on equal footing until a decision is made about the prenuptial.

And, truth be told, it's Ms. Turner who has the greater ability to relocate anyway."

"Objection!" Jack was on his feet. "There is absolutely no evidence of that. None! Mr. Bourne is alluding to Ms. Turner's father, and her father is not a party to this. There is no evidence they've submitted that Mr. Turner is ready to pour more money into this...*situation*."

Bourne shot back. "We filed yesterday our argument about Mr. Turner's income for her. A hundred thousand dollars to Ms. Turner that she conveniently omitted in her financial disclosure at the time of the prenuptial agreement. That's before the Court, Your Honor."

Jack countered. "Judge, there were three trips and numerous parties. Those expenses weren't going to be paid by Mr. Hadley. Not at all."

"Easy, take it easy," the Judge was waving his hands for both lawyers to be seated. "Here's what I'm going to do. I am ordering sole temporary use and possession of the home to Ms. Turner. It's a horrible idea to keep these two under one roof while they go through this. She's on the deed, and while we haven't decided the validity of the prenuptial agreement, I'm not going to ignore it either. This is the way it's going to be until further order of the Court."

The Judge brought his gavel down and recessed the hearing. Jack sensed Andrea exhale and slump forward in relief next to him. He turned to her.

"You okay?" He asked her quietly.

She looked up into his eyes. Her own eyes wet and soft. "Yeah. Jack...I can't thank you enough. I am so glad I can be away from him. You just don't know."

Jack nodded understandingly, and he gathered his papers to leave. He felt a deep sigh of his own as he did.

He walked Andrea from the courtroom downstairs. They spoke of details for the ruling. The Court hadn't specified how long Hadley was given to vacate, but Jack would push for ten days when he submitted the proposed Order the following day. He reminded Andrea as he had before that she shouldn't hesitate to call the police if she felt fearful or endangered.

When they reached the parking lot, she looked up at him, her smile bright. "Thank you so very much again. You don't know just what a relief this is."

"I'm just glad it has worked out."

She reached her arms out to him, and Jack felt a pang of apprehension. He briefly met her embrace and noticed her closeness much too well, he figured.

"Take care. Call me if you need me." He said it reassuringly, and she was still smiling to him as he turned and left. The sight of her soft blue eyes lingered in his mind.

The walk to his own car was light and surreal. He was ecstatic at things going as well as he could have hoped. He had felt confident, but one could just never be sure. You just never knew.

As he drove away, he took care of the next items he needed to be sure about. He pulled his phone up and dictated a short draft of the order he would want the Court to sign and file. He then dictated a letter he would want his assistant to draft to Bourne pressing Hadley to settle now that Andrea was in the house herself. The traffic was starting to intensify as he headed in the direction of his gym.

Jack maneuvered his SUV to an outside lane and continued his mental to-do list. He dictated again, and this time he was describing all of the things he'd done before the hearing to prepare for it that day, the attendance and trial of the hearing itself, and he described his brief time with Andrea afterwards. Then, he made a quick calculation of his time and he recorded his time entry that would be billed to her.

Next was a call that he savored. He rang Gene who was quick to answer.

"Yeah?" Gene's voice was ragged. On edge.

"She's in and it looks like she's in to stay."

"YES! Yes! Excellent, Jack, excellent." Gene was no doubt smiling on the other end. "How was she?"

"Uh, shaky, but very relieved."

"Okay. Well listen, good work. I'm going to call Bob right now. Go take a break this afternoon. You deserve it. See you tomorrow."

Jack found himself exhaling deeply again, still taking in the result. Such relief.

His cell buzzed aloud and he looked down. The caller's name was distinct.

"Andrea Turner."

6

ANDREA'S VOICE SOUNDED LIKE MUSIC.

"You were wonderful this afternoon," Andrea gushed. Jack could hear a smile on the other end of the line as she spoke.

"Yeah?" He couldn't help grinning. "Thanks, but you know, I think it was just a matter of the facts being on our side."

"Jack, I'm beyond words. You saved my life."

Admiration from Andrea Turner. The ultimate spoil of victory.

They had just left the courthouse within the hour, so Jack sensed more than just a congratulatory call. Jack's SUV sped past traffic on the interstate. "I'm sure you heard from him."

Her voice lowered and thickened. "Oh yeah, he's not happy. He's not in control. You know?"

"Hey, listen, remember you don't have to play his games or buy into his craziness. He only has the power you give to him." He wanted to gird her against the pressure Hadley would likely bring on her. Jack had seen too many situations where the fight waged outside the courtroom, and the wits of the psychologically stronger party sometimes made a difference. He wanted to prevent that here with Andrea's situation.

"I know you're right. It's just hard sometimes. That's all. Days like today help though. You standing up to him, helping me stand up to him. He really didn't expect that."

Jack passed several exits towards his gym and an early finish to his day. *Perfect.*

"As long as you understand that now is when it starts. That process of standing your own ground. The sooner it starts, the better off you'll be." He wanted to reinforce her progress.

They both paused and Jack started to wind-up the call. The intensity of the day had drained him. He was ready to decompress.

Before he could say anything, she spoke again, sounding softer, different.

"Um, we've talked so much about this house." Her voice definitely sounded different. Raspy.

Her voice lowered, but was clear. "You've asked a lot of questions about it. Maybe you should come by and see it."

His breath caught. His foot eased from the accelerator.

"Well..." Jack's mouth hung open as he tried to quickly calculate his response.

Instinctively, he knew he shouldn't go there, not now. It was midday. They had been in court. Court was over. She was his client. She was asking him to come to her house. *You know what's going on here.*

A kind of vertigo set in, as he knew just how badly he'd love to go there. He'd love to see her there. He realized he had questions and wondered about what it must be like there. A part of him thought that he could answer his own questions at the same time he answered questions about her case.

God, her eyes. Those deep, captivating eyes. Inviting. With this win today, the case is practically over. It'll be negotiated out. I've worked my ass off and this is what comes of it. Andrea. I want to see her. Whatever else I may know, I know that.

He exhaled. "Okay, I probably shouldn't right now, but if now works for you, then—"

"Great!" she chirped.

And, at that moment on that Thursday afternoon, Jack went in her direction rather than to the gym, out to get something to eat, or just home. *Why not? The case is as good as over now.*

The two-story suburban house sat perched on a hill. Several tall trees dotted the sides of the house, and large full bushes protected the front. Clean, white walls rose into the air and numerous draped windows squared the front. A wide drive climbed from the street off to the left. Jack pulled his SUV up as he peered at the house.

Jack stepped reluctantly up to the house that had previously been just an address for him. An inner voice screamed for him to leave. He rang the bell and without meaning to, he held his breath.

He stood there at the door in the cool afternoon air. *Leave, you idiot. What do you think you're doing?*

His mind conjured a question he could ask her to get her

to explain why the house was unique. *Yeah. Find out how this place is unique. This is all just fine.*

The door eased open. Andrea's bright, smiling face appeared from around the door.

"Hey." Her tone was muted. They stared at each other. She pulled the door further open.

She moved to her right and stayed poised a moment. She had changed from her courtroom clothes. Now, a thin white sundress hung from her shoulders. The top of it held two distinct points and the rest of it wrinkled in places. Casual, like she may have just slipped it over her head. Her feet were bare and her toes bore a crimson polish.

"C'mon in." She waved him forward.

Into the foyer, he followed her past a slender wooden armoire and mirror. She glimpsed over her shoulder to him as they entered the den. In the background, the sounds of classical music wafted about.

He reacted to its pull right away. "I like the music."

"It's Maurice Ravel." She touched the top of the long deep, brown sofa, as she glided past it. "I like reading in here."

She walked from the den to the adjoining kitchen. She took a couple of steps, where she looked to the cabinets, to his face, and then forward. Her path took her around a long quartz island that ran down the center of the kitchen.

They kept going, and left the kitchen into a wide dining room that stretched to a floor-to-ceiling window on the far side. She didn't even pause as she kept moving from the dining room to veer into an exquisite living room. Fine, well-crafted furniture was perfectly situated. He wished he knew more about furniture; these pieces appeared finely made.

He spoke up. "Nice."

She half-turned again, not stopping, but responding up to him with a delicate tone. "It was important to me that you come see this place."

They rounded the side of the living room and started up a staircase. Her small, pale feet climbed the first couple of hardwood stairs, as she talked from above him.

"The sound system goes throughout the house. It's one of my favorite things. I love having that."

His eyes couldn't help but follow her hips go from side to side as they ascended. Her feet took their time from one step to the next, and he noticed just how gauze-like her simple dress was. Perfectly smooth.

The hem of the dress stopped at her knees. Her calves showed lines of muscles with each step, her skin taut, and he cautioned himself not to peek higher as they neared the top.

"You were great today, Jack," her voice trailed up ahead.

His eyes betrayed him anyway, and the last few steps up gave him the view of her thighs as they disappeared into the dress. His chest raised and lowered, and a warmth descended over him, as she still didn't stop. She turned to him, motioned down the hallway with one hand, while drifting in the other direction.

"Down there are two guest rooms."

"I love your place." He followed her down the hall, her hand grazed a bannister to their right, her fingertips tracing the wood. "You're right about the sound system. Nice hearing that throughout."

She got to the doorway of a large bedroom at the end of the hall. He figured it was the master bedroom. He tried thinking of other things, but the sight of her turning to him and the effortless swish of the dress held him. When her half-open eyes searched directly up at him, his mouth fell open. He struggled. "Uh, this place is really something else."

A slight grin graced her lips, as her eyes darted back and forth on his.

He could feel his heart pound in his chest, while her eyes held his own. A lightness engulfed him. Something about her grin said she saw deep inside him.

He mumbled, "Andrea, I should probably get going."

Her tone was low. "This is the master bedroom."

He blinked a couple of times.

Her voice went to a half-whisper. "This is my favorite part of the house."

She turned and seemed to float into the bedroom. Her hands came behind her and one clasped the other, holding together as her bare foot eased further inside.

A huge bed centered the room, with a white, plush cover padding the top. A wide, curtained window stretched the far wall, and clouds dimmed the light from outside. Strings from Ravel's music downstairs slowed their pace. A lone flute wafted in the background.

She spoke slowly. "I guess everybody feels like their home is special."

"It's beautiful, really." He swayed in place a moment as she circled back around to face him.

"Well, I thought it was important you see this place we keep talking about, you know?" Her face rose slightly as she said it, and he noticed her upturned eyes—provocative, deliberate. She was smiling, looking directly at him. "Don't you think it helps?"

Jack stopped in place a moment and looked back at her. He

struggled to focus on what she was saying instead of on her blue eyes that danced as she said it.

"Well, it helps, but..." His voice trailed, as he struggled with what he needed to do. "Andrea, you know I have to go, right?" She didn't answer. She let a moment more pass where she looked straight up to him, and then she changed. He watched her bright, knowing grin fade into a more serious look. She was intense. Her lips barely parted, as she paused. She mesmerized him and he felt emotion swell within him.

He felt very aware that the dynamic between them had changed. He felt compelled by her. She looked at him longingly. His eyes fixed on her gaze until, seemingly out of his control, they drifted downward to her breasts, barely covered by her sundress. He imagined leaning over and kissing the side of her neck and drifting downward with slow kisses, and finally pulling away the scanty material that stretched across her breasts.

It was then, in a subtle move, she slowly brought her hands up. Jack started to react but wasn't sure how he would. Instead, he watched her hands go to her shoulders.

His heart raced. He turned toward the door. "I should go."

She walked past him before he even took a step. She stood beside the door and faced him directly.

He looked at her puzzled as she barely tilted her head, as if foretelling a decision. Her small hands went to the tops of her shoulders and each one brushed off her shoulders. He felt a reaction at once when the hands moved the small straps off her. The hands stayed up, but the straps fell swiftly down her sides.

His mouth parted as he watched the thin cover of her sundress fall away and down her body. Bare, tan skin was revealed as the dress came down, and he immediately noticed how no bra was in place. Her nude body stood revealed right in front of him. Smooth, pale skin. The two taut, pink nipples that raised and lowered with her breath. Her flat belly tapered into a mound.

They both moved at once, and all the tension and emotion of the past weeks came to the surface. Their mouths pressed together, and his arms wrapped around her. He was still savoring her soft mouth when her hands started working his shirt off.

Her face left his and her tender lips trailed down his neck. He gasped as her hands unspooled his belt, and undid his trousers. He put his hands in her soft hair and lowered his face into it. A whiff of lavender teased him.

She pushed at his trousers on his hips and they fell away. His blood surged and he drew a deep breath. His hands tilted her face up to his and he kissed her hard.

Her torso melded to him and she hopped, making her face bump their kiss. Her strong, lithe legs squeezed around his hips. Another surge raced through him and he was sure she felt it, too.

He moved them the two steps over to the bed and lowered them to it, their mouths still working at each other. She twisted under him, and at first he thought she was straightening. Instead, her legs rocked back and higher. Her knees slid further up his back. He was surprised by her eagerness, but it enthralled him.

Her hair fanned on the pillow underneath her, and they both could hear her soft moans. Her hands traced his cheeks and moved into his hair as she seemed to try to experience every-thing about him. They entwined and joined intensely.

Everything about her was soft and smooth. Her eyes narrowed with their intensity, while her mouth gaped and trembled. As much as she seemed vulnerable, her hands plied his shoulders and back. Her legs alternated between wrapping him and squeezing to him. Over and over, she surpassed any expectations or thoughts he had.

They tossed about on the bed, and he tried to savor every part of her. Whenever he thought he knew how she'd react, she surprised him. What didn't change, and didn't waver, was her focus. She remained present, absorbed, and attentive. He'd never experienced her kind of presence.

Afterward, she rested beside him motionless. She seemed so calm, he marveled. How very different from just weeks ago. They were so urgent and so furiously moving only just a bit ago, and now... now this. She tilted her head to the side just enough to glimpse him and to grin at him, and he reflexively grinned back. He had to fight a foolish giddiness that would have been very easy.

Remember this, he told himself, remember how she looks. Remember how this feels. Remember the birds you hear outside and a dog barking a couple of houses down. There's the blue openness in her eyes, and faint flecks of what can only be perspiration on her forehead. *Remember all of this.*

She looked up at him. Her eyes were all that moved, going from his eyes slowly to his lips and back. They were at once vulnerable and knowing to him, and he found this intoxicating. He swept a hand to her hair and lightly brushed it. It felt so soft to him, and she reacted so easily to him. Her chest rose and set to her deep breathing at being in this moment with him.

Deep inside him, underneath the comfort of being with her in her bed, he knew everything had changed. He had been her lawyer. He had acted for her and looked after her interests, and now he had made love to her. A clear line he had always known about and been told about was forever crossed and behind him. He couldn't change that fact and he couldn't help but regret it. *What have I done?*

ঔঔ

FRIDAY, APRIL 1, 2011

"Let's bring some of that Andrea Turner hearing magic to the Monica Henderson case." Gene grinned broadly as he said it.

Jack felt a pang in his stomach. He couldn't share Gene's enthusiasm. Jack stood in Gene's office doorway and relished catching Gene when he was available for a moment.

"Gene, I gotta tell you. I'm concerned."

Gene flinched a bit and then shrugged Jack off.

Jack persisted. "The other side is talking settlement, sounding reasonable, and Monica's having no part of it. She just doesn't care."

"She doesn't care?"

"Well," Jack slowed his words, "she doesn't care about the financial part of it. For her, it's all about the affair. She wants him to hurt."

Gene chuckled and nodded. "Listen, keep getting it ready. Meet with her. Tell her there's still plenty of time. This is just a temporary hearing. She needs to understand that we get this temporary order in place and then we can turn our focus to the conduct issues. This is just to set up temporary custody and

103

support. George Henderson isn't going to get away with a thing."

Jack returned to his office, and two different moods stirred him. He wanted badly to see Andrea. The sooner the better. Being with her energized him in a way he hadn't been in a while. At the same time, he needed badly to stay on top of his cases and his billing. This was a critical time for him. He mustn't let up.

A couple of hours into his day, a text message brightened his phone. "Good morning." He reflexively thought of Carla after he read it, but a further glance revealed Andrea had sent it. He grinned.

"Good morning to you." His thumbs worked away.

Her message came fast. "I think I had a weird dream last night."

He tried to imagine her at her house, texting him and probably in bed. "Yeah? What's that?" He asked.

"This hot guy came over and gave me a good going. ;-) Had to have been a dream."

He chuckled. His thumbs moved swiftly. "Sounds like an intense dream."

"Oh yeah."

"Maybe you'll get lucky and the dream will reoccur."

"Yeah?"

"Yeah. Definitely."

There was a lull for a while. Either Andrea was busy, she was contemplating what she'd say or she was tantalizing him. Or perhaps all three. He tried mightily to refocus on his work. He was poring over documents for Monica Henderson's case.

Monica's case could be won or lost in some of the details in these documents. Time was ticking by. *Focus.*

"Hmmm." Andrea's short text was welcomed by him.

She took her time it seemed. Then, before he could parry back, she texted again. "Maybe what I should do is nap at lunch today. Maybe my dream guy will come back."

"Mmmmm." His reply was deliberately brief.

But, he thought quickly. The thoughts were all involving her lips, mouth, and body. He punched at keys. "Entirely possible. Sounds like a good idea. Positive thinking and all."

"(grins)" She paused for effect. "So, I should get in bed for lunch?"

Her wit stirred him. He took a deep breath.

"Yeah." He answered. "I see."

Another pause, and Jack considered some witty follow-up rather than the legal questions on his desk laid out in front of him. Before he made some smart, sexy reply, she wrote him again.

"The door will be unlocked."

It was all her message said. He loved the daring of it, and inside he was ready to leave immediately. He stopped himself from firing off a graphic message that bluntly said what he was going to do with her. He was tempted but thought better. He kept his own message back to her short and direct.

"Will be there at noon."

He started to put his phone down and then considered at least some further tease back. He typed away.

"You should be ready for me."

Her response was fast. Almost immediate, and the quickness wasn't lost on him. "I will."

He exhaled with the effects of their exchange burning about him. He pictured her prone in bed and glancing at her cell with half-closed eyes. There was a satisfaction in knowing that behind her lively blue eyes she was thinking of them together. He glanced over to his watch and saw it was 10:24. He'd leave his office at 11:30. Now, he absolutely had to concentrate on the Monica Henderson case. He fretted that there were legal responses that should have already been sent by the other attorney. He whipped through the sections of the questions and requests, and he mentally checked for the areas of inquiry he needed to be there. Conduct, witnesses, documents, finances, and more. Ever present though was the image of Andrea waiting for him at her house. Readying for him.

The phone pierced Jack's fog of daydreaming about Andrea. It was George Henderson's attorney, Rob Patten, calling in.

"What's the word on our offer?"

Jack could feel his stomach tighten. "Talking to her today."

"Listen, she's probably giving you resistance," Patten paused. Jack didn't bite, "But, she needs to get realistic. There's enough shit here to smear everyone. Is that what she really wants? Let's resolve this damn thing."

"Monica just wants what's fair."

"No, she wants to hurt him. She wants his balls."

Jack clenched his eyes shut at the sound of his own words coming back at him.

"I'm talking to her today and will be back in touch."

Jack hung up feeling anxious. He immediately called Monica.

"Let's talk later today." Jack tried not to sound as tight as he felt with her.

"Yes, absolutely."

"Sounds good."

Jack returned to his documents. He knew his work was cut

out for him later that day. Fortunately, lunch would be a good break. When he thought it would never arrive, there was a ping from his cell that indicated it was finally 11:30. His computer showed an email from Richard Bourne. He scanned over it quickly, saw it was about discussing the status of the case, and winced. Any other time, his reflex would be to either return Bourne's call, or at least schedule a call back on his calendar. That's just the way he worked.

Instead, he hopped up. Grabbing his jacket, out the door he went. He would get back to Bourne later.

◈

He went to her at lunch.

Jack's SUV lumbered about the suburban side streets to get to Andrea's subdivision. Even leaving just before lunch put him in traffic. It gave him too much time to be anxious. He was excited to see her, but it troubled him to be taking a block of time from his routine like this. It wasn't that he didn't want to. He was determined to. It just put him outside his orderly ways. He reminded himself that he must make up this time for his cases.

He put in a quick call to an opposing attorney in a case about some documents, and then texted a time entry to capture the billing for the call. He started to make one more call in the time he had when a text came in. It was Andrea.

"You have to get over here. I need you." A sly grin escaped him as he relished the thought of her so anticipating his coming over. Just as he was himself.

"Nearly there." He punched his response.

The streets in her subdivision were as he remembered them, and with two quick turns he was there. No one appeared out in the neighborhood even though it was midday, and he was glad for that. His SUV was in the drive and he hopped out quickly. *Finally. Here with her.*

He bounded up the walk to her front door, and he paused, seeing her front door ajar. He slowed only a moment. She had said her door would be unlocked. There was something provocative in her not just leaving it unlocked, but also slightly open. He pushed it forward and called her name. There was no answer.

He climbed the staircase that started right in the foyer. He could not possibly forget her alluring tour of the house. He easily remembered his way to her bedroom.

He stepped to the partially closed door and eased it open. He stood there in her bedroom doorway and took a deep breath. He was facing the bed. The sight of her shook him.

She was staring right at him. An intense hungry glare. Atop the bed, she was laid back. Her arms were reaching behind her head and up to the posts at the head of the bed. Her hands clasped the posts and held tight. Following the sight of her hands, arms, face, torso, and on down to her waist and legs, he marveled at how lithe and supple her completely nude body appeared. She was truly a gorgeous woman.

For a couple of moments, he stood taking her in. Then, she broke his trance. She didn't say anything, but her knees lifted from the bedding and her feet drew just towards her. Rather than having her legs straightened out, they bent upward even though she still laid back. Then, she made the slight adjustment. Her knees shifted just a bit, parting slightly.

His blood surged. He didn't wait any longer. Urgently, he

stripped his white dress shirt and dark blue trousers.

Once on the bed with her, they moved fervently. He wanted to sense every part of her. Her skin felt delicately soft. Muted moans came from her. They were soon pushing and rocking furiously. It was as intense as anything he had ever experienced.

For the next hour, they ravished each other. Off and on, they alternated between physical connection and low, simple conversation. It was just them and time was for them. Nothing else mattered.

He eventually had to walk over to the master bathroom, and only then did he check his watch. He found himself not wanting to leave, but knowing he must. *Just a few more minutes.*

He crawled back in bed next to her. Her eyes danced back and forth on his. Her lips curled into a grin. Their exertion left her hair tossed and wild.

She half-whispered to him. "You're amazing."

He smiled back at her.

"I can't believe how close I feel to you."

He blinked. "Yeah?"

"It's like I can be completely free and open with you."

He swallowed hard. "You can."

Her eyes faced up to the ceiling and her look languished there.

"It's so tough with everyone else."

"It is?" He couldn't hide his surprise.

"Whether it's Jim or my Dad—" She brushed her hair with her hand and drew a breath. "Someone's always trying to control me, make me be a certain way. I almost can't bear it sometimes."

For a moment, it was completely quiet in the large house. The afternoon sun seeped in through the window, but otherwise there was stillness.

Her voice lifted a bit and her eyes found his. "It's unbearable, because I have so much to give of myself. No one in my life—not my Dad, not Jim, not even my Mom really—has ever taken my love of acting seriously."

Jack flinched. "Yeah?"

She turned on her side to face him. Her face rested in her propped-up right hand and her left hand drifted over to tease at his chest. When it did, the sheet slipped half off her chest to where her left breast leaned exposed to him. She did nothing about it, instead her voice picked up the pace.

"Acting is my *life*, Jack. Have you seen 'A Doll's House' by Ibsen?"

"Um, no."

"I'm in it. I love, love this character, Nora. I *am* Nora." She grinned.

Jack's eyes didn't stray from hers. "Tell me. Tell me what it is about 'Nora.'"

His interest moved her and she went from just leaning on her side to pressing her hand into the bed and sitting up. The other hand hooked her blonde hair behind her ear. Now both her breasts leveled freely towards him. He hoped she didn't see him gulp.

Her words rushed to explain. "Nora is one of these people... There are some people, just a few I guess, who absolutely *must* discover themselves. Like it's life or death, or something. The play's essential, Jack. It's as true as anything you'll experience."

She drew close to him and he fixed on how close she came. She brought her index finger to his bare chest, and she traced a soft line from his neck to his right nipple, grazing it tantalizingly.

Her next words came slowly. Something about her precise touch, and yet detached tone, gave him a start. In that slice of a moment, he glimpsed a calculating part of her he hadn't fathomed. Instantly, he regarded her as someone with more depth than he had thought.

"I do have talent. I'm more than just 'another blonde.' I really am."

"Uh, uh, yeah. I know, Andrea. I mean, I see that."

Her eyes considered him carefully. He thought he saw her eyes suddenly moisten.

"Life is very short. It's a gift, really...You must seize it and you must savor it. For all that it is worth...nothing should stop you from going after what you want. Nothing. You only live once. It's up to you."

Jack realized his mouth had dropped open listening to her share with him. She started easing away from him.

"You should get back to the office," she said softly.

7

"YOU SOUNDED POSITIVE ON THE PHONE."

Monica Henderson's eyes stayed locked on Jack. He could feel their glare. She flicked strands of hair from her face.

Unease coursed through Jack. He realized she had popped up thirty minutes after Fran had told her Jack could speak to her at three. It was 2 pm. And she couldn't sit still.

"Yes, I think it's very positive. I talked to Rob Patten. He's changed his approach. Now, instead of fighting and conducting discovery, he wants to see if we can reach an agreement."

"Oh, he does, huh?" Her chin tilted up defiantly.

"Yeah," Jack waited on Monica to express either relief or satisfaction at Jack's news for her. "You know, they've wanted to be difficult and argumentative up to now. So, this is positive."

"They have your requests and discovery questions you've sent them, right?" Monica braced, now sitting higher with her head cocked backward. "They're finally feeling some pressure. That's what it is, right?"

Jack nodded slowly. "Well, yeah. You're exactly right. They have the discovery. They're feeling some heat from that. But, Patten described a serious offer. We need to give it some thought."

"What is it?" Monica's tone seemed more agitated than interested, and Jack became concerned. He had always anticipated that Monica would want the matter concluded once she could get good terms she and the kids could live with. Now, he was uncertain.

"They came across pretty well actually. Sixty percent of the assets. Solid support of $36,500.00 a month for ten years. You and the kids stay in the house until both children graduate, then you refinance or sell it. It's a good offer. It helps get you through a transition. There's about $9,500,000.00 of it that's liquid, so you have choices. You can go back to school, or start a business. You get a new start, you know?"

Monica glared at him. "Jack, a new start is not the point." Her words sounded cold and distant. Her lower lip trembled. "I didn't want a new start. I just wanted my family. I wanted him doing what he stood before God and everybody else and said he was going to do."

Jack lowered his voice and tried to meet her disappointment with help. "Listen, Monica, I understand that. All of that. I really do. But, you know, things happen in life, and this is one of them. You have to move on. You absolutely do. Besides, how would you ever trust him again? With what has happened and all the lies already, how would you get back to being able to trust him?"

"That reminds me." Her attitude became more enthusiastic.

"What have we learned about the mistress? Do we know who she is?"

Jack paused as he took in her reaction. He had expected at least some excitement, some appreciation. There was no question that Monica relished talking about the adultery much more than working out a settlement. Her eyes brightened. Her energy increased. She cared more about the affair than about favorable settlement terms.

"No, we have been working on it, but they've been very careful. Raised objections and obstacles."

"I want to know who it is as soon as we can."

Jack grimaced. "Okay, I'll be sure to let you know when we know." He drew a breath and tried to reign her in. "Monica, at the same time, I want you to give some serious thought to this offer. I really do. I mean, they are offering a lot. Even with the identity of the mistress, we could maybe get some more, but I really don't think it would be enough to warrant the risks of a trial. Don't forget, he's going to argue you had been distant from him for years. You admit yourself the two of you had stopped being affectionate. Stopped being physical, right?"

"So, he gets to do this? Are you still with me on this, Jack?"

"Yes, Monica. Of course, I'm with you. I have been from the start. But it's also my job to be straightforward with you. Look after your best interests. I think we need to seriously consider what they've put out there. We need to respond. And, we need to do it soon."

Monica stirred in her chair. She crossed her arms and spoke haltingly. "Let me know what you think we should respond with. But Jack," her eyes bore into his, "I want to know who it was. That matters to me. It really does."

Jack nodded back. "Okay, Monica."

After they said their goodbyes, Jack wasted no time and called up Rob Patten.

"Hey, it's Jack. Just wanted to give you a heads up. I have met with Monica, and we're still talking to work up a response. I'll get one over to you."

"How do things look?" Patten asked evenly.

"I've got some work to do on my end. I think we can get it worked out, but she's still way upset over the affair. She wants to know who it was."

"What? That's a better offer than I wanted to make myself. I advised my guy against it. Is she crazy?" Patten was incredulous.

"Hey, it's a twenty-year marriage. Her life and her children's lives have been rocked. Let me work on it. I'll get back with you."

"Okay. But, don't take too long. My client could change his mind, you know."

"I know. I'll get back with you."

Jack hung up, and he twisted over to his computer. He banged in the time entry for the meeting with Monica as well as the phone call with Patten. He was typing time amounts, but he was ruminating over the reaction from Monica. She had seemed reasonable earlier on, but now he worried. She was fixated on this affair, who it was with, and her own pain. Jack had seen this before on occasion, and thankfully he had usually been able to talk clients through it. But now, with Monica, he wondered whether she would be responsive.

He figured he'd keep being torn about it until he did something more, so he picked his phone back up. He dialed Monica's cell, and she was on the line at the second ring.

"Hi." Her voice was alert.

"Hey, just wanted to follow up." Jack made it a point that his tone was firm. "I've already been thinking on the response to make. I'll make some notes and email them to you."

"Okay."

"And, I was also thinking it'd probably do a lot of good overall if you got something set up so you could talk with someone about all this. A lot has happened, and a counselor can help you work through all this."

Monica was silent at first before agreeing reluctantly. "Yeah, I understand. Help me get more answers on the affair, okay?"

Jack bit his lip. "Okay."

⤩

Andrea hadn't been looking for someone like George Henderson; he found her.

She sat at her make-up mirror, readying for the night's performance of the play, and this truth swirled about her. *Why did he have to show up at the same time as Jack?* Timing sometimes confounded her, but she wouldn't let it deter her.

Still, the memory of George and that first night she met him charged her so. Everything stayed so fresh and clear for her. His piercing eyes, the set jaw. The direct push of him into her dressing room after he had seen her performance.

She smirked to herself sitting there, as she thought of how she had left with him that night. Gone with him to the airport and they couldn't keep their hands off one another. His solid chest and jasmine-like musk lingered in her mind.

He had promised to whisk her away with him the next time he traveled. She had asked to where, and of course, he teased her. First he only said 'an island.' She demanded to know where. He grinned and evaded. And only when she pleaded, only then did his gravelly voice share, 'BVI.'

She didn't recognize it at first. He explained it was the British Virgin Islands. *Of course.* He had a place there.

It was time for her performance and she stood to leave. The audience was in place and the rest of the cast awaited. Awaited *her.* A last glance in the mirror told her she looked perfect and was ready.

Now, she just needed him and that island.

"This Henderson hearing is going to be the death of me." Jack surveyed the documents strewn across his desk, as David's voice came through over the speaker phone.

"You say that for every hearing."

"I mean it this time."

"You'll be fine. You always are."

Jack jotted a note on Plaintiff's exhibit 3 and his tone raised. "David, this client is dangerous. She just can't let go of this... bitterness."

"Well, that happens right?"

"Yeah. It does. But usually, and I mean almost always, I can manage it. You know? Hell, this is their life on the line, and if I tell them to maintain their temper in front of this judge, they damn well do it."

"And you think this one won't?"

Jack shook his head hard. "I think she believes she's got it

117

figured out. She can get what she wants and punish him. You know, that's really my problem. She wants him to hurt for what he's done, and it's like that trumps everything else."

"Sometimes it does."

Jack chuckled. "I also got a bad feeling, because this lawyer on the other side—he's no bullshit."

"He's not, huh?"

"No, no, no. And the real problem is that I don't have hardly any discovery."

"Huh?"

"Information. The evidence and the proof the other side has to give me according to the law. The process is supposed to keep you from getting ambushed. Showing up to trial and getting your ass handed to you."

"And?"

"And this hearing is coming up so quickly and she absolutely wants it now. Just can't stand it."

"So you're not really ready."

"Well, I'm where I can go forward. This is what's called a temporary hearing, and it just sets things up for the time being so that everything is stable until the divorce trial can happen."

David's voice softened a bit over the speaker. "You're worried about her swap coming out, aren't you?"

"No, I'm really not. These temporary hearings aren't supposed to be about conduct. They're about the essentials—the children, the house, paying the bills. That sort of thing."

"Custody?"

"Temporary custody. But hey, Monica's been the one at home with their boys. So, hopefully it won't be an issue."

"Couldn't they try to sling the sex evidence to smear her as a mom?"

"Guess they could try. But, you know what? The kids were nowhere around that night. And, George himself was around. According to her, he instigated it. So, I think it'd be stupid for them to try that. And listen, Patten's not stupid."

"How about the financial part of it?"

"So long as we're fine on custody, the financial issues should fall into place. I mean, the judge isn't going to let the family of a successful construction magnate struggle."

"Jack, sounds like you got it under control. You do. Just remember, focus. You know?"

"Yeah, focus."

As Jack hung up, he resisted a fact that lurked in his mind. All these talks with David helped so much. He liked David's feedback. Yet, none of the talks got into the break-up with Carla or the affair with Andrea. No need to search for why he didn't want to bring these things up with David. Jack well knew David wouldn't approve.

Jack's eyes caught the image in the color photograph at the corner of his desk. There against a backdrop of playground equipment in some happy park, two young boys sat close and beamed up at the photographer.

So innocent.

FRIDAY, APRIL 8, 2011

Monica looked striking in her fitted black dress. Her thick, mahogany hair and the way it was drawn back accentuated her radiant face, with her high cheek bones and sparkling eyes. Jack could easily see why George Henderson had married her years ago.

Still, Jack grimaced. *I told her conservative, dress conservative.* Modestly, like the good wife and mother she is.

They sat in court awaiting the judge, and Monica could absolutely not resist stealing glances over to George at the other counsel table. She was willing George's attention, it seemed. And, of course, he denied her.

At any moment, the judge was going to arrive at the bench, and Monica picked this moment to act out. She eased her chair just barely away from the table, and this made it possible for George to look over and see clearly Jack leaning to the table.

Monica spoke just a little louder than necessary, no doubt drawing George and his lawyer's look to she and Jack.

"Jack, let me ask you this."

She brought her head closer to his, and when she did her left hand shifted from her own lap and grasped Jack's leg at mid-thigh. The feel of her hand there made Jack flinch. It didn't help when she inched it just higher.

Jack whispered sharply. "Monica, stop it!"

She smirked. "Oh, sorry."

The bailiff cried out. "ALL RISE."

Judge Daniel Thompson took his seat on the bench, perched above everyone else, and the hearing got under way. It took Jack's own opening statement and part of Patten's opening for the distraction of Monica's hand to recede, but it finally did. Jack's attention jerked into place with one particular sentence from Patten's opening.

"Your Honor, Mr. Henderson seeks temporary custody today."

Jack got to his feet. "Objection."

Both Judge Thompson and Patten turned to look at Jack, and for a brief moment, he realized he didn't really have an objection as much as he just had a problem.

"Your Honor," Jack stammered, "this is the first I've heard of custody being an issue. I mean, Ms. Henderson has been the one home with the children. Mr. Henderson runs a huge construction business."

Patten chuckled and looked up to Judge Thompson. "Judge, the answer and counterclaim we filed clearly sets forth our claim for custody. Now, maybe they didn't take that *seriously...*"

Judge Thompson motioned them to move along. "Proceed, counsel. Let's hear some evidence."

Jack started to call Monica as his witness, and inside he heard bells and whistles sounding. Patten was too savvy and too experienced a trial lawyer to press the lever of custody unless there was support for it. Patten wouldn't risk his credibility, nor that of his client, by staking out a frivolous position. No, something was there. *This is fucked up.*

His mind reeled. The dilemma was that Jack's entire case for temporary relief rested with Monica. Monica showed every indication of still being volatile.

Jack quickly considered a change of course. He could call George as his first witness for purposes of cross examination. No one expected that. But that was highly risky, too. What if George came across reasonable? Credible? Then, Jack would have led off his case with a witness that hurt him. No, it must be Monica.

Judge Thompson barked down at Jack. "Mr. Adams, call your

first witness, please."

"Your Honor, I call Monica Henderson to the stand."

Monica got up and approached the witness stand with the deliberateness of a person who had been waiting to be seen and admired. She took her time, shooting stares at the table where George sat composed.

It didn't get any better when the bailiff swore her in. As the bailiff read the oath, Monica locked her eyes onto Judge Thompson. The Judge didn't follow her eye contact at first. When the Judge did look back at her, she was staring at him.

Jack winced. It was so off-putting. *What is she doing? She didn't need to do that.*

He started his direct-examination slowly and carefully. He established the basics with her. Name, address, age, date of marriage, children's names and ages, and more. She finally appeared to be settling down.

Jack proceeded with his questioning of Monica with renewed vigor. Custody was now an issue. Patten had raised the stakes. *Focus, focus.*

Jack built his basis for temporary custody. He hit key points. Historically, she had been the primary caregiver of the boys. George had to put in huge amounts of time and energy into the construction business for it to be as successful as it was. Monica had the judgment and good health to be the primary caregiver of the children. It had been Monica who George had relied upon to care for the children.

Monica's testimony flowed until Jack asked her whether the boys also were used to her being the one to provide them primary care. First, she nodded, but now words came. She gulped hard. Unexpectedly, she had caught herself in the thought of them, and perhaps their being the focus of this hearing, and emotion roiled her. She paused and dabbed at her eyes.

"Excuse me." She cleared her throat. "Yes, they do. I mean... they are used to me being there with them each day."

And like that, Jack saw authenticity from her. Jack saw the vulnerable Monica who had sat in his conference room unable to finish watching the surveillance video that first morning. Jack sensed this regained Monica a lot of points with Judge Thompson.

Having finished with his custody questions, Jack pivoted to the financial issues. He clicked through the questions they had gone over time and again. He talked to her about the needs she had identified in the financial affidavit she had filed with Court. His questions and her answers led methodically up to the ultimate question when he would have her ask for the support of $10,000 a week.

Together they reached the crescendo, and Jack set the question for her. "Now, Ms. Henderson, what is it you're asking the Court to order as support on a temporary basis?"

"I'm asking for $25,000 a week."

Jack froze. His stomach churned hard. "Pardon me?"

"I'm asking that he pay $25,000 a week."

Jack heard rustling in the courtroom and it sounded like Patten blurted a cough of air out behind him.

Judge Thompson leaned over the bench to look first at Jack and then at Monica. "Uh, Ms. Henderson, your lawyer said in his opening statement that you were seeking $10,000 a week in support."

Monica spun to face the Judge. "He needs to pay $25,000,

Your Honor."

Judge Thompson braced and stared at her.

Monica spoke rapidly, knowing her next words would draw an objection. "Judge, he's running around with some slut. He can't be trusted."

This did bring Patten to his feet. "Objection! Adultery isn't an issue for today."

Monica shot right back at him. "It damn sure should be."

Judge Thompson started banging his gavel. "Order, order!"

Jack swayed on his feet and took in the sight of his client there on the stand. Monica enjoyed a smug look, satisfied she had found a way to inject George's affair into the fray. *Monica, Monica.*

There was a quick decision to make. Try to rehabilitate her testimony and fix their discrepancy, or leave well enough alone. She had already gone off their plan with the $25,000 a week surprise.

What's next?

"That's all at this time Your Honor." Jack said.

Now it was Patten's turn.

Jack's stomach rolled. He watched almost helplessly as Patten's cross started. Sure, he would object when he could. The balls of his feet were planted into the floor ready to push him up as soon as the need arose. Otherwise, he had to wait. And watch.

Monica sat on the small chair in the elevated box. Her hands didn't know where to stay. Her eyes darted about the courtroom.

Jack knew she had never been on a witness stand in her life. Here she was on display in front of the people in the courtroom, the Judge, the lawyers, her husband, and God. She could not sit still. Patten fiddled with a keyboard. But Jack knew better. The veteran lawyer was making Monica wait. Patten raised his voice with the very first question. "George is a good father; isn't he?" He declared it, not asked it. Monica flinched. "Well, uh—" she wanted time to think, "he can be...I mean, he has—"

"George loves the children." Patten's hands went to his hips.

"Well, yes. He does. I never said he didn't *love* them. It's...I care for them."

Patten squinted his eyes. "*You* care for them?"

Monica blinked uncontrollably. "Yes."

"Ms. Henderson, the truth of the matter is that you have used au pairs. Isn't that true?"

"Well, on occasion—"

Patten leaned backward while he held her in his stare. "Occasion? You've used them for years."

Monica's mouth opened, but no words immediately came.

Patten stepped over to counsel table. He picked up a sheet of paper. He glanced back to her.

"I have a list of the au pairs you have used for the last eight years. Must I really take the Court's time and read them to you?"

Monica shot a look to the Judge who was staring at her. She looked back to Patten.

"Um, no. We've used them."

Patten paused. He paced back over closer to the podium that

faced the witness stand. He took his time.

Monica waited and her fingers fidgeted with the cross that hung from her neck.

Patten's voice again sounded full. "These au pairs are a great help to you, are they not?"

Monica shook her head slightly. "I don't know that I'd say that."

"You don't?"

Her lips moved with no words. Patten spoke up.

"On those nights when you've been out late, the au pair is always there the next morning, isn't she?"

"That does not happen that much."

Patten didn't slow down.

"George comes home some afternoons to care for the children. Isn't that true?"

"George has a full office in our home and travels with at least two assistants, so—"

Patten again chortled. "So your testimony is that he doesn't come home in the afternoons to see the children? I mean, we have au pairs listed as witnesses, Ms. Henderson."

Monica glimpsed Jack before speaking in a lower voice. "I suppose."

"Do you suppose you have been on your afternoon tennis team for years?"

Monica's mouth opened. "What?"

"You play on an afternoon tennis team. You have for years, haven't you?"

"Well, yes. But...it isn't the way you make it seem."

"Seem?" Patten cocked his head. He fired another question right away.

"The point is that the children are used to George seeing them often, aren't they?"

"Well, I guess."

"George takes them to doctors' appointments?"

"Uh, yeah."

"He takes them to the dentist?"

"We both do."

"George goes with them to their soccer and baseball practices?"

"Mr. Patten, we both do those things."

Patten stiffened in his place. "Yet, you are asking for almost all the children's time, Ms. Henderson. Eighty percent of the time with the children, that's true now, isn't it?"

Monica blinked again.

Patten didn't wait. He marched over to counsel table. He gathered a large photo.

Jack saw that Monica sat riveted to Patten bringing the photo to the podium. He started thinking about excuses for a break, but he doubted the Judge would permit it.

Patten looked down at the picture in his hands as he asked his next question. Jack knew Patten had no doubt seen this picture many times. Patten wanted the Judge thinking about the picture.

"Ms. Henderson, you want all this time and custody with the children, and you claim you are in good health for that responsibility, right?"

"Yes, of course."

Still peering down, Patten mimicked her words first before another shot. "Of course. And...you claim you have the good judgment to have custody of the children."

"Yes." Her voice sounded thin.

Patten brought his head up to face her and then his voice pierced the silence in the courtroom.

"Ms. Henderson, George has pleaded with you to enter rehab, hasn't he?"

Her mouth dropped open and spectators shifted about in the audience, causing a rustling sound while all waited.

She shot a nasty look at George and then to Patten.

She tried unconvincingly to sound indignant. "Perhaps Mr. Henderson should be the one to enter rehab."

Patten forged ahead. "George runs a highly successful commercial construction business. I'm asking about you. George has repeatedly asked that you do something about your addiction to alcohol and Valium, hasn't he?"

This time spectators gasped and Monica jolted backward and then forward. "I am not. I..."

Patten smirked. "Ms. Henderson—"

Jack bolted onto his feet. "Objection! He must permit her to answer."

"Sustained. Ms. Henderson, go ahead with your answer."

Monica reeled. "I...I am not addicted. Not to alcohol or Valium."

The Judge tactfully interjected. "The question was whether Mr. Henderson has asked you to enter rehab."

Monica feigned a smile and looked back and forth from the Judge to Patten and back again.

"He's doing that because of this divorce. He's posturing."

Patten leapt at her words. "He's posturing?" "Yes." Her hips squirmed.

Patten stepped from behind the podium, kept facing her,

and put his hands behind his back, still clutching the picture.

"Ms. Henderson, you recently had a car accident, didn't you?"

Monica froze, and Jack saw it. It was the wide-eyed look one gave when cornered.

"Uh huh."

"Ma'am, the court reporter needs you to answer 'yes' or 'no.'"

"Yes."

Jack cringed inside. *Why? Why? Why has she not mentioned this before?*

"Your car accident happened on a Saturday afternoon?"

"Yes."

"It happened after you had spent all day at the pool at the Club. Isn't that right?"

"It was a fender bender."

"You had been at the Club pool, isn't that true?"

"Yes."

"Was your son in the car?"

Monica stared at Patten. Jack tried to decide if her look was more anger or she was intensely trying to decide how to answer.

Patten repeated his question. "Your son Brandon was in the car with you when you had your accident, wasn't he?"

Her eyes appeared to moisten at her son's name spoken aloud.

"Yes," she replied meekly.

Patten glanced to the Judge. "May I approach, Your Honor?"

"Yes, you may."

Patten approached her and didn't divert his eyes from hers as she glared at him.

"This is Respondent's Exhibit Number One. Is this a picture of Brandon?"

129

Jack tried not to flinch at his counsel table. The picture wasn't horrible after all. It showed the bright smiling face of their son. Monica's head tilted, as she adored the picture.

"Yes, that's Brandon."

Patten gestured the photo into the air. "Move to tender Respondent's One."

Jack responded. "No objection."

The Judge followed up. "Respondent's One is in evidence."

Monica looked about at their exchange and then tried to orient back to Patten. He started back to the podium but he really only moved a couple of steps. He crossed his arms.

"You had been drinking all day long that Saturday, hadn't you, Ms. Henderson?"

Jack had no choice. He bolted upward again. "Judge, I'm sure you understand, but I have to invoke privilege for Ms. Henderson. The privilege against self-incrimination. As her lawyer, I have to instruct her not to answer the question."

The Judge looked back at Jack, and a moment passed where the Judge likely resisted any number of quips available to him. The Judge obligingly turned to Monica on the stand.

"I expect you will follow your counsel's instruction, Ms. Henderson?"

Monica nodded. "Yes, sir."

The Judge returned to Patten. "Proceed."

"Ms. Henderson, that Saturday, you had been at the pool with your children?"

"Yes."

"You drank four chardonnays and a margarita that day, did you not?"

Monica's mouth fell open again.

Jack jumped up. "Don't answer that." He pivoted to the Judge. "Privilege again."

The Judge was back to Monica as Monica tried to keep up. "Ms. Henderson, do you follow your lawyer's advice and exercise your privilege against self-incrimination?"

She shot her eyes to Jack and her hand pressed against her chest. "Yes, Your Honor."

Patten seemed to stand taller as he lifted his head to peer down his nose at her.

"You paid for yours and the children's drinks and lunch that day with a Club charge, didn't you?"

"Yes."

Patten marched over to counsel table where he jerked up a document. He headed back to the stand.

"You signed this receipt at the Club."

Jack blurted. "Objection. I mean, privilege."

Patten stopped and outstretched his arms. He grinned wickedly. "Judge, I'll save the Club bill for George to swear to. He paid for it after all. Of course, he wasn't there at the pool that Saturday. He was working."

Jack recognized the nausea churn in him.

Patten leaned against the podium and snarled at Monica. "Chardonnay is your drink of choice, isn't it, Ms. Henderson?"

Monica snapped back at Patten. "And George likes scotch, bourbon, and California reds, too."

Patten straightened at the podium.

Monica shook as she sat there and tried to rally. "George is the party person, Mr. Patten."

When Patten smirked, she leaned forward to him as if dared. "Ask Mr. Henderson about his Saturday night coke parties."

The courtroom murmured and Patten put his hands back to his hips. "Coke parties? George?"

Monica batted her eyes and bit her lip. Jack imagined her instantly getting just how self-defeating it was to accuse her high-earning spouse she was suing for support of snorting cocaine.

She stammered. "He went there first with all this addiction business."

Patten crossed his arms over his barrel chest. "You're the one here who likes cocaine, isn't that right?"

She choked a desperate, affected laugh. "No, it's not me."

"Are you telling this Court you don't use cocaine?"

Jack, dying inside, started to stand, when she blurted her answer.

"It's George who likes cocaine." Monica flashed her eyes over to Jack and Jack knew it at once. She had hurt herself badly.

Jack swayed briefly on his feet. Since she had answered, there was nothing more to do. His hands found the table and he lowered himself into his chair.

Patten swiveled on his heels, and for a moment, Patten savored a glimpse at Jack. The hook had been set into the prize, and now Patten would finish. Both of the lawyers knew it.

Patten clicked keys on the podium. "Ms. Henderson, is this you in the video on the monitor above?"

Monica half-turned to look at the big screen positioned behind her, as did everyone else in the courtroom.

The video opened with a shot of Monica sitting at a table squeezed between two other women with a half-full wine glass before her. Monica appeared dazed onscreen.

On the witness stand, Monica's hands yanked up to cover

her mouth. There was a muffled shriek.

Patten skipped to another question. "That's your entertainment room at home?"

The witness stand seemed like it might not hold her, as she started trembling. Tears rolled down her cheek.

On screen, a woman sitting next to Monica hands her a rolled-up hundred-dollar bill.

With an unforgettable lack of hesitation, the Monica on the screen took the bill and leaned down. There on the table was a slender white line of powder. The bill traced the line and the powder disappeared.

The onscreen image was clear. Monica pulled up and looked straight at the camera. She grinned.

8

THE LEATHER COUCH CRADLED JACK AS HE SPRAWLED OUT. His head rested back, but not totally facing up. He was more reclined than anything.

Normally, he wouldn't strike such an unpoised position in front of Gene. But after all, this wasn't normal. The Monica Henderson hearing had been awful no matter how you looked at it. And after all, it had been Gene's idea to meet for drinks anyway.

Gene picked just the right place, of course. *Ozzie's* had a well-stocked bar, soft jazz, and dim lighting that soothed Jack perfectly. The occasional sight of an elegantly dressed woman drifting by rounded out exactly the respite Jack needed.

The tart taste of the bourbon languished in his mouth as he listened to Gene figure out how to fix what had happened.

"Let's be glad it wasn't worse." Gene smiled gently. "Judge

Thompson could have taken the children away altogether. Maybe some shared custody will be a good thing."

"I don't know, Gene. Monica shifted between stunned and livid."

"She has no right to be stunned. You tried to diffuse that whole thing. It was all avoidable."

"Thank you. But, she's got this craving for some twisted vengeance, and until she gets it, nothing's going to be right."

"Is she going to get that counseling?"

"She's supposed to. Says she will." A tall blonde woman in a fitted evening dress distracted Jack a moment. "She kept talking about how he had violated her all over again. First, the affair. Now, he brought up 'partying.' She swore she could have gone there herself first at the hearing. His 'coke Saturday nights' and all."

Gene chuckled.

Jack continued. "Instead, she knew he has a reputation to keep with his business and all. Couldn't kill the golden goose so to speak. Well, he crossed that."

"She won't do something stupid, will she?"

The wail of a saxophone wafted from the other room where the band was.

Jack shook his head. "No, I don't think so. I mean, she's smart. She knows she and the kids have got to have that huge income. At the same time, she's going to find something. She absolutely will not relent."

Gene drew a long drink of his scotch. "Let her calm down. Dig more on the adultery. But, sit her ass down, and tune her up. We extract eight figures from George in a settlement. Her revenge can come with a dollar sign, okay?"

Jack nodded slowly.

"Hey, maybe this was a good thing," Gene finished his drink. "This temporary hearing can serve as her wake-up call. She may think George is so very guilty, and that he should pay and all. But, she needs to get it. It is possible to fuck this up."

Jack drained his glass as well. He closed his eyes for a moment and listened to the saxophone fade. He let the image of Andrea form in his numbed mind.

◦ℐℓ◦

Andrea loved George whisking her away to another world.

The journey had started even before the play. George had called her and said to bring an overnight bag, a swimsuit, and her passport to the theatre. He wanted to take her away afterwards.

She couldn't help but wonder if her entire performance that night had been more vibrant. The adventure that awaited made her pulse race. She couldn't stop grinning afterwards.

The driver took them straight from the theatre to Peachtree-DeKalb Airport, directly onto the tarmac. The pilot and co-pilot awaited them. Andrea liked that they were familiar with George.

As soon as they had boarded, the door closed and they were off.

Andrea walked the aisle of the plane with her eyes wide. The white leather seats looked plush. Forward and rear facing seats. Wood paneling stretched smoothly on the sides.

The flight attendant smiled as she approached and quickly introduced herself—Kelli.

"May I get you something to drink?"

"A water and...a Chardonnay."

"California?"

Andrea regarded her for a moment. "France."

Kelli nodded. "Alright."

Andrea walked past the conference table where George, his female assistant, and the burly guy huddled. George had his laptop out and up, and female assistant quickly caught up, doing the same.

George openly patted Andrea's butt as she passed, and neither she nor George reacted at all. Neither of the assistants dared.

Andrea got to the rear of the jet and Kelli came with her drinks.

"Thank you."

In the last row of seats, Andrea perched in a window seat. The oval window gave a panoramic view of the Atlanta skyline as they passed.

A large-screen television had powered on to a business news channel and Kelli reappeared beside Andrea. "Would you like something to eat?"

"A salad would be great."

"Absolutely."

Kelli disappeared and Andrea sipped her wine.

Whatever fatigue she felt from her earlier performance eased. She surveyed the luxurious interior once more, and a lightness buoyed her.

She grinned to herself. *I can get used to this. I love this. This is me.*

A fleeting thought passed. She could count on one hand the number of times her father had traveled in the last ten years.

How despicable.

All his money and all his success and he didn't enjoy it. Not really. Why didn't he take her mom places? It completely escaped her how he could miss out. How he wasn't *really* living.

She popped up and returned to the back of the plane. Kelli stood in the galley, slicing the tomatoes and avocado for the fresh salad. Kelli was making it just right. Andrea knew she would like it.

Andrea turned and headed back up the aisle. The spacious seats and leather and comfort all pleased her. She couldn't suppress a grin. Her fingers dangled at the skin where her throat met her chest.

I want this. I'm going to have this. This is my destiny.

George and his people stayed glued to their work as she slipped past. It didn't matter, the lack of attention. Not this time.

She drank her wine and weighed her options. There was her performance with Jim that would work against Jack and his firm. But that wasn't enough.

That wasn't close to enough.

It was only a start. A good start, but a start. Eight million that Jim expected her to split. And, they had to pay the lawyer a third before that. This just wasn't Gulfstream IV level enough. For that, she needed much more.

She wondered whether, even when she got the 'Jack money,' her dad would stop controlling her. As much as the plane and the luxury, she wanted the freedom. The independence. This would require more.

Her dad preached doing whatever it took. He had done every single thing. Everything "necessary." How many times had he boasted of that?

George sat there across the plane from her, and she marveled at him. He had this. She wanted this. How could he help her? George had such a presence about him. He barely moved or gestured but he exuded strength. Suddenly, it hit her. *Another performance.* A performance for George. He would help her. He didn't know it, but George was going to get a performance from her tomorrow. There, in the British Virgin Islands, she would perform and ascend to the level at which she belonged.

She was sure of it.

આ

SATURDAY, APRIL 9, 2011

Pure white sand and crystal-blue water laid out before Andrea. She faced into the cool breeze blowing in from the water and smiled. There was no better place in the world than the British Virgin Islands.

A few sea grapes and almond trees shaded the sides of George's pool that stood between Andrea and the beach. The pool had been just a touch cool earlier and she would revisit it after her talk with George. For now, she wanted to share with George. She had given a lot of thought to what she wanted to say and how she wanted to say it.

She turned slowly to face him and her blonde hair whipped about as she did. No doubt it created a wild look about her. She fixed on his intense, blue eyes. Her heart raced.

George wore some weathered t-shirt and khaki shorts. Her own blue bikini felt incredibly thin. Her hands rested on her hips where the bikini strings crossed.

She sensed relief when his eyes drifted about her and she paused to permit it. It signaled a good start. She couldn't help the points protruding from her bikini top, but she figured he might as well see them.

She sucked her lower lip a second just before she spoke up. "This whole thing between you and my dad has to do with Palisades, doesn't it?"

She didn't really expect a response and he didn't give one. She continued carefully. "I've heard parts about all that."

George took a swig of beer, glanced over to the surf, and then returned his hard eyes to hers.

"That whole thing reminds me of a story I heard one time."

Andrea brought a hand to her face to pull stray hair away, but it wouldn't keep.

"Back in the nineteenth century, these two members of the gentry had a big falling out. The younger one thought the older one had insulted his honor."

Andrea slowly shifted on her feet to face George more directly. George's eyes stayed glued to her.

"The younger one challenged the older one to a duel to restore the younger one's honor."

Still facing George, she brought her arms up to get her hands behind her neck. Her fingers found the strings holding her top. She started untying them.

"The older one refused, and the younger one said," she pulled the straps forward and down her front and the top slipped straight away, with the cool air meeting her bare breasts, "it's either a duel or I'm going to shoot you right here."

George's eyes roamed over her exposed hard nipples.

Her hands descended to her hips and played with the strings

of her bikini bottoms.

She continued. "There was a sheriff nearby who said nothing." When Andrea pulled at the strings on both her hips, George shot a look around to be sure the staff was in the house.

A final tug loosened the bikini bottoms and they collapsed to the ground. Andrea paused for a moment fully nude there on the lawn in front of George.

"The story goes that the younger one shot the older one dead." She stepped towards George seated before her and George's eyes lingered at her middle.

She reached to his t-shirt and lifted it up his torso. She spoke evenly as she did.

"So when I heard the story, I asked what happened to the younger one who shot the older man."

Andrea knelt and tugged George's shorts from his hips. He lifted himself to help her and she got them over his hips. She brought them down his legs where they pooled at his feet.

George sat back, nude now himself and obviously ready.

"I was told that nothing happened to the younger man because it was about his honor and getting his honor back."

In a swift step, she climbed onto his chair, facing him. She planted a knee on one side of him and then swung her other knee over his lap to place it opposite his other hip. Her left hand clasped the chair behind his shoulder.

"Are you prepared to do something about Palisades," her right hand reached between them and found him there, "other than just fuck his daughter?"

She held him in place and lowered herself. She arched her chest and her head tilted back. A low moan escaped her.

George closed his eyes.

↢↣

FRIDAY, APRIL 15, 2011

Like a mighty storm approaching, everything became very still in Jack's office, and a sick feeling hit him. The air was being sucked from the room.

Fran buzzed him. "Richard Bourne is on line one."

Cold fear hovered about Jack. He froze as he stared at the phone. *Why don't I think this call is about them settling the case?* He reached for the phone.

"Hey." Jack managed.

"How are you doing, Jack?" Bourne's tone bellowed deeply, commanding an authority that Jack at once resisted.

"Good, thanks." Jack looked about his computer screen as he went ahead and started his time entry for this call. "And you?"

"Good here, too. Just staying busy is about it."

Jack noticed something just a bit stiff with him, he thought.

"Calling on the Turner case?"

"Yeah, I am. Listen, we're going to need your client's deposition. I'll have my office call with convenient dates and times, but I wanted to give you a heads up, because it's going to have to be soon."

Alarm rocked Jack. This wasn't supposed to happen. Cold pangs shot deeply in him. Affidavits, yes. Depositions, no.

"A bit over the top, isn't it, Richard? Affidavits ought to cover it."

Jack heard a pause on the other end of the phone and he immediately knew he'd struck the wrong note in this exchange. Bourne was experienced enough to know he had landed a heavy blow asking for a deposition.

"Nah. I want this woman under oath." Bourne couldn't have been colder.

Why didn't I give this possibility more consideration? He shook his head as he realized he had just breezed through this contingency in the beginning. He had made a quick but horrible miscalculation, he now knew. The last several prenuptial agreement motions had been made using affidavits. He had expected early on that this case too would follow such a course. Surely, it would, he'd thought at first.

Only now it wasn't.

A tightness formed in his chest as his ego chimed in. He was a trial lawyer and he would find a way out of this. Still...Jack followed his apprehension on out to its logical points. Depositions meant sworn testimony. Sworn testimony meant Bourne questioning Andrea under oath. Questions for Andrea could include conduct. Conduct meant sex and affairs involving Andrea. And now, questions about Andrea and sex meant involving Jack in the testimony. It meant a mess and a scandal. It absolutely could not be permitted.

He felt a horrible anguish at having landed in this morass. Just the same, here he was. He had to work his way out of it. He had been pushed by circumstances before to strive and to struggle. Was this really any different? Sure, he shouldn't have let things come to this, but this is where he was. He had to fight his way out of it.

Jack knew immediately his solution. The path out was narrow, but it was there. He had to manage Andrea.

૭IՐ

This can be fixed.

Jack needed Andrea to remain calm and let him handle the other side. She might not understand this whole 'deposition' part of the case. He took Bourne's request for what it was. The tactic was a parry from the other lawyer in a fight the other lawyer was losing.

Jack walked up front to accompany Andrea back to his office, as was the routine. He braced himself some. He would be 'on' for the next hour. He would explain to her and help her understand. Hopefully, she could throttle the whole playfulness routine. They would need to be discreet a while longer, at least.

As Jack entered the reception area, he saw Andrea seated on a sofa in the middle of the room. Behind Andrea, Monica Henderson stood talking to the receptionist, way early for her appointment time scheduled for just after Andrea's. Jack headed towards Andrea.

Andrea smiled as he approached her. In a slow, fluid gesture, she lifted her hands to her hair and ran them through her hair, pausing a moment with her hands still in her hair as she stared at him enticingly. Jack looked over and saw Monica notice.

No, no, Andrea. Don't pull this now.

"Hey, Andrea." He smiled to her, extending his hand.

She brightened and stood. He tried to gauge who else might be watching their 'hello' without looking around self-consciously. He knew at least the receptionist noticed them.

"Hi there, Jack." Her words came slowly, and, in Jack's mind at least, they came lusciously. He told himself he'd enjoy her voice even if she were reading the phone book. It was that rich to him.

She stood and accepted his hand with her own. She held onto his hand more than a moment and they both knew it. Anyone watching would notice, he realized. They paused with eyes fixed just longer than to be expected. He was sure of it.

"How are you doing?" His tone was cordial and polite.

She tilted her head just slightly as if incredulous at his apparent formality. "I'm good, Jack. And *you*?" She said teasingly.

"Fine, thanks. Come on back." He led them down the hall, the same way he'd led clients back to his office for years.

At his office, he took a deep breath and held the door open as she entered. Her lithe frame passed close by him with her hair trailing just back. Her lips held a trace of a smile. He noted the poise in her stride and he was entranced. A light scent of roses and jasmine remained in her wake.

He closed the door behind her, as she made her way to her chair. She naturally picked the one that was situated just a little closer to him than the other. There was almost an unfolding to her, with her arms going to the sides of the chair and her small feet in her heels comfortably forward. One leg gradually crossed over the other.

He eased into his chair as he had many times before. As if by instinct, his body assumed his typical pose behind the desk. His arms propped on the desk and he leaned forward.

To his surprise, Andrea spoke first, purring in a soft, low voice. "I like that suit, Mr. Adams."

Her eyes invited playful banter that Jack knew he couldn't afford on this day.

Before he could answer she jousted again. "Do you like this blouse? I thought of you when I decided to wear it." Her lips curled mischievously.

Jack cleared his throat. "So, you doing okay?" He immediately worried about his tone. He knew he sounded too relaxed, rather than displaying the professional air he had intended to maintain.

"Jack, just seeing you today is making me much better." She grinned broadly. The emphasis on 'much' in her answer stabbed him.

"Andrea, I appreciate that. I do." He paused for just a beat and saw that even the slightest gesture by him registered with her. She braced just a bit.

"What's wrong?" She said it lightly but her eyes blinked quickly.

"No, no. Nothing's the matter. I just need to be ... serious some. That's all. Go over the case."

"Serious?" Her face tightened some. "What's the matter, Jack?"

He held his hands up, signaling her to hold on. "No, I just have to talk about a couple of things in your case is all." He regretted his words at once. He should not have minimized what he was saying in the least. He knew that. He had meant he just couldn't be as informal or flirtatious as they might. That's all.

"Well, everything's alright with my case, right?" Her eyes now held fear. Her hands looked like they couldn't be still.

"Andrea, everything's going to be alright. It is."

"But?" Her eyes narrowed. She was reading a tentativeness about him. "But, it's not okay right now, you mean?" She was hanging too closely to his words. He tried reestablishing his control over their conversation. "Listen, the opposing attorney is being asinine, that's all. Happens a lot."

She twitched her head, both anxious and not understanding. "How can he do that?"

"Well, he's asked for your deposition..."

Jack watched her face tense into a tight grimace.

"Andrea, first of all, it's not happening yet, okay? He may be just trying to exert some pressure, you know?"

He watched her taking breaths. She appeared to be trying to calm herself. "Why? Why would he be doing this? You said it should be straightforward." Her head shook a couple of times with frustration. Her voice got thinner. Whatever calming progress she had just made evaporated instantly. "This isn't sounding straightforward."

"That's what he's wanting you to think. That's what he's wanting you to feel." He shot a quick grin. Aimed to lighten her up.

"And I do, Jack." She squinted her eyes. "I don't know. I feel like it's not right anymore." She suddenly acted like she was struggling to contain herself. Her shoulders twisted back and forth and she shifted sharply in her chair. "You're going to stop him, right? Don't let him do this." The words left her mouth in a pout.

"Andrea, the more we try to act like there's a problem or evade this, then the more he'll push this."

"Yeah?"

"Yes."

Andrea's lips and chin trembled. "But he's ALREADY pushing it, right?" Her voice rose to a level Jack didn't like.

Jack paused for the right response and she shrieked.

"JACK!" She didn't even sound like herself. The volume from her made him physically recoil. "Tell me!" It came out as a demand.

Between her emotional outburst and his utter surprise, he felt unsteady. "Tell you what?" He felt out of balance with her reaction. His own tone was thin.

"Tell me I don't have to answer his questions."

"Let me work on it, Andrea." His voice sounded more plaintive than he wanted.

"Jack, can he ... you know," she looked over at him frightfully. Eyes wide. Her breaths hissed in and out.

Jack shook his head. "Can he what, Andrea?" He really wasn't following her.

She bent her head just down and forward, but she still looked to him. Her voice shook. "Can he ask about us?"

"Andrea, depositions are routine. It's not a problem, okay? Just something the lawyer may be covering as part of the process."

She jerked her head about, even more concerned. Jack couldn't remember having seen her this way.

"Listen, it's just a chance for the other lawyer to see you and hear you. Find out what kind of witness you'd make. You're smart. Attractive. You'll make a great witness."

Her mouth fell open. It was like Jack had asked her to perform a miracle or something.

"WHAT?" Her voice was loud. "This wasn't supposed to happen. It wasn't supposed to come to this. You acted like it was going to settle." Her eyes bulged.

Unfortunately, Jack lingered without saying anything, and this affected her. She started acting desperate. Her hand went to her mouth and covered it, then went back to her lap, and then came up again. She gasped for air. Jack was shocked by her melting composure.

Her bottom lip quivered, and he had an inkling of what would come next if he didn't fill the quiet void with words.

"Andrea, absolutely do NOT let this guy stress you like this. He can't hurt you with these questions."

"NO! No, he's not!" The words were shouted and this time Jack jerked backwards. "He is NOT going to ask me any questions. Tell me, Jack. Tell me he's not."

"Andrea, stop it. Get yourself under control."

"What all is he going to ask me about?"

"Well," he looked around some, defensively, he knew. "Um, about Jim. About the prenup. About..."

Jack didn't mean to let his words trail. But, he was busy keeping an eye on her, because he had no idea how she'd react next.

She blinked hard and looked into the short space between them, obviously conjuring the worst.

Her eyes darted straight to his and she leveled her question. "Tell me. Will he ask me about sex? Can he ask about us?"

He hesitated, looking directly at her, and it was like a switch flipped. Her eyes bugged wide open and her mouth formed an oval. Her chest drew in a deep breath, and then she unleashed it all with a harsh scream.

"Andrea! Stop it!"

The piercing scream only subsided for her to draw another

breath, and then she pushed from deep in her chest again, yelling with such force that his ears rang. Sprays of spittle shot from her mouth.

"Andrea, you've gotta stop it. NOW!" His hands went up and forward, palms towards her, as if this would help.

Her eyes narrowed and her entire body shook, but her throat found more breath and the yelling still came.

"Calm down, Andrea! *Please*. People can hear you. This is ridiculous."

She kept trying to scream, but now she was hyperventilating and there were too many desperate sobs mixed in. The noise remained too loud.

Only a moment passed and urgent raps were hitting his office door.

Jack rose from his chair, and he tried once more. His hand was outstretched gesturing her to contain herself. "Please, please stop it."

She pulled hard to collect air and then screamed as hard as she had before.

The office door swung open.

People had gathered outside, as another associate stood frightened in the doorway.

"Everything okay? What's going on?" The young man's voice was loud and highly concerned.

Andrea kept facing forward, balled her hands into fists, and punched them downward as she kept up torrents of screeches.

Jack watched the associate yell over his shoulder to no one in particular. "Someone call 911!"

Andrea lost the air to keep her screams at the volume they'd been, but she kept rolling sobs coming. That was how she rocked back and forth when Gene burst into Jack's office.

"What in the hell is going on?"

Andrea kept choking loud sobs while now shaking her head from side to side.

Gene looked over at Jack, and Jack raised his shoulders and opened his palms upward.

"She's panicked. We were talking." Jack couldn't find better words at first.

She slowly bent forward in her chair at her waist, and her hard crying was unrelenting. Gene patted her back very slightly, and tried softly to soothe her. Andrea half-turned to Gene and leaned into his arms. Her face nestled into Gene's shoulder. Gene motioned for Jack to leave the office, and Jack eagerly did so.

He had never seen anything like it. Ever.

Jack scrambled from his office, and he drifted over to Fran's desk.

Fran looked aghast. Fran had a great rapport with Andrea, and she was clearly concerned.

"What in the world is the matter?" Her voice cracked.

Jack shook his head. "She got very upset talking about possible depositions. That's all."

Jack glanced about at some of the people milling around nearby. He spoke softly to Fran. "Help me disperse these people. I don't want them all lingering around when the EMTs get here."

Fran nodded and asked. "What if people ask about what

happened?"

"Just tell them it was some kind of panic attack and she's going to be fine."

Jack and Fran went about discreetly getting people to leave the area. As they had just about cleared the area, the EMTs rushed down the hall and entered Jack's office.

While the EMTs were in Jack's office, Andrea's loud sobbing could be heard. Gene came out and half-whispered to Jack, "Go on down to my office. I'll be there once they get her out of here."

Jack walked down the hallway to Gene's office in a daze. He had trouble believing that Andrea, as poised as she had always been, had lost it.

Jack entered Gene's office and collapsed into a chair.

In only a few minutes, Gene appeared. "What the ...???"

He looked at Jack quizzically, while closing the door firmly. "Jack, how the hell did that happen?"

Jack only stammered at first. Gene interjected, "walk me through it."

"Well, she and I were meeting about possible depositions in her case. Bourne has demanded her deposition. I told her it was just a hardball tactic. That she was going to be fine."

Gene stood angled away from Jack. He looked off into the distance out his window. Suddenly it was as if Gene was distracted.

"Okay. What next?" Gene bit his bottom lip.

"Let's see. She started raising her voice and questioning how they could get away with this. I told they were just trying to pressure her and not to let it bother her, because that was what they wanted—to bother her. And Gene, it was like the more I tried to calm her the more hysterical she got."

Gene's face tightened as he crossed his arms over his chest. He took a few steps closer to his window and looked out over the Buckhead landscape. Various office buildings and hotels were in his sight and Gene seemed to look past all of it.

"What else did she say?" Gene's voice was tight.

Jack tried to recall the events. "That's really about it. She stopped making sense at that point. I've never seen anyone break down like that, Gene."

Still looking out the window, Gene spoke in a low tone, almost under his breath, as he wagged his head. "Unbelievable...I called Bob Turner and told him right away, and it seemed like Bob was able to talk her into calming down some before the EMTs took her away."

"How did Bob take it?" Jack asked.

"As best as he could, but we were in the middle of it. He's going to meet her over at the hospital now. I had better go over there as well."

Jack took this as an opening to depart, and he seized upon it. He got to his feet and talked as he moved to the door. "Please be sure and let me know how she is doing, and if there is anything I can do," Jack said.

Gene was still gazing out the window with his back to Jack, as Gene asked a final question. "Did Andrea mention anything in particular?"

Jack paused in place, then slowly asked, "I am not sure I follow... 'mention anything in particular?'"

"When the two of you were discussing the questions that would be asked in the deposition, what kind of questions was she so worried about?"

"Well actually, she was worried about any questions

regarding her sex life," Jack said.

"Did she say anything more than that?" Gene's words were barely audible.

"Uh, no. She didn't."

It struck Jack that Gene was worried about more than he was letting on. Jack considered whether to broach the subject further, but decided against it.

"I'll call you from the hospital later," Gene said abruptly.

Jack let himself out of the office and felt more confused than when he had entered. He wondered why Gene wanted to know so much about what Andrea said. What was it that Gene was so worried about? Surely Gene hadn't been involved with her, had he? The thought confounded Jack. It also repulsed him.

9

GENE WAS ABSOLUTELY SERIOUS LOOKING. There was an assistant present and sitting off to one side of the room, and another partner sat beside Gene. The assistant and the partner were taking notes, both acting like they wanted to be anywhere else.

Gene spoke evenly but intensely. He wasn't asking questions or looking for Jack's responses. It was all about Gene talking to Jack. Nothing more and nothing less. For his part, Jack didn't dare offer a word anyway. Jack sat bolt upright, listened closely and slowly felt parts of himself die inside.

"Andrea has talked extensively with her doctors, counselors, her family, and new counsel."

Gene's eyes burned into Jack. Jack felt as if he was indeed melting.

"Andrea has said that you and she had an affair. She said it happened while you were representing her in her divorce. She also said you were going to have her testify at her deposition even though she was scared about questions that were to be asked her about conduct, specifically adultery."

Jack slowly shook his head side to side. He knew there was no use in replying. He didn't speak at all.

"The stress she experienced caused her to collapse and suffer a nervous breakdown. Her family has hired new counsel to represent her in her divorce case. Her family has also hired counsel to bring claims against this firm for her damages caused by your representation of her that occurred during the course of your employment with this firm. This same counsel representing her for her claims against the firm will proceed to seek sanctions against you with the Bar Association. They intend to seek your disbarment."

Gene paused and showed the only concern for Jack he would show at this meeting. Gene looked away for an instant, jerked his head in disgust, but then turned back to Jack and finished his script of items to relate.

"This firm will retain separate counsel for your representation in this matter, and this separate counsel will only represent you and your interests. This will be discussed further with you by the administrator later. We will apprise you of developments, but you should know at the outset our intent is to address promptly and discreetly all claims and issues with a view of trying to resolve this matter with a containment of the risks and the attention that could result."

The words were starting to escape Jack and he was losing his focus. It was all too much for him. His world was crumbling. Gene was picking up on Jack's state and he started drawing everything to a close.

"You are suspended until further notice. We will review this matter and contact you further."

Jack could barely look straight ahead at Gene, and he struggled to keep his composure.

Gene's voice dropped lower and asked genuinely. "Jack, do you have any questions right now?"

"Gene, I am so very sorry. You have done so much for me. I'm sorry."

"Jack, take a couple of days and let's talk again."

Gene stood signaling this meeting was over.

Jack stood, too. "I'm sorry." Jack repeated, and then turned and left.

As he drove home, he struggled to process what had just happened. How had he managed to fall like this? How?

He once glimpsed his own eyes in the rear view mirror. He barely recognized himself. *How did I get so lost?*

FRIDAY, APRIL 29, 2011

Jack approached his old office building with nothing but misery inside his chest. He knew he had to do this, but that didn't make it any easier. *Just one more thing you have to do.* Gather a few belongings, sign some things, say a few goodbyes.

Like many times before, he drove the SUV to the parking deck. He found the same area where he always parked. He pulled himself from the vehicle and trudged his way around to the front entrance. He knew he would see people he didn't really want to see.

He made it to the front entrance of the building without

seeing a familiar face. But then it happened. The door swung open. The woman making her exit stopped right in front of him. They both stood shocked.

Jack and Andrea stood face to face on the sidewalk.

Jack's face brightened. "Hi."

"Hello, Jack."

He found himself happy to be looking into her eyes and to have her looking up at him. His happiness dissolved when her face went from a friendly smile to more of a stare. Her eyes narrowed, and for the first time since he had ever met her, she acted cold. Her face looked determined. Not sweet.

She didn't try to avoid him. She did look over to the side, and her look acknowledged someone else. He followed her gaze and saw the person waiting across the street.

Jack did a double take, unsure about who he saw.

Jim Hadley stood waiting outside of a black Town car, ready to whisk them away. A driver sat in the front and the car was running.

He turned to her perplexed. *What the hell? Jim Hadley?*

"How are you doing?" His voice was thin and strained, as he struggled to make sense of the situation. "Is everything okay?"

Andrea tilted her head and assessed Jack. She feigned a smile. "Please, don't worry. I'm actually fine."

His eyes widened and arched.

She nodded quickly twice.

He stumbled on some words before he managed a coherent question. "How's your treatment coming?"

Andrea stayed silent. Stared.

Gene said distinctly she was in some kind of treatment. She had broken down. Wasn't it a nervous breakdown?

Her eyes darted about his face, and she gave the impression she was trying to decide something.

Jack grew more concerned. *Am I getting dizzy?*

"Hey, listen. Don't worry about me. I'm fine. And I'm going to be fine."

When Jack's mouth dropped open and no words came, Andrea turned the question to him.

"How are *you* doing?" She was trying to change the focus.

"Umm," he strained for his bearings, "I'm coping. The fallout has been tough." His voice almost broke and he shot a glance over to Hadley, then back to her. "I'm really not sure what I'm going to do."

She grimaced as if perturbed, which didn't fit with what he had just said. *I'm lost, Andrea.*

She forced her words. "You're strong. You're going to land on your feet. You'll be fine."

Jack looked at her, and it set in for him that she really was just fine. He was having trouble. She simply was not.

Jack scanned to Hadley who was now visibly impatient with waiting. Jack dropped his eyes and searched for more information.

"Have you guys really reconciled?" His voice was low.

"Yes, we're together Jack. Hadley and I are staying together. We love each other." Her tone was adamant.

"You do?" Jack was shocked.

She nodded vigorously.

"Listen, take care of yourself..." She started but he interrupted her sharply.

"How long have you been back together?"

She acted evasive, and her shrug said she didn't want to get into all that.

Jack smiled warily and took a step back.

"I have to ask you something," he said anxiously.

"Jack, we have to get going."

"This won't take a second, and then you're gone."

"What's that?" she replied.

"Were you ever really apart?"

She didn't say anything to him. *That stare.*

"You're kidding." Jack stood there flabbergasted.

"You two were never apart, were you?" He implored her.

She remained silent and she just looked directly at him.

He blinked a couple of quick times and then grinned in realization.

She returned his look with a small, tight grin of her own.

"Unreal," he said.

"I have to go," she stated matter of factly.

"Andrea, please, you have to tell me. Did you and he stage all of this? Seriously?" Jack felt disoriented.

She paused and then finally answered slowly. "I'm not about to say I did something wrong or fraudulent, you know? Because obviously, like... I wouldn't do something like that."

She hesitated more, looking around. Jack felt like she wanted to say more to him about it. She looked back over to Hadley himself, who was tapping his watch. Andrea returned her eyes to Jack.

"I'm truly sorry about the pain I've caused you, about wrecking your life. I didn't want that. I did care about you. I still do. It's just..." She acted agitated that Jack was getting her to open up, but she did anyway.

She spoke evenly. "Every moment under my father's control was excruciating. I had to stop it. I wanted my freedom with everything I had. Every fiber of my being."

"And now you have it." Jack interjected.

"And now I have it."

She took a deep breath and started around him. "Good bye Jack."

She walked away from him, towards her car.

After she had taken a couple of steps, he called out to her, "Andrea?"

She turned to him, an affected cute grin spread back across her face. "Yeah?"

"Go fuck yourself."

Her face turned hostile. She swirled around and stomped away.

He swayed from side to side and then staggered into the building lobby like he'd just been punched hard in his gut. He hadn't been punched though. It hurt far worse than that.

Jack entered the building in a daze. His encounter with Andrea left him reeling. His mind was sorting through her revelations when Andrea's lawyer, Gloria Andrews, walked out of the elevator. Andrews took a couple of steps before seeing Jack right there in front of her.

For a few seconds, they both froze. The short, stern plaintiff's lawyer took in the sight of the tall, wounded, former divorce lawyer standing right before her. She didn't seem frightened or apprehensive really. There was more a look of sympathy about her, and Jack recoiled when he realized it was for him. He felt there was something condescending to it. More importantly, he thought it misplaced.

She briefly acknowledged him with a nod and then started to walk past him. As she rounded the side of him to leave on her way, he shook his head and found himself unable to resist. He had to speak to her. He couldn't let this opportunity pass. He just couldn't.

"You're wrong, you know." His voice sounded odd, even to him. He didn't know where those words had come from. He just knew, instinctively, that there was something he must tell her. Something he wanted her to know. It screamed importance to him.

She stopped. Still facing away, she appeared to contemplate continuing on to leave. He saw she was torn. What good could come from engaging with this man she had had a hand in damaging, albeit rightfully. At the same time, Jack figured she couldn't resist. She no doubt considered there was likely value, some sort of good, in letting him vent and have his say to her.

Gloria took a step more, but then turned back to him. She kept a distance, but she faced him squarely. Others ambled about in the building lobby, but Jack and Gloria stood fixed in front of each other. Her eyes looked directly to him, and Jack sensed he wouldn't have her attention long.

"I'm wrong?" She said it more in a doubting manner than truly in a questioning way.

"Yes, Ms. Andrews. This is not at all how it seems." As soon as he said this, he knew this was probably something she heard quite often in one form or another. "I mean, you don't have the full picture. I just ran into Andrea." Jack winced inside, aware he was struggling now with getting this out. He knew he had to press on while he still had the chance.

"Yes, Andrea and I were just upstairs. We had documents to sign." And settlement checks to pick up, Jack thought to himself. "You probably already know this, but you should really keep a distance from her now."

Jack chortled at this. "No kidding." He shook his head vigorously at the implication he would do anything but keep a distance. Then regret struck. He hadn't intended to get sarcastic with her.

"Well, I should get going." She moved to turn away, and when he spoke up, she stopped.

"I ran into Andrea, and she had Hadley along. They were together."

Gloria considered the idea of it, then just shrugged.

Jack continued. "You really don't have the full picture, because..."

Gloria interrupted him, her patience now thin. "I do have the 'full picture,' Jack." Her tone became sharp. "What else is there?"

"Andrea is not who you think she is. She's no victim here. She and Hadley...They had this planned all along."

"What are you talking about? No, Jack, they didn't."

"Yes, Gloria, they certainly did. I just saw them, and she admitted as much."

"Listen, Jack—it comes down to this. You had a duty here. You know that. Every lawyer does." She gazed intensely at him. "You had a duty to protect her. A duty to take care of her. As lawyers, clients look for that from us. They need that from us. She came to you in one of the worst times of her life."

"I know that. I know all of that. You're not listening to me."

Gloria shot right back. "And you're not listening to me. Jack, when you took on her case, you were making a promise to her.

When she came to see you, it's as if you made a promise to her to be loyal, to protect her and to help her get the best result you possibly could. Most of all, you promised she could trust you and you would not harm her interests. That you wouldn't take advantage of that trust. You violated all of that."

"And something you don't get is that she also made promises to me, Gloria. You see, it's like any other relationship. Every other relationship really. People make promises to each other. Implicitly."

Gloria's eyes squinted. Jack kept going.

"She promised to be loyal and trustworthy to me as well, to be honest with me. She had a duty she owed back to me. It was basic. We were *both* supposed to act in good faith with one another. She didn't do that. She did the opposite. She harmed me, abused me. And she used the role I took on with her to do it."

"Promises to each other?" Gloria didn't seem quite as emphatic, quite as certain. She genuinely considered the notion.

"Yes, promises to each other." Jack in turn was emphatic, and he was certain now. He was never more sure of anything. "Promises to trust each other, and be trustworthy and honest. You know, it's true I broke mine. She couldn't have succeeded in her scheme if I didn't. But there were broken promises here by each side. You should know that. There absolutely were."

Jack watched Gloria, as her expression changed. She visibly softened. Her face took on a mixed look of being stunned and finding some insight. She silently stared back at him, her mouth barely open. He had reached her.

"Do you even know what all I've lost? I've worked four years of college, three years of law school, a two-year clerkship, and five years at this firm—I want those back."

Jack thought he saw some comprehension from her. He appreciated that, if nothing else, then maybe at least Gloria Andrews got it. Understood. To some extent, perhaps.

She was still looking to him when he pivoted away. He walked on, leaving her standing there. In this devastated state he found himself in, it was no small thing to at least have this satisfaction.

Jack rode the elevator up to his former office, and he started feeling a lightness he hadn't ever experienced. His breathing was smooth and deep. He sensed a calm that hadn't been with him for as long as he could remember. He didn't try to figure it out either, except to know that the interaction with Andrea and then the exchange with Gloria had both changed him.

The elevator emptied him into the lobby of his old firm, and the reception by the people he used to work with was just as he had expected. Awkward and tense, there were looks and whispers that were inevitable. Jack eased his way about the task, doing what he must to sign the papers he needed to sign, gather some belongings and answer questions a couple of people had about matters pending that he knew about. It was the last in a series of meetings like this for him, but this time incredibly he felt no inhibition or tension himself. He simply took care of the visit.

The receptionist checked with him about one last item before he left.

"Mr. Adams, I'm supposed to confirm your meeting with Mr. Hatcher. Does tomorrow night at seven still work for you?"

"Yes," he answered, "that'll be fine."

"Thank you."

"Sure."

The elevator ride back to the street was instant, it seemed. A passing thought struck him that this was likely the last time he'd ever visit this office. He had spent much time here, but that time had now passed.

He tried to imagine where he'd land from all this, and nothing specific formed in his mind. He sighed and stiffened his back. *Damn it. I'll get past this.*

The elevator doors opened. He went forward into the sunlight of the day.

ℐℛ

After Andrea and Jim had said their goodbyes to Gloria Andrews, their car took them home. They hardly said a word on the way home. When they both walked into the house, the tension didn't dissipate at all. Now that they were truly alone and both could speak freely, the atmosphere grew more strained.

Andrea tossed her purse into one of living room chairs. Jim went straight to his favorite chair in the family room and slumped into it. Where he would have sometimes instinctively switched on the television, this time he just looked over to Andrea as she followed him into the room.

Andrea glanced to him and then looked away. She chose to stand in front of the floor-to-ceiling windows that lined the wall, and she pondered things as she gazed out onto the trees lush beyond the deck outside.

Jim blurted simmering concerns. "You should have denied everything to Jack."

Andrea skipped over his criticism.

"You know, maybe you shouldn't even be here." There was a tone in Andrea's voice as she said it. Andrea meant it contemplatively. She could see Jim took it as cold. He shook his head hard.

"Maybe I shouldn't be here?" Jim's voice rose from the start of the question to the end.

He appeared shaky to her. He looked about the spacious home. She was glad it remained deeded in her father's name.

He then almost spit his words. "Hell yes I should be here. Why are you even thinking like that? You worry me sometimes."

"Worry you?" Andrea looked hard at him. "Things are going right, but this isn't *complete,* you know? We shouldn't be getting cocky." Her words were sharp.

She folded her arms over her chest and then paced around the living room. "You heard Gloria."

"Yeah, I heard Gloria." Gloria had called them on their way home, right after Gloria's confrontation with Jack. "Jack's pissed off. No real surprise there. At all, Andrea." He arched his eyebrows with what he added. "I also heard Gloria say the firm had agreed to the ten million. The transfers are made, and we're there. Just as planned."

"Jim, no question we're almost there. But, you have to believe me. This thing isn't done until the money's cleared the bank. You know that."

"What? His firm wants all the scandal of one of its lawyers botching a prominent divorce case? He'll shut up, because they'll tell him to shut up."

"All I'm saying is let's be careful. We're talking about a substantial sum of money. We're dealing with a disgruntled lawyer. Let's make sure this goes right. That's all." Andrea tried to convey in her face she was being cautious.

"I hear what you're saying." Jim leaned towards where she stood. His voice softened. "Put yourself where I'm at. I'm almost divorced, and I have no protection in this. No back up. You have this house. You have your family. Now, you have this claim. I am totally at risk here. I need something to rely on."

Andrea recoiled. "At risk?"

Her eyes went wide with disbelief. "Who do you think you are you talking to Jim? Who has fucking been there for you for eight years now? You need 'protection?' From who? *Me*? I can't believe this."

"Andrea, you have no concept, no idea, what it's like for me to sit around and wait. You don't. I need reassurance."

"Jim, what do you want me to do? Prick my finger and write it in blood? Don't go getting paranoid on me now. Don't. I have enough on me as it is."

He stood and paced. After a few steps, he stopped.

He narrowed his eyes and fixed on hers. "You've been seeing someone." He watched for her reaction.

Andrea froze at first. Her impulse was to look away and she fought it. "Seeing someone? Seriously? You mean other than Jack?" She left her mouth gaping open.

"Don't play games with me, Andrea. Don't. I'm very serious about this. My future is at stake here."

Andrea didn't like his tone or the intense look on his face. She couldn't remember him ever having looked at her like this before. "Jim, I don't have any idea what you're talking about. Of course I'm not. Are you losing it?"

"No, I'm not losing it...I know. And...I'm not losing on this. You can believe that." Jim's words hung in the air.

Andrea couldn't believe what she was hearing. "Jim...Jim."

She waited until his eyes settled fully on hers. "It's me. Stop that."

She eased to him. Stopping squarely in front of him, she peered up at him. She used her best grin.

"What can I do to prove my loyalty to you? Huh?"

She grinned wider and he fidgeted.

Her right hand rose to his chest and lightly played at it.

"I've been thinking."

She could see him gulp.

"We shouldn't stop here. Not now."

His brow knotted.

"This little project with Jack went so well. This was just a warm-up."

He tried to grin back, but his face tensed helplessly. "What?"

"I say it's time for another *project*."

"What in the hell are you talking about?"

Andrea brought her other hand up. She alternately straightened his shirt and caressed his chest there.

"This was okay, but really what are we looking at?"

He stared down at her.

She spoke softly. "After Gloria's attorney's fees, there's less than seven million. Split that in half. Less than three and a half each?"

He blinked several times.

"Is that enough for you?"

Her hands drifted down his abdomen.

"Do you want more?"

Jim shifted on his feet and she smiled that he was clearly rattled.

She stopped her hands on his belly just before his waist. Then her hands went to his hips and rested.

"What are you talking about?" he half whispered.

She almost laughed at how raspy he sounded.

"Let's go get forty, fifty million dollars," she exclaimed.

Jim froze. "What the *fuck*? What are you talking about?"

She inched just closer to where their bodies almost touched. She figured she had to be doing well with Jim if she was so affected herself. Maybe it was saying out loud 'fifty million dollars.'

Jim's voice squeaked. "Where are we going to get forty or fifty million dollars?"

Andrea traced her fingers over Jim's beltline. "What if I can show you how?"

Jim shook his head. "Andrea, are you alright?"

"Jim, my father taught me a long time ago that you have to get your hands dirty...I am my father's daughter and his only child. Um, he's already told me he's got his estate set up with everything coming to me. He's gonna leave it to me to take care of my mom."

"Huh?"

"I'm saying my dad has me set up. Set up to be his sole heir. I'll just need to take care of my mom. That's *if* something happens to him."

"Andrea, that's way out in the future."

She sucked on her bottom lip and let her hands dangle against the pockets of his jeans. The touch was light but certain. Jim's middle was a zone where she hadn't ventured in a while, but it was impossible for it not to have registered with Jim.

Her words fell to a half-whisper. "Jim, Dad has had heart problems."

Jim closed his eyes, shook his head once slowly, and then glanced back to her.

"Andrea, have you lost your mind? Are you serious?"

Andrea rose up to her toes and went to whisper in his ear. He flinched when her body rested against his as she lifted.

Her mouth drew close to his ear and she whispered to him. "Anti-freeze poisoning has the same symptoms as heart failure." She lowered back onto the balls of her feet but she kept her face close to his. She saw his face had gone pale. He looked like he was holding his breath. He could barely speak aloud.

"If you're willing to kill your own father, where does that leave me?"

SATURDAY, APRIL 30, 2011
As Jack moved about the restaurant, he saw Gene Hatcher, who stared at his cell phone. He was engrossed in his emails. Jack walked up to the table and took a quick moment to absorb the sight of Gene seated there. Jack had known Gene for a several years, and now this was likely ending for him, too. Gene was impressive just sitting and waiting as he was. Jack knew that he owed this man a tremendous debt, and the realization that Jack had disappointed Gene pained him.

Gene shot a glance up to Jack before Jack had spoken. "Hi!" Gene actually stood and the men shook hands. "How are you doing? Have a seat." Gene held a hand toward the chair across from Gene, motioning Jack to have a seat. Jack took the seat and abject anxiety welled inside him. This was terrible.

"I'm hanging in there, Gene." Jack forced a smile.

Gene looked intently at Jack. Gene's eyes held concern for Jack. For his part, Jack was struck by this. Jack instead had anticipated anger from the older man.

"Well," Gene forced a smile, too. "That's what you have to do. You know?"

"Yes, yes."

A server appeared at tableside. "Sir, would you like a drink?" Jack looked over to Gene's drink.

"I'm having a bourbon." Gene informed him.

Jack looked up at the server. "I'll take a beer. A Corona with a chilled glass and a lime."

"Yes sir."

As the server slipped away, Gene studied Jack carefully. "Thanks for coming out."

"Of course. Absolutely." Jack appreciated the courtesy.

Jack looked about the upscale steakhouse. Jack wasn't the least bit surprised that Gene had picked here for them to meet for dinner. He was surprised, at least somewhat, that Gene had even wanted for them to have dinner.

Jack had tried to think about what Jack and the whole sordid episode with Andrea and her breakdown must have cost Gene and the other partners. He could never bring himself to put numbers to it. Of course, there was the payout on the settlement itself. Jack estimated it to be at least seven figures. Paid straight up, quietly, and before any lawsuit was actually filed, the firm had been liable for its associate, meaning Jack, and the firm hadn't wanted any part of any attention or focus on how the whole affair and breakdown played out. Their lawyer had gotten involved with a client, and the affair had harmed the client, horribly, and at the worst time for the client. The firm had wanted it over. This was the cost before one even estimated what the likely loss of Bob Turner's business with the firm had been.

"Like I said the other day in your office, Gene, I am so very sorry. I can't possibly say how sorry I am that all this happened."

"I appreciate that." Gene spoke directly. "Listen, this isn't easy for either one of us, meeting for dinner. I know that. We needed to talk some more, and it was better to be away from the office."

Jack nodded, but he was uncertain exactly what more Gene wanted to discuss. The server brought Jack a beer. Beer had never tasted as good as it did right then.

Gene graciously let the conversation take its own measured pace. Unlike the office where the efficiency and press of business kept matters going briskly, Gene was keeping dinner more casual. Like Gene had already noted, this was not easy for either of them, but it was even more difficult for Jack.

Some brief small talk about sports and news kept the atmosphere comfortable until they had their entrees and second drinks. Jack then went to a sentiment he had wanted to be sure to convey.

"Gene, I want to make sure I say... how very much I appreciate everything you've done for me. I've learned so much from you. You've been great."

Gene smiled warmly. "Thank you. Hey, you did a lot of great work for the firm. That's not lost on me, and it shouldn't be lost on you either."

"I feel absolutely horrible about the harm I've done. I still can hardly believe all this has happened. I never fathomed it."

"Well, it is a horrible situation. No doubt about it.

Unfortunately, part of the price to be paid is your dismissal, of course." Gene frowned.

Jack took a deep breath. "I understand." He absolutely expected this, but it still struck him hard. It was not abstract anymore.

Jack hesitated, but he wanted Gene to understand that there was more to this than appeared, given what he had learned running into Andrea.

"Gene, this is going to sound strange, I know, but there's another level to this. I ran into Andrea and talked with her. She and Hadley had this planned all along."

"What?"

"Yeah. She was with Hadley after they came by the office with Andrews. I talked to her and I asked her point blank if they planned it."

"Oh yeah? And what did she say? Did she admit it?"

"Well, not exactly. But, she didn't deny it. It was obvious. Let's put it that way."

"Jack, what proof do you have, huh?"

Jack was silent and Gene leaned toward him. "Listen, let's be really blunt. This all doesn't happen if you don't have sex with her, right?"

Jack started to speak, but held up. He stayed quiet and nodded slightly.

Gene shrugged. "Hey, what you did was wrong. That's all there is to it."

Jack needed Gene to understand. "Yes, I was wrong. Absolutely wrong. But there's more," Jack leaned in and fixed his eyes on Gene's. "Something more was at work here, Gene."

Gene swigged lengthily from his drink. Jack tried for his best tone.

"In this situation—hell, in any situation—there's a principle where the two people are acting in a certain way. A relationship is founded upon BOTH people promising to be fair and honest with each other. It's just basic; it really is. BOTH people are obligated." Jack shook his head. "Other than that, we're just a bunch of fucking animals." Gene chuckled and leaned in himself. His smile was not necessarily nice. His voice came across as tight and instructive. "Jack, some people would say we *are* just a 'bunch of fucking animals.' But," Gene slowed and tried for a gentler tone, "you're a lawyer and a man, and you've just gotta guard yourself against that. You just do. And the fact is...in this instance, she got this. She understood you were supposed to do this. Now, whether it was by duplicity, fraud, or whatever, it just damn well doesn't matter. More is expected of you." Gene let his words hang there, and Jack shifted about in his chair. He nodded once, but he pressed his lips. Several things ran through his mind. He wondered how he could make his idea about this clearer.

Gene looked around the restaurant, likely giving Jack a brief respite before finishing. "Listen," Gene softened his tone and tried to assuage Jack, "you will land on your feet. I'm seeing to it. But this has to ... go ... away." Gene's slow words emphasized their import.

Gene's pause was not lost on Jack.

"The firm is damn well exposed here, and we will not have it. This must be handled. You have to understand that. And you have to be on board. No other option. Remember this comes from what you did. So, this stuff about 'promises' people have makes sense, but we're talking about damage here, real harm." Jack looked down, down past his plate, feeling himself sinking in his own hell. He expected that Gene probably worried about him. Worried about his judgment in these circumstances. Jack raised himself back up to maintain some figment of poise.

Gene furrowed his brow and changed direction for the conversation. "It's probably early on yet, but have you thought much about what you're going to do next?"

"I'm not sure, Gene."

Gene brought a folded envelope from his inside jacket pocket and placed it on the side of the table.

"This is six months of severance."

Jack froze. He hadn't imagined this kind of consideration. With the chaos and the fallout from this fiasco, he never anticipated any generosity. Jack figured this had to have been the result of Gene's efforts.

"Gene, thank you. Thank you so very much. That is so very kind and I certainly appreciate it." Jack's voice was thin and strained.

Gene spoke on. "I've also talked to some people with the Bar. Looks like we can work out a six month suspension, and then you can apply for reinstatement."

Jack was completely taken back by this. Jack's eyes widen and he slowly shook his head. "Wow. Thank you. I'm at a loss. I am so grateful."

He looked to Gene, looked down at the table and then around the restaurant. His mind swirled as he considered the mix of the harm he'd caused and yet the unexpected consideration from Gene and the firm. Jack concluded he didn't truly deserve this help. The conclusion welled emotion inside him that he immediately regretted.

Gene must have noticed Jack close to getting emotional, and Gene reflexively chided him. "You got a six-month break and then it's back at it. You've used up a big fucking chit here, but you'll be back." The tone was not as harsh as the words. It was stern but respectful.

At once Jack braced himself and curtailed his reaction. "Forgive me. You're right. I just really appreciate everything. I will forever be in your debt."

Gene smiled reassuringly. "Don't worry about it. Just part of how it is, that's all."

"Yeah?" Jack couldn't resist some curiosity. "But why? This is more than I anticipated, that's all."

Gene looked a bit pensive then shared more.

"First, I look at it as I'm still your mentor. The way I look at it, I don't just disown you because you made this mistake. You're human."

Jack gulped inwardly. "Thank you very much. That's good to hear right now."

"Well listen, there's a bit more." Gene tensed somewhat. "This stays here, okay?"

"Absolutely."

"People do make mistakes. Whether it's sleeping with a client, missing a deadline, forgetting something. Hell, we're all human. Hopefully the damage isn't too bad or the mistake too great, but stuff does happen."

Jack nodded gratefully.

"And another thing ..."

Jack hung on Gene's words. The candor surprised him.

Gene tossed back a slug of bourbon. "Listen. I'll share this with you. But it stays right here."

He took another long swig. "Andrea and I have a bit of history, too. Now... I didn't sleep with her. It didn't go that far. But... let's just say she teased me along and had her fun aggravating me. So, believe me. I get it."

Jack sat stunned. His mouth was agape a moment. But he rebounded quickly.

They both smiled.

Gene swished about the remaining drops of bourbon and ice in his glass. "Anyway, no substantial harm came from my... lapse... but it could have. Easily could have."

There was brief silence before Jack offered quietly.

"Thank you for that, Gene."

Gene stood and they shook hands. "Good luck to you, Jack. Stay in touch."

10

DINNER WITH GENE HAD DRAINED HIM. Jack just wanted some peace and quiet. *How did things get this bad?*

Jack drove from the restaurant back home with little patience. His SUV hurried up the interstate to Johns Creek, leaving lines of traffic to his right crawling along in comparison. It seemed later to him than nine-thirty.

Gene's message rocked Jack. Gene had to look after the firm, of course. But still, the very idea that Jack wouldn't practice law for six months—how would he cope?

Jack tried to just concentrate on traffic. He rubbed his face and watched the exits slipping by. Wouldn't be much longer.

His cell phone buzzed. The screen flashed "Carla."

Jack frowned. He really didn't want to replay his dinner with Gene. He just didn't. He needed a break and he needed it badly.

He would let her know quickly he was okay and that he'd get back with her. He tapped his phone.

"Carla, I... His words trailed when his phone buzzed again. He looked at it and froze.

It was a text. From Andrea.

"Must come quick. It's urgent."

He sat there shocked. He reread the text again. Andrea was the last person he expected to hear from, and this was the last thing he'd ever expect to hear from her.

He went back to Carla's call.

"Gotta call you back. I have to go."

"No. No, Jack don't go." Her voice was tight. "What's the matter? Are you okay?"

He shook his head. "I can't get into it. Everything's alright. I have to go now."

He thought he heard her sniffle, but he was already moving to click off. He rerouted his SUV. He hurried towards Andrea's subdivision. His mind raced.

A fleeting, desperate thought shot through him. Perhaps Gene had called Bob Turner upon letting Jack go formally at dinner, and Bob could have called Andrea. Had she felt some remorse for the havoc she had caused? Had she reconsidered?

He reached the entrance to her subdivision and drove faster.

Two easy turns, and suddenly his SUV was whipping into her driveway. It struck him right away that only the foyer light was on downstairs and her bedroom light upstairs. He hurried from the SUV.

He went quickly up the sidewalk and to the door. Immediately, his eyes fixed on the sliver of light from the foyer that showed through the slit where the front door was ajar. He smiled with the instant memory of the other time he had happened upon her front door ajar.

The intensely satisfying lunch and afternoon they had spent in her bedroom that time remained utterly unforgettable. How completely clever of her to recreate that circumstance now. He rushed right in, and as he bound the staircase, he called out for her.

Of course, she didn't answer. *She didn't before either.* Rather, he had walked into her room to find her reclined and ready for his arrival. Here he was again.

He whisked through the short hall upstairs and her bedroom door was open. His chest swelled with excitement and his face drew a broad grin. He readied to announce 'here you are.' He passed through the doorway and managed two steps into the bedroom.

Her body tilted away and angled awkwardly back on her side. Dark red circled the sheet at her head. Her eyes stared open and absolutely did not move.

All his breath left him. The room felt extremely bright. He heard himself cry out an unintelligible sound.

There was a look of terror fixed in her eyes.

Oh my God.

Dizziness struck him hard. His shoulders pitched from side to side, and he was aware he might fall. His searching eyes saw the side of her head unnaturally misshapen, and his chest heaved strongly. The pungent taste of his own vomit erupted into his mouth, and his hand jerked there to try to block his spitting out.

He thought he might collapse, and he saw a decorative chair to his side. He stumbled over and fell into it, all the while looking for any movement or sound that there may be life in Andrea. Her body stayed absolutely still.

Think, think, think. Your phone. Take out your phone. 911.

His hands moved and he fixed on them. Somehow there had been blood splatter on the chair and now slick red stains streaked his hands. He didn't dial his phone.

Suddenly, the sounds of sirens broke the fog about him. Louder and louder they sounded until there were then steps moving on the staircase outside the bedroom. He was aware his eyes were blinking, and he wasn't sure if he was actually crying or had only thought he was going to break down.

He just could not steady his thoughts, as Andrea's lifeless form sprawled in front of him. None of this made sense. Over and over in his head, he heard himself saying, 'no, no, no.'

Jack sat motionless. Activity stirred about him. Police officers.

"He's disoriented." One officer told another.

Jack's mind blurred various thoughts. *Andrea's dead.* His mind was incredulous. *Andrea's dead?*

Uniformed police officers moved about in his periphery vision.

SUNDAY, MAY 1, 2011

The next morning, Jack just ached, lying about in the stillness of his dark house.

He loathed his wrong turn. The straight trajectory that had been his life bent horribly the day he went to Andrea's house. There was no question that he had erred. Now, he felt mired in the awfulness of it.

And she was dead.

Why?

Incredibly, her death made no sense to him, and yet it simultaneously seemed inevitable. Young and talented, she had so very much. Yet, she had this reckless fury; maybe somehow she had smashed into her fate.

But she was too strong and powerful to have shot herself. He didn't think he would ever accept that. *Was there a note?*

Each time he contemplated her having taken her own life, he blanched. *Impossible. The same Andrea Turner who thought of herself as 'Nora?' Driven to discover her true self? No.*

But if it wasn't her, then who? That answer came to him quickly and repeatedly. *Jim Hadley.*

It was the only explanation that made sense.

The entire morning, back at his house, all he managed was dragging himself from room to room. Silence and no television or music. Bread. Water. And quick flashes of what she had looked like when he found her.

He traded text messages with David and with Gene. They were concerned, and he told them he just needed to rest and process it all. Gene also suggested a counselor.

Later in the day, Gene sent a text that abruptly changed tone. The others were gentle. This one was stiff.

"We need to meet."

Jack stared at the screen a moment. He knew sooner or later he was going to have to engage again. Venture out. That time had come.

Jack texted back. "Was about to go for a walk. What did you have in mind?"

Gene was quick in reply. "Where's your walk?"

"Webb Bridge Park. Know it?"

"Yeah. Sounds good."

Jack was surprised. "Will head on over."

"Will be there in forty-five minutes."

Jack couldn't resist adding another message. "Must be serious."

Gene fired right back. "Yeah. It is."

Something about Webb Bridge Park always soothed Jack. Beautiful green trees abounded. A creek etched through part of it. Birds, squirrels, and countless flowers all around. A couple of soccer fields centered in the bottom of the park, while a wide path circled just over a mile around the upper cusp of the place.

Jack had made one lap around the path when he found Gene sitting atop a picnic table. Wearing some older jeans and a polo shirt, Gene slouched over and forward. A youth soccer game played out in the distance, but it was clear that Gene paid it no real attention.

Gene's eyes locked on Jack's as soon as he appeared at Gene's side. The men shook hands. Jack hopped up and took a seat beside Gene.

"Is there anything you have to tell me?"

Jack blinked a couple of times. It was like he had been punched in the gut. He spoke slowly. "Seriously? I can't believe you're asking me that."

"Jack, don't make it even worse for me than it is. I have to ask all the hard questions at this point. Tell me what happened."

Jack tried to take his time to explain. "Well," he stretched out his hands, with his cell cradled in his right hand, "I was almost home after you and I had dinner last night. Uh, I was on the phone with Carla, when I got a text."

Jack was trying to make sure he covered everything.

"The text was from Andrea."

"Andrea texted you?"

"Yeah. It said, 'Must come quick. It's urgent.' I mean, here." Jack handled his phone and scrolled to the exact message. He presented it to Gene. Gene didn't take it from him."

"Take a screen shot of it." Gene said. "Now, email a copy of the pic to your email."

Jack sent it right away.

Gene spoke evenly. "Okay, so Andrea texts you to come over. What next?"

"Um," Jack looked around the field. "I went to her place. I got there and the door was ajar." Jack swallowed hard. "I knocked and called for her, but she didn't answer."

"She didn't answer. Okay."

"So I went on in."

"Huh?" Gene turned in place and stared at Jack.

Jack suddenly realized how it must have sounded.

"Gene, Gene... It's weird to have to admit now, but I had actually gone inside like that before."

"What?"

Jack frowned. This was awful to have to explain. "Gene, one day at lunch, I went to see her. She had left the door open for me."

Gene squinted. He pursed his lips, looked like he started to say one thing, but then appeared to change his mind, and said something else. "Alright. What next?"

"Well, I hurried upstairs." Jack lowered his voice and decided on being very candid. "Gene, the time before when the door was open, she was upstairs and waiting in bed."

Gene swayed his head as the realization of what had occurred that night to Jack sunk in.

"Yeah, I went right up thinking she was waiting again."

Gene stared off at the soccer game on the field and let Jack finish.

Jack's words came thin and forced. "Gene, I got up there, and ... she was dead. Uh, shot in the head. I'll never get that image out of my head."

The two of them sat there on the picnic table a moment before Jack finished his explanation.

"I could barely stand it. Collapsed into a chair. Before I could call 911, the police got there."

Gene rubbed his hands and sat there at first. When he spoke his voice started off a bit muted.

"The police said there was some blood smeared on your hands."

"Gene, there was, like, blood splatters all over that side of the room. When I hit the chair, I must have put my hands in it."

"They said the pistol was on the floor." Gene took a deep breath. "She had fallen onto her side on the bed, but the gun had dropped to the floor."

Jack thought for a moment. "I don't really remember the gun. I don't know."

Gene glimpsed at Jack and then gazed back at the field.

Jack looked out over the field, too. "Gene, did they find a note?"

Gene looked back over to Jack as if perplexed. "Huh?"

"A note. Did she leave behind a note or something?"

Gene drew in another long breath. "Jack, I don't think you understand."

Jack stared at him.

"Guess you wouldn't, since you haven't yet talked to anyone."

"What's that?"

"Jack, the police say the gun angle was downward. Usually, with a suicide, the gun angle is up. It actually looks more like someone was standing over her."

Jack furrowed his brow and tried to process what Gene was saying.

Gene continued. "They're also saying that suicide shots are at contact range or near contact range. A close shot like that will leave a burn mark around the wound. Plus, it should leave gunpowder residue. That didn't happen with Andrea."

Jack tilted his head and kept listening closely.

"Jack, there was also no gunpowder residue on Andrea's hand. If she had shot herself, there would have been."

Jack braced his hands onto the top of the picnic table to steady himself. He muttered under his breath. "Holy shit."

"Yeah."

Jack looked over at Gene with complete seriousness. "That damn Jim Hadley. I can't believe he fucking did this."

Gene blinked quickly and cleared his throat. "Jack, the police have concluded it wasn't a suicide. But they haven't said anything more than that."

Jack slowly nodded but was dazed.

Gene spoke carefully. "Jack, I'm worried. Really worried. I'm like you—I think it had to have been Hadley. But..."

Jack put a hand into his hair and pulled back, gradually stretching taut his forehead. "Oh, Gene. ...Gene. No, you're not thinking they..."

Gene shrugged.

"Suspect me?"

Gene spoke up. "I hope not. I damn sure hope not, but we don't know. We just don't know."

Jack lowered his face into his hands. For a moment, he couldn't even think. Chills shot through him.

Gene's voice rose to more of a level and firm tone. "Hey, I'll find out all I can, and we'll go from there. That's what we'll do. We'll take this one step at a time."

Jack brought his hands away from his face and held them forward with palms up.

"This is crazy. I mean, I didn't do anything. I just found her."

"Step by step, Jack."

Jack looked out onto the soccer field, his mind reeling.

Gene's tone stayed steady. "Let's go ahead and be ready. There's a guy. He's been doing this more than thirty years. Very good. His name is Jacob Weinberg. Go ahead and call him this afternoon. Let's be prepared."

MONDAY, MAY 2, 2011

Of course, Gene had fully apprised Jacob. Jack learned as much as soon as he met with Jacob the day after seeing Gene in the park. There was no time to waste.

Jacob's office had a cozy feel. Several green plants adorned shelves and tables about the Buckhead office. Pictures of children and grandchildren were all over. Jack figured that Jacob was in his late sixties or early seventies and had seen a lot. Big, bushy grey hair groomed perfectly in place. As could be expected, Gene's recommendation had been impeccable.

Jacob started carefully and worked forward. They covered much of Jack's history, and they bore into detail when they discussed Jack's assignment of the Andrea Turner case. Jack already appreciated the importance of Jacob knowing everything, and Jacob reminded him of this. Jack spared no fact about the affair with Andrea, and he repeated a couple of different times how things unfolded the night of Andrea's death. Jacob took detailed notes.

Jacob folded his hands in front of him on the desktop and took a deliberate tone.

"Listen, from this point forward, you talk to no one else about this. The prosecutor's office will have my number for contact. If they seek to indict you, they will call me."

Jack flinched. "Hey, I'm just being cautious here. I realize they may call me in and want to ask me some questions. I get that. But…"

Jacob studied Jack a moment and then spoke with his voice just higher than before.

"Jack, the reality is that they are likely coming after you. They're going to prosecute you."

Jack chuckled but the sound was shaky. "Look, I didn't do this. This is crazy."

"They are going to arrest you and they are going to prosecute you. You were seen enraged with her, and then you turned up at the murder scene. You even had blood on your hands, Jack."

Jack's mouth dropped open. He stammered. "She ... she texted me. Um, somebody texted me. I'm not some killer. Jacob, if anyone killed her, Jim Hadley killer her. C'mon."

"Listen, I think it was Hadley, too. But that doesn't change where we are right now. I mean, Hadley wasn't at the scene *with blood on his hands.*"

A chill washed over Jack as Jacob continued.

"We're preparing. I think you must prepare yourself that they are going to come after you."

Jack slowly shook his head. "Alright. Let's see where this goes."

Jack drove back home, and he almost had time enough to change clothes to go to the gym when Jacob called his cell.

"Jacob?"

"Jack, I just heard from the DA's office. They're going to give me the courtesy of walking you through."

"Huh?"

"I've spoken to Gene. He's on his way to my office. He'll pick me up, and then we're going to swing by and get you. We'll be there in about an hour."

"Wait, wait. What are you saying? 'Walking me through?'"

"Yes, they're going to process you through. They're letting me just bring you in and are handling it less harshly."

"All this just for questioning?"

There was brief silence on Jacob's end.

"Jack ... they have decided to prosecute you for Andrea's murder. This is your booking, your arrest."

Jack yelped. "What?"

Gene drove along Georgia Highway 400 quietly, with Jacob in the front passenger seat and Jack in the back. They were headed to the county detention center downtown. Jacob prepped Jack.

"We just need to get from *here* to *there*." Jacob's finger jabbed into the air, making the points of *here* and *there*.

As Gene steered the German luxury SUV through traffic, Jack kept quiet in the back. He simply wanted to wake up from his nightmare.

Jacob continued. "It's a straightforward process. Fingerprinting. Mug shot. There may be some time waiting in a holding cell. Just have to process through."

Jack watched the traffic slide by and shook his head in disbelief.

Jacob half-turned to Jack and spoke directly. "Whatever you do, don't discuss the case. Don't answer any questions. You're represented by counsel. You want your counsel present."

Jack nodded. "Got it."

The monstrous white building spread across several city blocks. Gene pulled them up to the curb, and Jacob and Jack got out. In ten minutes, Jack was going with a deputy down a long corridor while Jacob waited up front.

The first locked barrier didn't involve bars at all. The deputy slid a card and looked to a closed circuit camera, and they passed through a couple of large doors. The doors banged closed and they were in a circular room with many other officers.

Jack cringed inside when another deputy rolled his fingers to get prints. A third deputy kept trying over and over to get his mug shot. Only when Jack felt exasperated and likely gave the worst look did the deputy accept the picture.

Jack was being led to another hall, when a plain-clothed detective appeared.

The detective dismissed the deputy. "It's okay, Harry. I got him."

The detective flashed an easy smile at Jack. "I'm Rafael Woods. How are you doing?"

"Uh, hanging in there."

"Here, walk with me."

Detective Woods took them down a hall in the opposite direction than where Jack had started.

Woods talked as he led them. "I'm not on your case. Detective Kisha Collerain is working it. She's good. Solid."

Jack spoke up. "Hey, I'm represented by a lawyer. I can't discuss the case. I just can't."

"Oh, I know. I'm not here to ask you about it. I understand you're a divorce lawyer."

"Yeah, that's right."

Woods had them turn into a break area. Coffee pots took up one counter, a sink and dishes sat on another counter, and a wall of vending machines lined the opposite space.

"Want some coffee?" Woods started fixing his own.

"Um, no thanks."

"Listen, the prosecutor, this guy Manford McCleary, he's tough. No doubt about it. A political shark, too."

"Yeah?"

"Uh huh. But, Collerain ... hey, Kisha's the very best. She's a true believer. Calls it like she sees it."

Jack looked around. No one else was there right then. He wanted to sit, but Woods hadn't sat, and Jack didn't know what was next.

"Anyway," Woods gulped at his coffee, "Kisha still thinks Hadley's a bad guy, you know?"

"Yeah? I think so, too."

"In fact, Hadley has already tried to get back in the house. Bob Turner wouldn't permit it. Evidently, he's on the deed, and not Hadley. Thing is, Kisha can't think of why Hadley would want back in."

Jack winced. "I'm sorry. I really am. But, I just … I just can't talk about the case. Any of it at all."

Woods put down the empty coffee cup. "Okay. I understand."

Woods started out of the break room. "We better get back."

Nothing else was said, and Woods turned Jack back over to Harry. Harry took Jack to a wing of the floor he hadn't been before.

When they turned a corner, floor to ceiling bars and meshing stretched taut. Before they proceeded, Harry had Jack remove his belt and shoes. Jack's wallet was already up front. Harry tossed plastic sandals at Jack's feet. The further down the hall they ventured, the louder the noise became—metal doors clanging shut intermittently, occasional shouts, and errant cries.

Jack braced and followed Harry along. The first quarter of the hall housed cells with doors, but the rest of the way had various cells with more inmates than comfortable space.

Jack could feel the eyes on him as he was led to the first rectangular holding cell on his right. Undecipherable shouts grew down the hall and Harry swung the cell frame open to have Jack enter it.

Harry spat words out as he turned from Jack. "Be back in a bit, counselor."

At first, Jack just saw several men standing around in front of him, most in the dull orange jumpsuits, but a few were like himself in street clothes and the plastic sandals. Jack edged in and Harry slammed the barred frame shut behind him.

There were too many men for the space and he felt crowded in the cell immediately. The toxic mix of sweat, urine and what smelled like rotten eggs made his stomach roil. He immediately tried to stand off to one side. He felt his hair lift on the nape of his neck and on his arms.

There were two bunk-like beds stretched across the sides and a stainless steel urinal in the back-right corner, only slightly behind a concrete barrier. The barrier only reached up a couple of feet. On the opposite side of the urinal was another stainless steel sink and counter. Inmates crammed the room.

An overly energetic older man saddled up beside Jack. The guy stood too close, but there was nowhere for Jack to go. The guy stared hard first before saying anything.

The man's eyes darted about. "Did he say 'counselor?'"

Jack couldn't get an answer out before the crusty man fired another question. "Whatcha in for, counselor?"

Jack's elbows pressed into his sides, like he wanted to withdraw himself as much as possible from this space. "They say I killed my client."

"What?" The inmate's mouth dropped open, but before he could say anything else, a large, dirty hand clasped the guy's shoulder and yanked him away. A tall, hardened figure took the older guy's place. This man stood easily a foot taller than Jack and leaned an angry face right towards Jack.

"You a lawyer?"

Jack looked about the room and realized the others all waited to see what unfolded. His heart pounded up into his throat.

"Yeah. I am." He hated how his voice trembled.

"Listen, man." The guy scowled and propped himself closer to Jack than Jack would've ever wanted. "I got busted with a brick in my Benz."

Energetic Man reappeared and looked to try to get a question in, too. "Hey—"

Angry Man pivoted and planted his right foot in the direction of the other guy. In a swift, instinctive move, Angry Man pumped his right fist into the older man's mouth.

The unmistakable *slap-thud* of flesh smacking flesh sounded, and it made everyone jump. Instantly, Energetic Man fell away. He couldn't fall straight down, because the room was too crowded, but other inmates moved away from him. His body bounced off the others nearby before falling into a heap on the ground.

Jack shot a quick glance into the hall, but no deputy was around. Angry Man re-focused on him.

"Anyhow, I was saying," the guy grabbed part of the steel support for the bunk he and Jack stood next to and the guy inched his face closer to Jack. He acted as if he was moving closer to be discreet, but his voice didn't soften at all.

"It was me and three other guys. We're riding along." Over the guy's shoulder, Jack watched as a heavy-set man in the back edged back to the urinal. "We get stopped and they arrest us all. How is that?"

The Angry Man's face screwed even tighter. He expected Jack to be as shocked by that as he clearly was.

The heavy-set guy in the back unceremoniously unzipped and dropped his jump suit and sat down at the urinal just on the other side of the concrete. Jack could not believe he had wound up here.

Angry Man growled. "They trying to put that brick on me. It was in the back. I didn't even know about it. Wasn't my coke."

Jack tried to raise his palms up. "I wish I could help. I'm a divorce lawyer. I don't really do criminal law."

The big man's eyes squinted. "Huh?"

Jack cringed. The man not only had a foot of height on Jack, but he had at least fifty pounds as well. The guy was likely quick. If it came to it, Jack probably couldn't faze the guy with his fists. Jack thought of the pressure points he'd have to use—eyes, ears, nose—anything Jack could put his fingers to and cause pain if he absolutely had to.

In the back of the cell, others started complaining and trying to get away from the man Jack had seen sit down there. The rustling and commotion pressed the big inmate in front of Jack even closer.

The man's breath was bitter. "They can't do that, right? How do I get that thrown out?"

Harry started back towards the holding cell and Jack saw him in his periphery.

Jack shook his head a bit and said all he knew. "Hey, I'm just a divorce lawyer. I really don't know. There was something back in law school about the 'equal access rule,' but I'm not even sure that applies."

Over Jack's shoulder, Harry started moving the steel door open. "Alright, counselor."

Jack squeezed out and stuck to Harry's side as they walked back down the hall. They turned the corner and when they reached where the open floor was again, Detective Woods stood holding some papers. Woods motioned him to follow along. Jack gladly accompanied him back to the same break room.

Woods again went with his easy smile. "Here. Have some water." Woods pulled a bottle from the fridge and made himself another coffee.

"Collerain doesn't get how you're upstairs. No signs of forced entry or anything."

Woods leaned back against the break room counter, and Jack took a long drink of the ice cold water. Jack was out of the holding cell, but he was only out of there because of Woods. Jack got it.

Jack drank more of the water. *I didn't do anything. Nothing. How do I get hurt by this?*

Jack spoke slowly. "She left the door open. Andrea had left the front door open for me before. She did that night, too."

"She left the front door open?"

Jack nodded.

"Hadley says the last thing he heard you say to her was to 'go fuck herself.' He really didn't expect you would have been there."

Jack looked blankly at Woods and searched for what to say. He had said too much already and immediately regretted it. If he brought up the text, Jack wasn't sure where things would lead. All he could do was shrug and shake his head.

Woods sipped more coffee and then straightened. "Okay, well at least I didn't ask you any questions. I mean, you're represented and all. Let's get going."

Woods led him up the original corridor but not down the hall that went to the holding cell. At the end of the corridor, they had his shoes, belt, and wallet. Jack readied quickly.

He was very happy to see Jacob and Gene had the SUV waiting outside.

On the ride back, Jacob gently checked on him. "How did it go?"

"Pretty rough, really."

"Sorry to hear that."

"Yeah, thanks."

"They try to talk to you?"

"Uh, yeah."

Jacob paused, and when Jack wasn't forthcoming, Jacob half-turned in his seat to look back at him.

"Please tell me you didn't."

"Jacob, the first time I didn't. There was this guy named 'Woods.' Said he wasn't on the case. "Asked me about Hadley really."

"Jack, Jack, Jack..." Jacob shook his head.

"Jacob, that place was hellacious. It absolutely was. But I got some info myself though. From Woods."

"Yeah?"

"Yep."

"What happened?"

"Woods says the lead detective is a woman named Kisha Collerain."

"I've heard of her. She's very good. A straight arrow."

"Woods says Collerain has a lot of questions about Hadley."

"He says that, huh? Well, I'm not sure what Hadley was up to this afternoon, but I'm pretty sure he wasn't in a holding cell. What else?"

"Woods said Collerain didn't understand how I was in the house. There were no signs of forced entry."

"Jack ..."

"I told him she left the door open for me. She had done it before and she did it again."

"He was just trying to get you talking."

"Well, that's all I said."

Jacob looked at Jack until Jack's eyes met his own. "Listen, no more. We can't take any chances. Okay? None."

Jack nodded. "I understand."

"Tomorrow, let's get started. We have a lot to cover."

Jack watched cars pass outside his window. "Alright. I'll tell you this. I can't go back in there."

Silence descended upon the SUV.

"I cannot go back to jail."

Jack drew a deep breath. His stomach stayed clenched. He strained his next words.

"We just have to win."

11

Jacob clapped his hands together. "Here's the thing."

Jack sat rapt in Jacob's office, notepad in his lap and pen at the ready.

"A case in the criminal system is sometimes said to be like a train trip. We started with the arrest. We next go to 'discovery.' Then, it's on to trial. Just like that."

"We have discovery on the civil side, in divorce cases, too. Much more involved."

"Yeah, I wish we got the same discovery you did, but it is what it is, right? We'll get all the information we can. It's going to be very important to get everything we possibly can on Hadley. What did they do? Who did they talk to? What did they find? We prosecute them for not prosecuting Hadley. What did they miss? Why not Hadley? Reasonable doubt, reasonable doubt, reasonable doubt."

"I'll be curious to see it myself."

"Yeah? Me, too."

"Why didn't they?"

"I don't know. But hey, they got her pissed-off lawyer at the scene with blood on his hands, Jack."

Jack clenched his eyes at hearing that again.

Jacob pushed on. "Let's talk about Jack's alibi."

"Good. What's that?"

Jacob permitted himself a small smile. "Jack, uh, that's my point. What do we have?"

Jack's eyes drifted about Jacob's office. "I left dinner with Gene. Was driving home when I got Andrea's text."

Jacob wrote notes.

"Wait," Jack remembered. "Carla called me. As I was driving home. That's right—she called me on my cell as I was on the way home."

"And?"

"She wanted to check on me. I stopped our call when I got Andrea's text."

Jacob rubbed his chin. His eyes seemed to dance. "Hmmmmm."

"What are you thinking?"

"I dunno. You get a call from your ex, to check on you as a result of your lover getting you fired, and the lover winds up dead."

Jack pondered it a bit and shook his head. "Nah, nah. You should see Carla. Couldn't harm a fly. She doesn't shoot someone with a pistol in the head."

"Not even Andrea?"

Jack watched Jacob to detect a grin, but none came. Jacob

201

volunteered, "'Hell hath no fury,' and all."

"I don't think so. But at least I was on the call with her."

"Okay, look. Let her know I'll be calling. I want to talk to her. She could help."

"Alright. Will do."

"Meanwhile I'll get the discovery and we can go over it."

"Great."

"Hey, from here, things will move fast."

Jacob opened his hands and gestured up, as he continued. "This prosecutor's swamped. I filed what's called a 'speedy trial demand.' He has to try you quickly, so the heat is on."

"Thanks."

"You bet. Stay out of trouble and let's get ready."

"Sounds good."

⁂

WEDNESDAY, MAY 18, 2011

Monica Henderson's voice shocked Jack.

"Hey, it's Monica. How are you doing?"

"Um, hanging in there. It's a pretty intense time."

Jack paced around his living room, wondering what would prompt her call.

Monica's tone turned deeply emotional. "I am *so* sorry you're going through all this."

The irony stung Jack. Monica now sympathized with him.

"Thank you, Monica. Thank you very much. Stuff happens, you know? You keep on moving. How are you doing?"

"Still nuts." She sniffed a couple of times and forced a laugh. "Dr. Misencik's been great. I'm really trying to get past all this.

I really am."

"Good. Good."

"I am having a hard time right now, though. My boys. He's turned them against me. It's ugly. Horrible."

Jack thought at once how her case was now Gene's case.

"Monica, it's really important you go by what Gene says. Follow what he says."

"Oh, I know. I do." More sniffles. "It's just... I know you cared. You fought really hard. I appreciate that. I should have listened more to you. I get that now."

"You've just got to hang in there."

"And Gene's great. Don't get me wrong."

"Monica, Gene mentored me. He's the best. Don't worry."

"Oh, I've screwed things up awfully right now. I get that. Sometimes my boys won't even talk to me."

Jack knew this had to hurt her at her core.

She continued. "You think I can fix this later? I mean, I get done with the divorce. You get your stuff straightened out. I mean, I can go back, right? A modification or something?"

Like some stray beam of sunlight on a wretched day, the notion of Jack getting to practice law again, live normally again, lifted him.

"Well, yeah, Monica. You have to take it a step at a time, have to rebuild your relationship with your sons. But it can happen. For now, you have to stick with what Misencik and Gene tell you, okay?"

"Thank goodness. Yes. Absolutely. I will."

"Hang in there, Monica."

"You, too, Jack."

Ouch.

✑

FRIDAY, JUNE 3, 2011

Jacob acted surprised at how soon the State got their discovery to them, but here it was.

"Here's what we have."

Documents were strewn on the conference room table. A separate duplicate stack was in a box for Jack to take with him. These are different reports, notes, materials on witnesses, and the like. There's a good bit here, but nothing that greatly helps us.

"There's not?"

"Let me explain."

Jacob went to a center stack of the documents and pulled parts out. He circled around to Jack and spoke evenly.

"These are the main documents on Jim Hadley. They interviewed him, looked into him deeply."

Jacob straightened into a stance with one hand on his hip and the other gesturing about the air between them.

"The essence of it is that Hadley was at his gym when Andrea was killed. They even checked his membership card with the gym management. He enters the gym forty minutes before Andrea's killed."

"And does it have him checking out later?"

"Actually, there's no use of the card by the gym member to leave. Hadley didn't have to swipe his card or anything."

"No?"

"Well, no. But here's the thing. They have a surveillance camera for the lobby."

"Good."

"Collerain, the detective, obtained the video. It doesn't show Hadley leaving in the forty minutes before the time of death."

"It doesn't?"

Jacob slowly shook his head. "It does not. In fact," Jacob crossed his arms against his chest, "Collerain watched the video five times. Over and over again. I mean, they have the video. No Jim Hadley. But..."

"But?"

"Well, Collerain didn't stop there. She got the rest of the night's video, too. Up until closing. Watched it five times as well."

"Really?"

"Really. They say it's 'inconclusive.' There's a big cluster leaving at closing, so they say 'inconclusive.'"

"But they can't show him leaving."

"They can't show him leaving."

Jack gradually nodded and felt hopeful. He watched for some reaction from Jacob to confirm his own take that this was a good thing. He got none.

Jacob went on. "I got our own investigator, Dan, going over there. We'll dig some on our own."

"Good."

"Yeah."

They were wrapping up, and Jack gathered his box of documents to leave with. Jacob had one last point to cover.

"Wanted to let you know I talked to Carla."

"You did?"

"I did." Jacob paused and shrugged. "She's very concerned, says she cares very much. But..."

"But?"

"She says she is scared. Has never been called as a witness for anything, much less a murder trial. She says she's also scared she might wind up hurting as much as helping."

"What?"

"Something about the abrupt way you had to cut the call short that night. Like you were upset or something."

"Ah, bullshit."

Jacob tried to offer a consoling smile. "I take it that it was you who ended the relationship, I guess."

Jack swayed on his feet and finally moved his head up and down.

"I'm not going to ask about the timing of that break and when you and Andrea started."

Jack lifted his eyes and face and tried his best to be positive. "Thanks."

♪♫

MONDAY, JUNE 20, 2011

Jack found refuge in his workouts at the gym. Like a sanctuary of sorts, the gym was the one place Jack could go and not have to think or engage. He put on his headset, cranked his music, and then let his mind find a distant zone.

Now and then, he treated himself to a smoothie afterwards. That or some sort of wrap or roll. It was a simple routine, but a very necessary one. It helped him relieve stress and he truly believed it was all that kept him sane.

Another routine developed where Jack talked with David each day. The entire ordeal made David fraught with worry and desperation. Time and again, David insisted on coming to Atlanta and being there for Jack. David would say he had to. Each time, Jack thanked him, took his time, and gently urged David not to come.

Jack shared with his brother that the strain was all he could manage. He was immersed in preparing for trial. He appreciated his younger brother's deep concern, he really did. He loved David, too. But he had to do it just *this way*.

Whether David truly understood or not, Jack didn't know. But David honored Jack's wishes on this. And for that, Jack was grateful.

જ

THURSDAY, JUNE 30, 2011

Jack paced about Jacob's conference room. It felt like there wasn't enough oxygen. The walls crept closer. He shook his head.

Jacob tried to explain further what he had learned. Jacob had been in the midst of relaying it when Jack couldn't sit still any longer.

"Dan, the investigator, feels confident about his source at Hadley's gym. A lot of people are familiar with Hadley there. Maybe something about Hadley being an old college tennis guy and all. I don't know."

Jack kept a steady pace.

Jacob took his time. "Hadley's been involved with a personal trainer there. He's supposed to be ga-ga over her, but she? Not so much."

Jack held up and looked to Jacob.

"Anyway, Jim's planning to leave town. He's talked her into going with him."

"He is?"

"Yes, he is."

"Is he under subpoena?"

"He's under subpoena, so he'll have to wait until the trial's over."

"He's going to leave without the insurance money coming in yet?"

"Oh, he can get the insurance money whenever it comes in, and get it wherever he's at. Until then he's got money."

"He does?"

"The money that came in from the scam against you and the firm went into a joint account Andrea and he had. Under Georgia law, he gets that. He has it and it's almost seven million. He's just fine."

"Sounds like a helluva motive to me."

"Yes, it does. And, believe me, it'll be used. But he's on his way out of town."

Jack and Jacob stared a moment and then Jack's phone sounded.

The number looked strange.

Jack figured he'd pick up, find out who it was, and tell them he'd call them right back—Jack wondered who it was.

"Hello, this is Jack Adams."

A strange silence hung on the other end.

Then a male voice tentatively spoke. "Jack, this is Jim Hadley."

Jack choked a breath. "Jim Hadley?"

"Surprised, huh?"

"You could say that."

"Hey, listen your lawyer's investigator has been prying around my gym, scaring the shit out of some people."

"Sounds like you're getting some bad information, Jim. My lawyer is a professional and so is his investigator. It doesn't help us in the least to scare anybody. So that's nonsense."

"I want it to stop."

"And I don't want to go to trial for murdering Andrea when you and I know I didn't do that."

"Well, that makes two of us."

"What?"

"I didn't kill her either."

Jack decided to take a chance. "Sit down and talk to me. Half an hour to an hour tops. Off the record."

"Off the record, huh? Right, like I'm to believe that. Besides, my lawyer's told me not to talk to anybody."

"Yeah? My lawyer's investigator will talk to everybody and fucking anybody we need to."

"You're trying to pressure me. You're also trying to talk to me when I'm already represented, too."

"Well, call the State Bar. I'll deal with that as soon as I get through being prosecuted for murder, Jim."

Hadley sighed on the other end of the line.

Jacob shifted four or five times quickly in his chair, clearly tortured at only being able to hear one side of an extremely important conversation.

"Listen," Jim's voice lowered and he sounded fatigued. "We talk for half an hour. On my terms. No one else around. You carry no weapon with you, no phone, nothing. After that, I never hear from you or anyone working with you again."

A moment flashed by and Jack couldn't think of any good

choices. At all.

"Okay ... Okay." Jack clenched his eyes hard as Jim finished their call. Jack wondered if he was entering into an impossible agreement, but he didn't feel he had any choice whatsoever.

Jim's voice pitched just higher as he gave the details.

"We meet tonight. Midnight. Jeju Spa and Sauna. No weapons, no phones, no friends with us. At the back of the second floor, there is a row of rooms. Two saunas, two ice rooms and two steam rooms. As you look from left to right, I'll be in the fifth room. You'll know it's the right room, because it'll be a steam room and the top third of it will be painted black."

"Wow. Okay. Anything else?"

"Yeah. Don't fuck with me." The phone clicked off.

Jack stared over at Jacob and he knew the blood had to have drained from his face.

Jacob implored him. "SO? What gives? Jim Hadley? Seriously?"

"I'm meeting him tonight."

"You're kidding."

"Nope, I'm serious. He's willing to talk for half an hour, but there can be no more prying by us around him. He's really serious about that."

"Hey, we've run out of clues around him anyway." As soon as Jacob let the words go from his mouth, it looked like he saw Jack's face blanch. Jacob immediately tried to fix what he said.

"For now, I meant." Jacob pressed a forced smile, and shifted gears. "Excellent news. We've got work to do. You sure you're comfortable meeting him?"

"Yeah. I'll be fine." There were no other choices.

◦‿◦

Jack felt like he was in a different city. In a different country. On a different continent.

He detected what he thought were three different languages simply passing from the lobby, through the men's locker room, and to the first floor of the expansive facility. Rumor had it the establishment changed after midnight to a younger and more Asian clientele, and while Jack didn't have any frame of reference, the moderately crowded area looked like it trended younger and Asian in demographic. Everyone went about their own business.

The signs instructed showering before use of any of the rooms on the three floors available, and Jack took a quick one. Then, he wrapped himself in his towel and slid on the sandals he had been provided upon check-in. Jack liked how immaculately clean and orderly the place was kept, and Jack hoped to return sometime when he could relax and enjoy it.

Jack made his way to the fifth room. Inside, thick steam swirled and there was one other guy sitting there. Jim sat waiting on him.

Jack started to sit beside Jim, but Jim needed to verify their other rules.

"Hey, uh, it's not like I wanna see your stuff or anything, but... I gotta see you're not wired."

"What?"

"Open up and turn." Jim drew an upside down circle with his finger at Jack.

Jack paused, but then undid his towel briefly, turned around completely, and then sat back down.

As soon as Jack sat, Jim started his spiel.

"I'm going to tell you three things."

"One, I didn't do it. I absolutely did not."

Jack waited a moment. Jim likely sensed Jack wasn't going to commit one way or the other to Jim's declaration, and Jim pushed ahead.

"I've been in some scrapes, but I've never killed anybody. And, Andrea..." Jim's voice trailed and he looked off out into a distance only he could see. He was still looking away when he finished the thought to Jack.

"Andrea was special to me. We'd known each other since college. We may not have been passionate like we had always been, but we did love each other. She was there for me. And I was there for her. No matter what, that wasn't going to change."

Hadley stared at his hands a second and inhaled hard. "I'm scared shitless. I don't sleep. I'm looking over my shoulder. Yeah. I got the money. But I feel like I have a bulls-eye on my back. I gotta get out of here and I gotta go far away."

Hadley bent his head to face Jack directly with his next point.

"Two, Andrea was involved with a heavy hitter. Very wealthy man. Don't know exactly who. A no-bullshit kind of guy. He was flying her places. I don't know where they were at with things, but if he thought she was pressuring him... "

Hadley shrugged. "I mean, if he took it that she was pushing him to replace me, and then get divorced and marry him, then yes, he struck me as the kind of guy that could do it, or have it done."

"You think she pressured him?"

Hadley tossed his hands in the air. "I've racked my brain on that one. Over and over. It wouldn't have been like her to do that. It just wouldn't have. In her mind, she never 'needed' anyone, you know?"

"I understand."

"Now, on the other hand, did this guy get the impression she was pressuring him? Or was about to? Or was capable of it? I don't know. *That* could be possible. Listen, in her mind, she could come up with shit. I mean, she came up with things I could never whip up in a million years. Never. Which brings me to number three."

Hadley looked about the steam room and then back over at him. Hadley's eyes bore into Jack's. His lips were tightly pressed at first, not wanting to speak.

"What I'm about to tell you is some deadly shit, okay?"

Jack started to smart off about the predicament Jack was already in, but Hadley looked much too far past any humor at all. Instead, Jack just nodded back.

"I mean, you gotta even think about how you would bring this up. I never would, myself. In fact, you can't say I said this, alright? I will absolutely deny it. Got it?"

"I hear you. It didn't come from you." At this point, Jack couldn't even reason out how he was using any of this, but he needed to hear 'point three' and Hadley needed to blurt it out already. Jack was past tired of sitting in a steam room with Jim Hadley in the middle of the night.

"Okay, here's the thing. You knew the sweet, loveable Andrea. I get that. She was absolutely special. No one else like her. Gorgeous. Captivating. Charming. But there was even more. When she looked at you, it was like no one else existed on the planet, and *Andrea Turner* was absorbed in you. I get that. I really do."

Jack tried not to show it outwardly, but Hadley had just nailed exactly how Andrea had made him feel numerous times. Jack didn't respond and waited on Hadley's revelation.

"But, let me tell you," even in the thick moist fog that hovered between them, Jim's wide, drawn eyes peered at Jack, "as much as she could seem vulnerable, she wasn't. Not at all."

Jack considered how true this was, but said nothing.

"Man, she didn't *feel*. She might act like she cared, or she might act like she was emotional," Jim shook his head, "but it really wasn't there. Take her toughness at scamming you and multiply it by ten. A hundred."

Jack looked at Hadley and Jack's face tightened. Hadley seemed to get that Jack didn't quite appreciate just how inwardly tough Andrea was, so he enlightened Jack.

"You did not hear this from me, but Andrea wasn't satisfied with the settlement money from you and the firm. That was pocket money to her. She had been around this businessman and all his toys and power, and she had decided she wanted it all."

"Wanted it all?"

"She wanted Bob's money, the family money. Evidently, she thought Bob had taught her she had to be willing to 'get her hands dirty.' So she came up with a plan."

"No. Her *father*?"

Hadley slowly nodded. "Bob's had heart problems in the past. She had this idea about poisoning him with anti-freeze. The whole thing was wild, sure, but she had a plan."

Jack swayed in place as he processed this. His head swam.

Hadley beat Jack to a thought just before Jack got there on his own. "Hey, what if somehow Bob got wind of that, man?

You think he'd let her take a shot at him? No way. I mean, he probably didn't find out, but hell, who knows?"

Jack wiped gobs of sweat off his face and shook his hand off to the side, spraying perspiration onto the floor and against the far wall. A question gnawed at Jack as they sat there. He leveled it at Hadley.

"Tell me something. Why are you giving me all this? Why do you care what happens? You've got some money. And more coming."

"Well, it's like this. Turner's right-hand man is an old military guy named McSherry. He's also done some investigative work for Bob. I've talked to McSherry. McSherry has let me know that Bob doesn't believe you killed Andrea. And listen, it doesn't take much of a stretch to know that if he doesn't think it was you, then he likely thinks it was me. Bob Turner's not going to let this pass—Andrea being murdered. He will deal with it. If he doesn't think you did it, he'll go after who he thinks did."

"So you're hoping I get this out there about the married guy. Steer the light off you onto him. Is that it?"

"Hey, it wasn't me, man. It damn sure wasn't. If it wasn't Bob, then I could die. Seriously. When your trial's over, Bob will kill me."

"And if somehow it was Bob Turner?"

"Then you've raised the prospect of the businessman having done it, which again takes the light off me. Turner will see I didn't raise a word about knowing anything about Andrea's scheme against him. Plus, if it looks like the businessman is the bad guy, then there's no reason to kill me. And look, I'll take off. He'll never have to worry about me again."

Jack put his face in his hands. They had been sitting there so long that he felt dizzy. Hadley must have also. As Hadley got up to leave, his words were clipped.

"Good luck, man."

12

JACK AND JACOB WORKED UP UNTIL TRIAL, and they struggled with the information Hadley had dropped on them. Jack had been encouraged by what he had heard, but when they analyzed it, they didn't have much. Jacob walked them both through the tactics of how it would play out.

The angle that pointed to Bob was way too risky. Jacob could hardly argue that the victim herself was maneuvering to murder her own father. It literally added insult to injury. And moreover, their source was Hadley. If they tried to rely on what Hadley said, they couldn't point at Hadley as a possible culprit, too. It just wasn't credible.

The theory about the mystery 'businessman' had to be discounted as well. It would again depend on Hadley. It was too much of a stretch. And included in the theory was Andrea's affair with the businessman. It just wasn't a good idea to focus on the victim's bad behavior as part of the defense.

Hadley's information tantalized them, but in the final analysis, it didn't give them an argument or proof they could use. They would keep it in mind just in case, but things would have to change *a lot* for them to be able to use it. They couldn't expect that would happen.

Jack wound up trying to explain all of this to David in their last daily call before the start of the trial. It took time and patience, but he accomplished it.

Jack also succeeded at getting David to understand why it was important to Jack that David did not come to Atlanta. As much as David wanted to help, Jack would feel enormous stress from David going through it with him. Jack explained to David how much it mattered for Jack to be able to focus. Jack promised David he would call him every day. David begrudgingly said he understood.

Jack failed at the one last thing with David that wound up being so very meaningful. The plea bargaining conference was a formality that Jack and Jacob appreciated as necessary but useless. Jack and Jacob had to meet with McCleary to discuss whether an agreement could be reached without going to trial. Jack and Jacob figured McCleary wanted prison time; in McCleary's view, this was a premeditated murder. Jack and Jacob went in knowing there wouldn't be an agreement.

Jack was explaining to David how the conference went, and all was well until one particular part that stopped David cold. David asked Jack what McCleary wanted to offer to get the matter resolved short of trial.

Jack answered candidly. "Life to serve 25."

The phone went silent.

David's voice trembled with a question. "Twenty-five years in prison?"

Jack said. "Well, yes, twenty-five years, but the reality is that parole is possible after seven. Possible."

"My God. What will he seek now?"

Jack paused but answered.

A couple of seconds passed with nothing, but then Jack heard a sound he hadn't heard even at his father's funeral. He hadn't heard it since he and his brother were boys.

David choked first a short breath and then a harder one. Then, the shrill of his brother's crying came through.

Jack pleaded. "Oh David, don't. *Please* don't."

In that moment, Jack loathed himself. David didn't deserve to suffer this pain Jack had now caused. Jack wasn't guilty for Andrea's murder, but he felt like he was responsible for the pain this caused David. Jack didn't see how he could ever forgive himself. Except to win.

Life with no possibility of parole.

WEDNESDAY, JULY 20, 2011

In an expansive courtroom packed with people, the somberness and the silence weighed heavily.

Monday and Tuesday's jockeying over jury selection was complete; it was time for the actual trial.

The Honorable Madeleine Claude went to her full voice to summon the lawyers to begin.

"Counsel, proceed with opening statements."

From the counsel table closest to the jury box, Manford

McCleary gradually rose to his feet. He deliberately took his time. All eyes in the courtroom, even those of the experienced Judge Claude, followed the prosecutor raptly, step by step until he stood facing the jury.

"Ladies and gentlemen of the jury, let me begin by thanking you for your service in this case. This is a case that is very serious to all involved, and I thank you for your time and attention.

"This is my opportunity to talk to you about the facts and issues in this case. It is a kind of preview, if you will. I strongly expect this to be straightforward.

"Tragically, Andrea Turner's life was cut very short. It didn't have to be. But unfortunately, she crossed the wrong man.

"I expect the evidence will show that the Defendant, Jack Adams, murdered Andrea.

"I also expect the evidence will be straightforward about the three things central to this case." McCleary's hand rose as he ticked off each element. "Identity, opportunity, and motive."

"The proof will show, beyond a reasonable doubt, that the identity of the killer is the Defendant. He was right there on the scene, Ladies and gentlemen. Now, he's smart," McCleary shot a contemptuous glance in the direction of Adams. "He's a successful lawyer. Well... he was—I'll get to that in just a moment."

McCleary walked across in front of the jury box, and all the jurors' eyes followed him.

"He thought he had staged this well as a suicide. So he was there when the police arrived. Now, I also expect you'll hear that he didn't call the police. Please remember that. He supposedly just happened upon Andrea dead, or horribly shot, and he doesn't pull out his cell and call 911."

McCleary's head slowly shook back and forth. "Nope, he doesn't do it."

"Someone else heard the shot and called. I expect the Defendant's plan was thrown off. You see, he didn't get to finish his work of positioning Andrea before the police arrive. You'll hear evidence that she wasn't positioned to have fired this shot herself. Before he could call, he must've heard the sirens. He was interrupted."

McCleary looked at the jury and then shot a long look at Jack. The jurors also peered over at Jack. Jack suddenly felt very self-conscious. He wasn't sure what to do. All he could do was stare back blankly.

McCleary turned from staring down Jack and addressed the jury again.

"In addition to being at the scene, he had the opportunity. He and Andrea had been lovers fairly recently. He knew the layout of the house, and evidently he knew how to get in. He either knew how to get in, or she let him in unaware of what was going to happen. You will not hear a word about any forced entry or break-in. The Defendant had the opportunity, and he seized it, ladies and gentlemen."

McCleary slowly walked back across the jury box, his hands up in front of him and his fingertips tapping at each other. In a deeper but still crystal-clear voice, he intoned his next point with a reverence that made it significant.

"Probably the most compelling part of this case is the motive. You are going to hear how the Defendant's world had fallen absolutely apart. His license to practice law, his successful practice, his luxurious lifestyle—it was all forever gone. In his outsized sense of *entitlement* and *ambition*, he had not just represented Andrea Turner, but he had also taken her as a lover. You may hear talk of some scheme or hoax or whatever, but none of that justified killing her in cold blood. Shooting her in the head and killing her. Of course not."

"But the night she was murdered, the Defendant had dinner with Gene Hatcher, his superior at his firm, and the Defendant learned in no uncertain terms that with his affair out in the open, it was costing him his license, his job, and his lifestyle. It was all gone."

"Ladies and gentlemen, THAT was when he went to Andrea's house. That was when he shot her and staged the scene to try to make it look like a suicide. He took from her everything she had or ever will have, because he figured she had done that to him."

♪

As McCleary took his seat at the table, Jacob Weinberg bolted up and around his own table. It was an energized move tinged with urgency, as would be expected from one who was eager to speak of what he had just intolerably heard. He planted himself in front of the jury box, and appeared to lean towards them.

"Ladies and gentlemen, we thank you for your service, too. This is indeed a serious and tragic matter for all involved. It really is. We trust you will give it the kind of attention and thought that it needs."

Jacob bowed his head a moment and then brought it back up, eying as many of the jurors as he could as he spoke carefully.

"We also continue to offer our respect and condolences to the Turners." For a moment, Jacob fell silent. His eyes gazed over to where the Turners sat in the gallery, but he kept it a quick acknowledgment. His attention came right back to where it should be, and that was with the twelve people watching him intently.

"Ladies and gentlemen, there are three points I raise and I ask that you bear in mind as we go about this case. Mr. McCleary is an excellent prosecutor and he certainly can argue. No question about it. But Mr. McCleary is trying to get you to convict Jack Adams of murder. And not just murder, but a horrible murder of a young woman Jack cared about.

"I first must ask you, and the Judge will later instruct you, that you base your decision at the end of this matter on the evidence and the law. No matter how eloquently Mr. McCleary argues, as he did just now, and no matter the emotion and sympathy we all feel about the tragic loss of Andrea, in this case, in this Courtroom, the question turns on the evidence and the law. It absolutely does.

"We are fortunate to live in such a country as ours, where our peers hear the evidence and judge, and we are governed by law. Please listen carefully to what the evidence is and just as importantly, what it isn't. Judge the case on the evidence and the law. I truly believe that when you do that, there'll be too many unanswered questions to say that there is no reasonable doubt.

"This brings me to my second point, which is that the prosecutor here has the burden of proving this case to you. Mr. McCleary must prove this to you, and—this is important—he must prove it 'beyond a reasonable doubt.' We'll be able to argue this point more at the end of the case, because right now is just my chance to set out the issues, but when it comes to deciding whether Jack is guilty, it is Mr. McCleary who has the burden of doing that and doing it beyond a reasonable doubt."

"Lastly, for now, I respectfully ask that you recognize and

use common sense. Just now when I said that we are lucky to live in a country where we are judged by our peers, I was in a sense also alluding to this. When I hear 'common sense,' I often think about that knowledge and sense we all have and share about what we hear and see. "

"We all know when something is amiss, when it doesn't fit. There will be those things in this trial, and I will leave you with one such thing that I expect the evidence to show you."

Jacob paused and gazed at the jurors. He gestured his hands gently open and forward like he was giving them something. The jurors hung on his words, waiting.

"The evidence is going to be that, yes, Jack was suspended from law, but the suspension was for six months. Six months, ladies and gentlemen. He had NOT, contrary to what Mr. McCleary argues, lost everything for evermore, as it is depicted to you. He still had a license and a livelihood to come back to. It wasn't over for him."

"Instead, there was someone else who was at much greater risk, and with much greater risk, and that person should be sitting where Jack Adams sits. Jim Hadley, Andrea's husband, should be sitting there, ladies and gentlemen."

Jack's mind whirled and his stomach churned from the opening statements. During McCleary's opening, a couple of times he tasted the recurrent pungency of his own vomit seep into his mouth, just as he had that fateful night when he found Andrea. He was living a nightmare he didn't see ending or getting better.

He struggled with focusing with the first couple of witnesses, and try as he might, he couldn't follow the words that came first from the emergency medical technician and then Detective Collerain. He heard descriptions about positioning and what the scene was like, but the substance sailed right by him as he reeled from the gravity of it all.

It wasn't until the name of the third witness was announced that he could bring himself to really listen. He felt bolstered by the sound of McCleary calling out the name "Jim Hadley." Rustling and muted whispers first murmured in the courtroom. Then the courtroom fell absolutely silent.

✍

"Where were you on the night of Andrea's murder?" McCleary directly questioned Jim Hadley.

The courtroom, though packed, stayed absolutely quiet. McCleary's tone implored Hadley to give him the truth.

Hadley looked straight back at McCleary. "I was at my gym. I was working out." As soon as he had said the words, Jim was looking directly over to the jurors, facing them.

"Did you go to Andrea's house that night?"

"No, I did not."

"Now Mr. Hadley," McCleary took his time with the follow-up question, "you are a beneficiary of a three-million-dollar life insurance policy on Andrea, correct?"

"We had three million dollars in coverage on EACH OTHER." As Hadley pointed this out, Jack appreciated the deftness of McCleary's tactic. McCleary had chosen to go ahead and diffuse this issue himself. Better to deal with it himself and directly.

This showed he didn't fear it.

"Mr. Hadley, did you kill Andrea Turner?"

"No, absolutely not." Jim Hadley looked straight at the jury. "I didn't kill her."

McCleary paused just a moment to shift topics and gears. His manner attempted a delicateness with the next line of questioning.

"What, if any, effort were you and Andrea involved in to obtain a large sum of money?"

Hadley looked sheepishly into his lap and then back up. "Andrea was making a claim against Mr. Adams and his firm for Mr. Adams having compromised her case by sleeping with her."

"Objection to the characterization, Your Honor."

McCleary rehabilitated the answer from Hadley. "You mean, allegedly compromising her case."

"I guess."

"Mr. Hadley, was there ever a time when you saw Mr. Adams upset with Andrea?"

"Yes. We had gone to Mr. Adams's law offices to fill out some paperwork, and he saw us coming out of the office."

"Did he and Andrea talk?" McCleary prompted.

"Yes, they did."

"Is this when Mr. Adams learned that Andrea had set up the claim for damages against Mr. Adams and his firm?"

"No, but it was the first time he'd seen her since he'd learned."

"And, how did Mr. Adams act?"

"He got extremely angry."

"What did he say?"

"He yelled at Andrea to 'go fuck herself.'" The expletive sent an audible shock through the room. "It was the last thing he said to her that day."

Jack didn't betray any reaction outwardly, but inside, he cringed. McCleary pivoted from the lectern smugly.

Right away, Jacob Weinberg was on his feet and moving swiftly to the lectern.

"Mr. Hadley, Andrea was divorcing you, isn't that true?"

"Yeah, but ... we planned to dismiss that."

Jacob pushed ahead. "Andrea had recently won an important ruling against you in Court. That's true too, isn't it?"

"Yes, but the case wasn't over. Plus, there was the claim against Adams."

"Well, you couldn't be absolutely certain about the damages claim. Nothing had been paid yet, right?"

"No, not transferred yet. It was going to be wired though."

"And the case wasn't going well for you."

"I dunno," Hadley weakly offered.

"There was a prenuptial agreement, correct?" Jacob asked sharply.

"Yeah, but we were fighting that. In the divorce and all."

McCleary could not have liked Jim's use of the word 'fight' there, Jack figured.

"Mr. Hadley, if you lost the divorce case, you were going to get nothing."

"Yeah." Hadley noticeably shifted in his chair.

"Now you stand to get at least three million dollars?"

"Yes ..." His tone conveyed serious wounding. The voices in the courtroom rustled from behind Jack "... but I didn't kill her."

"The divorce case is certainly over now that Andrea is dead, isn't it?"

Jim Hadley's head jerked and his mouth gaped open. McCleary wanted to object, but Jack knew that McCleary wouldn't want to call even more attention to the exchange and he certainly didn't want to be overruled. McCleary kept his seat.

Jacob Weinberg returned to his seat.

Judge Claude's voice resonated with a question to counsel. "Can this witness be excused?" It was more a formality, and the prosecutor replied yes.

Weinberg couldn't resist one last sneer at Hadley who looked around very uncertain of what was being said about him. "Yes," Weinberg uttered slowly, "nothing further of this... 'witness.'"

Weinberg twisted the last word in such a way that all knew Weinberg's abject distaste of Hadley.

McCleary stood and surprised the Judge. "Your Honor, we should keep Mr. Hadley available. Pending the Defense's case."

The Judge shrugged and turned her attention back to Hadley. "You are not yet excused. Remain in attendance and subject to recall. Mr. Hadley, I instruct you that you shall continue to refrain from discussing this case with others or permitting them to discuss it with you. Do you understand?"

The Judge said it to Hadley dismissively, and Hadley looked first to the jury who seemed to collectively look away from Hadley for various and sundry reasons.

"Yes, Your Honor."

Hadley self-consciously descended from the witness box. His head titled down, and for a split second he may have appeared almost sympathetic. Then, his eyes darted about, and his face tightened to where he appeared to suppress a mean side.

Jack watched Hadley closely, and when a couple of the members of the jury seemed to notice the same thing, Jack permitted himself a sliver of hope. Hadley resembled someone trying to figure out if they were getting away with something, and for that, Jack was very thankful.

Jack was still following Jim's exit from the courtroom when Jack noticed something subtle but profound. Hadley had cleared the front portion of the courtroom when Hadley glanced to his right. Jack traced Hadley's look and saw what Hadley was regarding. Bob Turner was seated on the end of the second row, and Turner's eyes were locked menacingly onto Hadley. Even from where Jack sat angled away from the exchange, Jack could still detect Hadley flinch. Turner looked like he could physically launch onto Hadley. Hadley hurried past Turner, and Turner struggled to breathe deeper, trying to calm himself.

Mindful of the jury's time and fleeting attention, McCleary efficiently called Gloria Andrews as his next witness. McCleary walked Andrews through the fact that she was a personal injury lawyer and that she had represented Andrea in her claim against Jack and the firm. Andrews held herself poised and displayed an authoritative air.

"Did you have occasion to talk with the Defendant?" McCleary formally asked.

"Yes, I did."

"When was that?"

"Andrea and I visited his firm's law office to complete paperwork. Mr. Adams was entering the building as we were leaving that day."

"Where did you see him?"

"In the lobby."

"Had he spoken to Andrea at that point?"

"Yes. I later learned that he had. I spoke to him just after he had confronted her."

"What had he confronted her about?"

"He had concluded that she had schemed the whole situation up where she made claims against him and his firm."

"Had she?"

"No, not to my knowledge." Gloria Andrews seemed to slump her shoulders a bit and then sounded a candid tone. "Hey, I can't be sure exactly how it all unfolded, but like I told Mr. Adams that day, if they had not slept together, then none of the problems would have occurred. I tried to get through to him that he had a role and a duty that he had failed to meet."

McCleary nodded. "How did he react to this?

Andrews looked right over to Jack, and she glared at him. "Not well. Not well at all. He went on and on about some kind of 'mutual promises' kind of thing. He felt Andrea had betrayed him. That there were 'broken promises,' and he was very upset."

"Did the two of you discuss anything else?

Andrews hesitated and then she added reluctantly. "I told him he shouldn't come around her anymore. That he should keep his distance."

"How did he react?"

"At the time, I thought it got through to him." She paused and it looked like her composure barely slipped. She brought a hand to her mouth as if she might become emotional. She managed to catch herself, and then she finished her thought. "At the time I really did think it had gotten through to him. It seemed like it had."

McCleary thanked her, and then it was Jacob's turn. He was quick and efficient with Andrews as well.

"Ms. Andrews, Andrea and Jim Hadley were both with you that day at the firm's offices, weren't they?"

"Yes." She shrugged.

"And they had been together throughout their purported separation, isn't that true?"

"I guess." Her eyes searched briefly around, uncertain. "As far as I know."

"And as far as you know, Jim Hadley knew all along that Andrea was going to have an affair with Jack."

"I guess. I mean," she stammered somewhat, "it sure seems that way now. But who knows."

"Andrea and Jim Hadley were going to receive over seven million dollars for their claims against the firm and Jack, isn't that true?"

"Yes."

"So when you saw Jack that day, he was understandably upset about the situation."

"I understood him being upset about thinking that it had been planned, but..."

"Jack made no threats, did he?"

"No."

"He did nothing to cause you to believe he presented any kind of risk, did he?"

"No."

"In fact, you took no precaution nor made any report fearing anything would happen, did you?"

"No, I didn't."

"That's all I have," Jacob's last words then had a bite, "for this witness."

❧

The gym couldn't quench Jack's anxiety the night after the first day's testimony. He rode the stair climber, hiked the elliptical, and pumped some weights.

Even the hot shower didn't work.

As soon as he left the gym, he rang Weinberg. Weinberg answered and did his best to try to reassure Jack. Jack reeled.

"McCleary's evidence is still thin." Weinberg's tone stayed even.

Jack couldn't sit still as he drove home.

"I've never understood why he came after me anyway. Don't people *always* suspect the husband?" He worried his tone was more of a whine.

Weinberg talked of being patient, but Jack had to *do* something.

"Jacob, I know we've talked about this, but things are really bad now. I have to get up there and testify."

"Jack, Jack..." Weinberg sighed.

"Jacob, I can do this."

"Andrea really damaged you. McCleary knows that. Your job. Your career. Your reputation."

"He just thinks his theory makes more sense."

"You know," Jack tried to handle his next point delicately, "you, Hatcher, really anyone who knows me—no one who actually knows me thinks I did this. They know it's just not me."

"That's all well and good," Weinberg interjected.

Jack shifted in his seat. "The reason no one who knows me thinks I did it is because when they get to know me, they know I'm not that guy."

Weinberg's voice grew thin—the first time Jack had heard

it do so. "Are you going to tell me the jury simply needs to get to know you?"

"Jacob, I know it's not that simple. I do. But..."

Jacob interrupted. "Jack, you'll be in a no-win situation." Jacob's words came sharply. "You come off sounding smooth, then they'll say you're a lawyer. They'll think you're supposed to come off well. In court and all."

Jack drew a breath in while Jacob continued.

"And hey, if you *don't* do well... Forget it. That's it. You're hiding something. You're guilty. It'll be over. We'll lose."

Jack's mouth dropped open and no words came. Weinberg finished the conversation.

"McCleary would put you on the defensive, and even though it's not how it's supposed to work, he'll have you trying to explain why you're not guilty. You can't do it, Jack. Way too much risk."

Jack's eyes glazed. He surveyed the dark sky and tried to get his bearings. He searched for something more to say. Jacob gently moved them on to other issues.

"Let's work together on some of these direct-examination outlines. I'll bring you copies of them in the morning. We can brainstorm them some more."

Jacob wasn't letting up at all. Jacob tried one last time to calm Jack.

"Hang in there. It's going to be alright."

THURSDAY, JULY 21, 2011

Gene Hatcher rocked side to side in the chair on the witness stand. He turned to one side and then the other. He couldn't get comfortable. Gene took a short glance to Jack at the defense table, and then he focused on the direct examination from McCleary.

"Mr. Hatcher, on the night of Andrea Turner's murder, where did you have dinner?"

"Hal's Steakhouse." Gene answered forthright.

"Who did you have dinner with?"

"Jack Adams."

"And what, if any, particular purpose was there for this dinner?"

Gene's head tilted slightly higher as he steeled himself to testify in open court about what was to have been a discreet meeting and topic.

"I had dinner with Jack to discuss what the firm was doing about the ... situation that was going on with Andrea."

McCleary stood closer to Gene at the witness stand, almost willing the jury to pay close attention to Gene's testimony.

"Mr. Hatcher, what are you referring to when you say the 'situation' going on with Andrea?"

Gene maneuvered again awkwardly in his seat but continued. "It had been discussed that there was an affair between Jack and Andrea. When it turned out that Jim Hadley's lawyer wanted to continue fighting Andrea's divorce case, and that this would mean Andrea's deposition, Andrea broke down. She broke down in Jack's office when he told her she'd have to testify."

"What did this mean for your dinner that night with Jack?"

"I'm not sure I follow you." Gene was defensive. He had to testify, but it was clear he did not feel he was there to help McCleary. To the contrary.

"Well, how did the situation with Andrea affect what your

dinner with Jack was about? Were you having dinner with him to discuss it?"

"Yes, I was having dinner with him to talk to him about his relationship with the firm, to let him know what had been decided."

"And what had been decided?"

Gene glanced down and then back up as he stiffened in the chair within the witness stand. He grimaced and pushed on.

"It had been decided that Jack was going to be discharged from the firm. This had been just too much. Andrea brought claims against not just Jack, but against the whole firm. It had the potential to be devastating to us. To all of us. We couldn't get past that. There was just no way." Gene's eyes reflected dismay. "I understood why he was being let go, but I did feel sympathy for him and what he was going through. It was my job to tell him he was being let go, and... I also wanted to try to help him."

"How? How were you trying to help him?"

"Well, the firm provided him a severance. I pushed for him to have a six-month severance, and the partners agreed. I let him know that night, and I also gave it to him. But I also tried to talk to him about how he could go forward. How he could get past it all. I felt it could be worked out. Over time that is."

"Did you get specific with him?"

"Yes. I did."

"How so?"

"I told him that he could take six months and then get back to practicing law. I believed that he could have his license reinstated and get back into practice."

"Was his license taken?"

"Andrea's lawyer had brought a complaint with the Bar. It was being suspended."

"So basically, Andrea, through her lawyer, had acted against his livelihood?"

"Yes, it was probably something that Andrews, Andrea's attorney, felt was consistent with what they were saying Jack had done, so they had filed a grievance with the Bar against him."

"So," McCleary turned to the jury and gestured with his hands upward as if to make his point clear, "as you're there having dinner with him, you're telling him that the firm is firing him and meanwhile the Bar has suspended him because of Andrea?"

Gene waited a moment. He didn't want to help McCleary, but he was under oath. "Yes."

Jack listened, noted the heavy silence in the courtroom after Gene's reluctant admission, and Jack experienced a sinking feeling.

McCleary built on Gene's testimony. "How did Jack take this?"

"It was an awful lot. Obviously." Gene valiantly took up for Jack.

"Yes, it was. But again, how did he take it?"

"How did he 'take it?'" Gene's tone was mocking. "He took it as well as could be expected, I guess."

"Oh, so he just said, 'okay, sounds fine by me?' He just accepted what you set out there?"

Gene shot a look over to Jack. It was brief, but it was certain. Gene had to be truthful. Gene looked back over to McCleary who stood squarely before him, waiting.

"Jack took it understandably. He didn't like it, and I didn't blame him for not liking it."

"But did he agree?"

Gene looked down and then back up. "He wanted to contest Andrea's claims. He felt she and Jim had concocted all this, schemed it against him. He didn't want her to get away with this. Or, profit by it, really."

"What did he say?"

"He felt she had broken a promise to him. The promise a client makes to a lawyer who has taken on their case and promised to defend them. It was quite a philosophical argument. He felt very strongly that she had wronged him, as well. That she hadn't been honest with him."

"So he didn't want there to be a settlement with her? For her to 'get away with it?'"

"No, he didn't."

"And did this matter? Could he stop the settlement with Andrea?"

Gene stared at McCleary. There was no way around it. "No. No, he couldn't."

"And why couldn't he, Mr. Hatcher?"

Hatcher's eyebrows lifted and his face expressed a candor about it. "Basically, I made it clear to him that the firm wanted to deal with this swiftly and discreetly. That's all."

"And he didn't like that?"

Gene slightly shook his head. "No, no he didn't."

"As dinner ended, how did the Defendant appear to you?"

Hatcher frowned. "Jack was fine. He perhaps didn't like exactly how this was unfolding. But he didn't seem out of control or anything either."

McCleary pressed Hatcher. "Mr. Hatcher, he didn't want Andrea 'getting away' with this and he was agitated, was he not?"

Hatcher braced and shot back. "He didn't act like someone

who was losing it, Mr. McCleary."

"Let's see. He was losing his job, being suspended from the practice of law, his very livelihood, and he was told by you that Andrea was going to be paid a lot of money by the firm for her claims. You were telling him in essence that she was 'getting away' with it, isn't that true?"

Hatcher stared at McCleary. His pause only made the answer's effect more potent. "Yes, I guess."

"Are you testifying that he wasn't agitated at this?" McCleary's tone was matter of fact.

Hatcher pulled in a long inhale and answered back. "No. No, I'm not."

McCleary was moving to his seat and Jacobs was up quickly on his feet.

"Mr. Hatcher, how long was Jack to be suspended for?"

"Six months."

"He was getting his license back?"

"Yes. Yes he was."

"And from what you knew he wasn't broke or destitute either, was he?"

"No. Absolutely not."

"In fact, that night at dinner you had given Jack a severance check had you not?"

"That's right."

"What was covered by that severance check?"

"It was for six months."

"Six months, huh?"

"Yes, that's right."

"Mr. Hatcher, did Jack's demeanor that night cause you serious concern?"

Hatcher thought back a moment. "No, not serious concern. I mean, he didn't like what was happening. But it didn't cause me 'serious concern.' No."

"Well, I mean, you didn't leave dinner that night worried about anything Jack might do, isn't that right?"

"That's right."

"Because you didn't do anything. You didn't call anyone or check back with Jack to make sure things were alright, isn't that true?"

"That's right."

When Jacobs was sitting back down, it was McCleary who bounced right back up.

"Mr. Hatcher, you had known the Defendant a long time, hadn't you?"

"Yes, of course."

"And you had had to tell him some very hard truths that night, what had to happen with the claims by Andrea. Isn't that true?"

"Yes." Hatcher's tone was unavoidably resigned.

"You left there concerned about Jack, did you not?"

Everyone saw Hatcher glance to Jack and the answer was evident before he even gave it. "Yes," Hatcher had to admit it.

13

THE NIGHT AFTER THE SECOND DAY OF TRIAL, Jack paced
from room to room in his house. The quiet halls barely held
him. The dimmed lights didn't soothe him.

His mind raced. Gene's testimony had hurt him. Jack knew
that. Gene had come off as someone who didn't want to testify
against Jack, but still had damaging things to say. Damaging
facts.

The jury wouldn't even look at him. None of them. That
couldn't be good.

The testimony was layering, where each witness built upon
the last and the testimony all bolstered the prosecutor's theory
of what had happened. McCleary's case had worked so far. And
it wasn't over.

From room to room, he drifted. He couldn't stop thinking
about Hatcher on the stand, and McCleary scoring points

through Hatcher, piece by painstaking piece. Jack was certain the jury noticed it all, just like he did.

The trial moved one day closer to the end, and Jack faced few alternatives. This reality weighed on him. There was simply no getting around it.

Jack reminded himself that Weinberg had said it was going to be like this. The prosecution goes first. They should be expected to gather momentum. It was the nature of the process. As a lawyer, Jack knew this as well as any client. Still, with his own fate in the balance, it was hard to take.

He got ready for bed. He first tried to read to get himself calm for some sleep. His mind wouldn't slow down. After just a few pages, he turned to some writing, but there was no relief in even just writing out the thoughts in his head.

Finally, he resorted to deep breathing. Slow, measured inhales and exhales. All deep into his stomach and then released out of his open mouth. There was some relief but no sleep.

He got out of bed. The only other thing he could do was wander the floors again. Maybe he'd tire more. He roamed to the living room, and then to the kitchen.

He resorted to the bottle of Crown Reserve he'd had pulled out earlier, but had not opened. He retrieved a tall glass, filled it with ice, and then poured half a glass of whisky. The rest of the glass he topped with water. He swirled it about as he walked to the bathroom.

Standing in the bathroom, he sipped the strong drink, savoring its initial smoothness and then the robust butterscotch and corn-like flavor. His eyes briefly closed as he followed the first sip with a longer pull. He tried to avoid a thought that hovered.

A sick question had followed him about as he walked his house. It haunted him. Of all nights, why had he thought of this?

Why had his father told him that?

Jack had tried and tried to remember when or where his father had mentioned it. For the life of him, he couldn't. All he knew was that it had to have been while he was young.

Once a Marine, always a Marine, and his father had often invoked this truth. His father served actively twenty years, but he would never stop being a Marine. He simply went on 'inactive reserve.'

His father always reminded him that there were two ways to do anything. There was the wrong way, and there was the Marine way, or the right way. Over and over, his father taught him that the Marine way was the right way to do anything.

But why tell him *this*?

Jack looked about the bathroom. On the bathtub sat the items he had arranged earlier. He had left them there and walked away. Now, they sat ready.

On the one side of the tub was the bottle of hydrocodone Jack had never used. Months ago, he had strained his back and been prescribed them. He had just never used them. There was a bottle full of the pills.

On the other side of the tub, a long hunting knife balanced on the porcelain. Unsheathed, it gleamed. One of the most expensive, and amazingly sharp, it had been a gift from a former client named W. A. Surls.

He hadn't run the water in the tub earlier, but now he eased it on. He adjusted it, so it would be hot when he got in it. He stood back up and pondered his question.

Why in the hell did he tell me that?

His father's words came back in the same clear and even manner he must have heard them so many years ago. The specific words weren't there, but the message was loud and clear.

The wrong way to cut one's self is from side to side on the wrist. That is messy and inefficient.

No, the right way, *the Marine way,* was to begin the cut at the soft part of the skin of the arm where the crook of the arm was opposite the elbow. Right there beneath the crease. Then, you just drew straight down to the wrist. The blood would rush from such a cut. It would be fast and very effective.

Oh, and you do this in a tub. Do not leave a mess for others. The Marine way was to have some water and be in a tub, so that it was easy to clean up.

Why tell a kid this? Why? Why?

Jack braced. He drank a hard gulp of the whisky before he bent and shut off the hot water. It felt perfect with just a light mist rising from the water.

He picked up the pill bottle and unscrewed the cap. He felt his throat tighten and his chest squeeze with one possible answer to his question coming to him.

Maybe he equipped you with this. Maybe you were supposed to know this all along. Maybe this was how this was supposed to work out all along. Maybe this is the answer.

He took two pills from the bottle slipped them in his mouth, and then he chugged at the whisky.

A blissful lightness washed over him.

His eyes fluttered. He would have maybe twenty minutes of alertness when he downed the whole bottle. He stepped into the hot water, and after he got used to the water, he laid on back.

Of course, it was then that he realized his glass was low on his drink. He smirked. *I guess I could fuck this up.*

The smirk turned into a grin, and the grin widened to a smile. *No.*

He laid his head back to rest on the tub.

That cannot be my fate. Just can't. I won't let it.

The rest of his drink was the best part of all. He didn't linger in the tub with two painkillers at work inside him.

At least now maybe he would sleep.

His trial awaited.

FRIDAY, JULY 22, 2011

McCleary sat frozen a moment at counsel table, and Judge Claude had to ask him a second time to proceed. The delay drew more focus and drama to what McCleary did next. McCleary raised to his feet slowly, seemingly reluctantly.

"The State calls ... Genessa Turner."

There were audible gasps in the courtroom at the summoning of Andrea's mother to the stand. Even Jack couldn't resist turning to watch the older woman's entrance into the court-room. There was no way this couldn't be sad, he realized.

The still-mourning Genessa Turner made her way up the aisle of the courtroom with a delicateness that no one missed. Her head was bowed and her eyes looked heavy. While her husband had made their family extraordinarily wealthy, no one could be envious of her at that moment. She climbed into the witness box clumsily and plopped down. She was sworn in and she looked straight at McCleary.

"Let me begin by saying I am very sorry for your loss."

"Thank you," she answered softly.

She looked at McCleary respectfully, but she was aloof. She appeared so distraught that she no longer felt she was even one of them. She would sit in their courtroom and answer their questions, but she was not one of them or even really among them.

They just could not possibly know her loss. Not even close. Yet, they wanted to ask her questions about it. Have her talk about it. They were all too simple to understand this tragedy.

Her eyes looked at them. A weariness showed. Her Andrea was still gone and would always be gone. Mrs. Genessa Turner seemed there, but not there, at the same time.

She steeled herself. The most important thing, as far as Genessa was concerned, was for it to be said—to be known—that her Andrea had not committed suicide.

Her Andrea did not do that.

"Mrs. Turner, on that night," McCleary tried in his own way to be gentle, "what communication did you have with your daughter?"

"She texted me."

"Was it customary for Andrea to text you?"

"She did on occasion, but it wasn't the norm really." She explained it as a matter of fact, as though it was to be expected that her daughter would not just text her.

"On this night, how many times did you get a text from her number?"

"Well, there were two."

"Mrs. Turner, I apologize, but I have to ask you. What was the first message?"

Genessa Turner didn't immediately respond, and Jack sensed she may slip with her composure. She spoke carefully when she proceeded.

"It said, 'I've made too much of a mess of things.'" Tears formed in Genessa Turner's eyes.

"And the second?"

Mrs. Turner's face bent to stare down at her lap, as she fought to stay articulate. When she glanced back up, her face had the unguarded look of one who was starting to cry and give in to their emotion. "It said, 'I love you.'" And with that, Mrs. Turner sobbed earnestly.

The Judge gave her a moment, and then asked if she'd like to take a break. She told the Judge she'd like to get this over with. Jack suspected that there was no one in the courtroom who blamed her.

When she had rallied to regain herself, McCleary proceeded. "Were these sorts of texts typical of Andrea?"

"No, absolutely not," the response was terse. "Andrea would never send a text about such things. She would have called me. Or come by."

"Mrs. Turner, on those occasions when Andrea did text you, was it her tendency to use shorthand when typing? Would she ever type words out completely?"

"Like a lot of younger people, she used shorthand, not complete words."

McCleary paused, again building some suspense to his last couple of questions. "On these occasions *that night*, what were the texts like? Shorthand or complete words?"

"They were complete words."

"Like an older person would send?"

Jacobs was on his feet. "Objection, your Honor!"

"Sustained."

Jack knew the damage had been done and the point made. It was more likely an older person—a lawyer—had sent the texts, rather than Andrea Turner. Jack didn't look around to check, but he sensed that many of the eyes in the courtroom were bearing down on him.

Weinberg kept his time very limited with Mrs. Turner.

"Mrs. Turner, I too am sorry for your loss."

"Thank you."

"Please forgive me, but I must ask. As we sit here today, we do not know who it was that sent those texts, do we?"

Mrs. Turner first gulped for some air. Then, shook her head slightly. "No. No, we don't."

Jacobs then did the smart thing, and thanked her and sat down.

When Mrs. Turner had extricated herself from the stand and was leaving the courtroom, Jack jotted Jacob a note. "Please get me a meeting with Bob Turner ASAP."

As court recessed, Jacob discreetly made his way to Bob Turner in the courtroom, and Jack made a hasty move to get outside into the hall. Jack stepped urgently down to the restroom. Once inside, he surged into a stall. His hands gripped the sides of the stall as he bent over, vomiting violently everything he had.

Jack didn't know how long he fought and shook in the stall, but eventually he heard Jacob's voice just outside the stall door. "Jack, is that you? You okay?"

Jack swayed lightheadedly inside, but managed to reply weakly. "Yeah. I'm okay."

"Hey, we're meeting with Bob tomorrow morning."

"Okay, good. Thanks."

⁂

On Saturday morning, Jack thanked Gene profusely. The evening before, Jack had called Gene to see if he would accompany him to the meeting with Bob, and fortunately Gene had agreed.

Jack had let Jacob know that it was probably best for Jack not to have his lawyer with him. Maybe it'd help with Bob's level of comfort, Jack thought.

Jacob had warned Jack. Jacob didn't think it was a good idea, but he relented and told Jack to let him know how it had gone afterwards. Jack appreciated it.

As Jack and Gene stood by their cars before going into Bob's office, Jack tried to explain further to Gene where he was coming from. Jack believed at his core that this was important for him to do.

"I have this gut feeling that I need to talk to him. See what he thinks. I don't know." Jack looked around shaking his head. "Maybe I'm just desperate, but I just feel like it's important. Plus, I'd like to get into that house. Look around."

"Alright," Gene nodded reassuringly. "Hey, let's just see."

The two men walked into the quiet of Bob's office. Bob didn't move from behind his large desk across the room. To Bob's right sat his private investigator, John McSherry. The tall, serious looking retired Marine acknowledged Gene and Jack, but he didn't move towards them either.

"Good morning," Bob blurted gruffly. "Come on in and have a seat." His hand motioned towards the two chairs that faced the desk, and Jack and Gene took their seats. "This is John McSherry, my private investigator," he gestured.

Jack wasted no time getting started. "Thank you for seeing me."

He paused, but Bob didn't really offer anything back to him. He sat fixed across from Jack with folded hands resting on the desk.

"Mr. Turner, I wanted to come to you and to tell you directly. I didn't kill Andrea. I swear it. I cared for her and about her. I absolutely did not do it. For reasons I don't think I can even explain, I just felt like I should come to you and tell you that. That's all. I don't know if that makes any difference, but I hope it does."

Bob took a long look at him and then spoke evenly.

"I appreciate that. I do. I'm sure it wasn't easy for you to come to me and say that. I do appreciate it." Bob paused and took a breath, and for the briefest of moments, Jack thought he discerned a vulnerability to Bob, where Bob was truly affected by all of this.

Bob opened his hands and offered more. "You know, I've thought it over a lot. There are always hunches and instincts, I guess. And then there are facts. But, with it all, I've just never thought you did it."

Jack's entire body sagged hearing Bob's words. They were unexpected to him, and they struck him profoundly. Jack couldn't think of any other time when someone had come right out and said this basic kind of acknowledgment—that they didn't think he actually did it. Even Gene hadn't conveyed that level of confidence in his innocence. Moreover, this was Bob Turner. The significance and the relief were considerable. Jack had to temper his optimism at thinking that, if Turner didn't think he was guilty, then maybe others didn't think so either.

"Mr. Turner, thank you very much. I can't begin to tell you how much that means to me. This process has been extremely difficult."

Turner slowly nodded.

"I had this deep-seated feeling that I should come tell you directly I didn't do it, but I also needed to come to see if I could get your help."

The investigator McSherry shot a look to Turner who returned it without revealing anything overtly. Turner directed his attention back to Jack.

"I'm not sure I understand. I don't know that there's much I can do really."

"Uh, I've been thinking about that. I realize this is pretty unusual, me coming here and all. But I'm really needing some help. Everything's at stake. I don't know if you would consider speaking to McCleary or maybe even testifying."

Gene shifted uncomfortably in his chair and looked down. Jack took it that Gene probably didn't like these suggestions, but Jack almost didn't care. Jack was desperate. There wasn't much time. If there was anything that could be done to help, he needed it sooner than later.

"Let's see," Turner's words were careful and contemplative. He looked to the desktop where he rubbed his hands. "We're this far along in the trial. I can't think of McCleary doing anything differently than what he's doing. He may be feeling good about things."

Jack winced and lost some of his buoyancy he'd just felt moments ago. Turner continued carefully and thoughtfully.

"I would consider testifying, but you know, what would I really say? I can't just get up and say I don't think you did it, right? Can I just give my opinion like that?"

"No, no you can't," Jack answered. Jack's eyes darted about the room. He searched frantically now for something. It hit him what a rare opportunity he had at this moment in front of Turner, and he didn't think he was maximizing it. There had to be something he could think of. Something more to say.

Jack put his hands to his face and unguardedly rubbed at his eyes, wiping at them for relief.

"Listen," Turner tried to sound reassuring, "let me speak with John." Turner's hand gestured over to the investigator. "Maybe we can come up with something."

Jack's eyes widened. "Thank you. That would be great." Jack looked to McSherry and then back over to Turner and a thought came through. "Let me ask you, you took the house back over, right?"

Turner's eyes narrowed as he instantly considered Jack's thought. "Yes. I bought the house for Andrea originally."

Jack glanced to McSherry and then back to Turner. "I wonder if you would mind my going over there. I'm not sure that it will help. But the lawyer in me says to look over the scene again. Just check things out." Jack's eyes opened wide and pleaded with him.

Turner inhaled deeply and again looked over to McSherry. After a brief moment, McSherry gave the slightest gesture, tilting his head barely and lifting his eyes in a manner that said 'why not?' Turner brought his attention back to Jack.

"I don't see why not." Turner gazed closely at Jack. "I'll send John along, too. Hopefully, he can help. Two sets of eyes and all."

"Great. Thank you very much." Jack saw it as added help and was grateful. Gene likely saw the oversight that McSherry provided for Turner by being along, but Jack was just glad for the help at all.

Jack also looked over to McSherry. "I appreciate it."

McSherry nodded.

When Jack sat forward to begin to rise from his seat, Bob spoke quickly. "Jack, one more thing."

Jack waited and no one stirred to leave yet.

"There's something I want you to do for me." Turner deliberately maneuvered in his large chair, turning from facing Jack around to the credenza behind him.

He picked up a leather satchel from the top of the credenza and rotated back around again towards Jack. His hands gently placed the satchel on the desk top in front of him. "You don't have to, of course."

Jack found himself seriously perplexed. His words came stammered. "Okay, sure. What is it?"

All three men watched intently as Turner's fingers worked the zipper at the side of the satchel. The zipper released the leather top of the satchel as it rounded three quarters around the circumference of the satchel. Turner's hand moved the top open, and a handgun was revealed nestled inside. Turner left it open and looked across to Jack.

Jack sat wide-eyed and gazed back. He could not make sense of what was happening. All three men sitting around Turner shifted audibly in their chairs around the desk.

"What is it?" Jack's tone was thin.

Turner spoke cautiously. "I want you to pick up the pistol."

A collective gasp in the room sounded, and Gene spoke up. "Bob, stop this. He can't..."

Turner abruptly cut Gene off and raised his hand to silence Gene.

"He doesn't have to! He doesn't." Turner's agitation was distinct. "I'm just asking that's all."

Turner tried to reassure Gene with a more open look to him. Gene grimaced and looked over to John. John was alert and concerned. John's eyes darted about all of them, keeping an eye on the whole situation. John looked ready for anything.

Turner's eyes came back to Jack. Jack's pulse throbbed in his ears. A rush of emotions swirled about him and he fought to steady himself. He sat forward and then thought better; he'd better stand to do this, he figured.

Jack reached his hands to the edge of Turner's desk and held there as he raised himself from his chair. As he stood in front of the desk, he stared down at the open satchel. The pistol looked shiny and absolutely dangerous before him. Jack brought his eyes from the gun to Turner who was watching him closely.

"Just pick it up?" Jack's voice was shaky.

"Just pick it up." As shaky as Jack's words were, Turner's were sure.

Everyone followed Jack's hands to the center of the desk. One hand held the side of the pouch and the other hand hovered to the pistol. He blinked hard several times.

With an inhale, Jack clasped the handle of the heavy pistol and he lifted it straight away. His fingers wrapped to secure it in his hand and he let the barrel stay pointed downward. His hand lifted gradually higher and stayed. He was careful not to rotate it or position it unnecessarily. With it in hand and over the desk, Jack looked questioningly back at Turner.

Turner quickly eyed the gun and Jack, and he then nodded. "Okay."

"Just put it back?"

"Just put it back." Turner's tenor was firm.

Jack's hand abruptly descended and he wanted the gun out of his hand. He wasn't even sure the gun was exactly replaced like it had been, but he didn't really care. It was out of his grasp.

As Jack exhaled, he wondered if anyone noticed Turner do the same in relief. Turner likely noticed Jack did not ask if it was loaded, did not check to see if it was loaded, and he had not wiped it when he put it back. They probably all saw Jack's utter discomfort with the exercise. Turner verified his view that Jack hadn't killed Andrea.

Turner stood and he was then joined by the others standing around the desk. "Thanks Jack." His voice sounded just lower than before. "I just wanted to check a hunch. That's all."

Jack nodded along. "Yes, okay."

Turner looked around the room and concluded the meeting. "Okay, John, you go with Jack over to the house. You guys see what you can find. If you need anything, let me know."

"Thank you, Mr. Turner." Jack extended his hand and the men shook.

This is it. This is my last chance.

Jack focused. His first thought was that it was Saturday late morning. Court resumed on Monday at nine a.m. His clock was running.

He needed answers. He needed proof. He needed a homerun today. Time was almost gone.

He said goodbye to Gene, who offered to help in any way he could. Jack asked Gene to let him know if he came up with any ideas. Gene assured him he would.

Jack turned to John McSherry, who stood ready.

"What do you have in mind?" McSherry's words were gentle but direct.

Jack swallowed hard and thought for a moment. He had considered several approaches and ideas while shaving and showering that morning. He had kept coming back to a basic task he now wanted to cover most.

"Let's go to the house." They turned to Jack's SUV. "I need to walk the scene."

"Great idea. Good place to start."

They made the half-hour drive to the house Andrea had shared with Jim and they were mostly silent. Jack's mind was buzzing with thoughts about what all they should do, and in what order it should be done.

It struck him that he should be taking more advantage of McSherry as a resource. Jack got McSherry talking about his work with Turner and his experience in investigation generally.

McSherry was polite and considerate. He answered Jack's questions and talked about how he had mostly looked into people's backgrounds, checked out companies and areas, and performed surveillance.

Jack got him talking about surveillance, because that fascinated Jack. Then Jack quickly reconsidered. Jack thought it better to brainstorm with McSherry. Two heads are better than one and all.

"Hey, let me know what you think." Jack looked to McSherry, who was visibly concerned. "Time is short. Any ideas are really appreciated."

McSherry slowly nodded. "The house is a good place to start. See what we find. Maybe follow up with Hadley. See if he'll talk some more. Go by his gym, too."

"We reached out to Hadley several times. He wouldn't talk to Weinberg or Weinberg's investigator. I tried to, but... wasn't much help." Jack felt horrible about minimizing the talk at the spa. Jack would come back to it at some point perhaps. He was at a loss for how he could possibly now say what Jim had said— that Andrea may have discussed killing Bob.

"He talks to me. He knows it's important to Bob. Bob had me speak to him a couple of times, but there was nothing."

"Has anyone ever mentioned any friends Andrea was close to? Someone she may have confided in?"

"We've checked. She didn't have any close female friends. She was very close to her mother. That's who she'd speak to. Her and Bob. Other than that, she really kept her own counsel."

The SUV made its way into the subdivision and Jack felt chills. Every other time he had traveled these streets, he had done so with giddy anticipation of soon seeing Andrea. Her death still moved him.

With McSherry being talkative with him, together with the fact that Jack had little to lose, Jack decided to be very candid and direct with McSherry.

"I have to ask. What do you think? Honestly." Jack kept as soft and respectful a tone as he possibly could.

"About Andrea's death?"

"Yes."

"Hadley killed her. He lost his faith in her and he panicked. He went with the chance at the seven million. Hell, it's like ten million with the insurance."

Jack braced. The certitude and the simplicity provided great encouragement. McSherry made it sound so credible, so easy.

But Jack knew it was still just supposition. He couldn't possibly rely on that. He was glad it sounded great, but he had to have more.

The SUV climbed the incline of the driveway. The house loomed in front of them. Formidable. Eerie even.

McSherry opened his door and started getting out and Jack forced himself to do the same. McSherry slammed the door on his side and was already half up the drive as Jack stood beside the SUV.

Jack paused. Slow down. Pay attention. Slow down.

That night... someone had walked this drive. Entered this house. Take the steps yourself.

He ran his view from his side slowly across his front. Bit by bit. The side of the house had trees and some shrubs that formed a faux wall from the neighboring yard and house. The homes weren't on top of one another, but there wasn't a lot of distance either.

The neighbor in the house to the left had been interviewed by the police, as well as by Weinberg's office. They had not been home. The neighbors in the house to the back of the property had heard nothing.

Jack gazed to his right. Take your time.

Jack started turning to face across the street. He couldn't remember any meaningful mention of the neighbor directly in front of Andrea's house. The police detective dropped by but the neighbor hadn't been home. The notes said the neighbor customarily went to Florida in the winter and was staying down there later than normal this year. That was it.

Jack stood looking at the house directly across the street, and something struck him. The driveways were almost, but not quite, aligned. The developer of the subdivision had prided herself on making every single house in the subdivision face in the most optimal way to provide for privacy, he remembered hearing. Yet, now as he paid close attention, there was this one particular feature. The two drives were closely aligned.

Jack froze. Staring at the neighbor's garage he trembled with excitement. His pulse raced. He asked himself a couple of times if he was truly seeing what he thought he was seeing. He restrained himself from immediately breaking into a run across the street.

"John!" Jack's voice pierced the midday quiet, and McSherry stopped fumbling for the front door key on the porch.

McSherry looked over. Jack was entranced. McSherry immediately hustled over. He got to Jack and turned to face across the street.

"There. Over the garage door," Jack exclaimed.

McSherry followed Jack's stare, and his mouth soon gaped open.

"Yep." McSherry confirmed he saw it.

There, perched over the garage door, was a small surveillance camera.

The men immediately started walking across the street. Jack's steps had a bounce. McSherry initially thought of reigning in any expectations Jack had, but he decided to stay straightforward.

"The neighbor's name is Sam Matarazzo. A retired CPA. Spends his winters in south Florida."

With a quiet hurriedness, Jack led them straight to the front door. He tapped at the doorbell and held his breath. A couple of seconds passed with nothing.

Then, the door swung open.

After a moment where Jack simply stared, McSherry started cordially talking. Jack worked to stay calm as McSherry gently and deftly disarmed Sam of any concern.

They needed help, McSherry explained. They were across the street checking on things. McSherry described how he worked for Bob Turner. Bob Turner owned the house across the street.

Sam started nodding and volunteered that he was sorry to hear of Andrea's death. McSherry thanked him and shared how very difficult it had been for the Turners. McSherry engaged in just enough polite conversation to keep Sam interested, but soon directed questions to which Jack could barely wait to hear the answers.

The surveillance camera. Had anyone asked about it?

Sam shrugged. "No, and haven't they already caught the guy anyway?"

Jack resisted cringing at Sam's words, and McSherry got to the heart of it. As McSherry asked more, Jack again held his breath. Emotion swelled inside him.

McSherry asked whether the camera had been operating the night of Andrea's death.

Sam answered, "Sure," and Jack almost grunted aloud. The words he heard next were clear but sounded more distant, as the air grew thin for Jack.

"Was the footage preserved?" McSherry asked.

Sam started his head forward and backward in a friendly nod, and Jack's world changed. He became lightheaded. He swayed in place. He could barely maintain his composure even though Sam was noticing his unsteadiness.

"It's kept digitally."

Sam was fine with them looking at it online. Right then.

The three walked over to a laptop on Sam's dining room table. There was no way of knowing yet what it would show, but Jack felt exhilaration. This would be it. He just knew it.

They huddled in front of the screen and waited. As it booted, McSherry asked a couple of more questions, but Jack stayed riveted to the screen. This was it.

Once online, Sam navigated to the site and typed in a user-name and a password. There was silence and stillness in the home while Sam entered the date and time when Andrea was thought to have been killed.

Footage appeared of a vacant driveway and most of the front of Andrea's house. Jack knew Sam noticed when Jack drew air deep into his lungs and waited.

Just as easily as the driveway had appeared, the screen went suddenly dark. Jack grunted out loud. There in the middle of the dark screen a circle flashed and it began rotating clockwise. Underneath the circling image, the word "loading" stood forth.

Percentages calculated. First in the twenties and then methodically higher. Jack suppressed a cry when the circling hovered in the eighties.

"It sometimes does this," Sam said softly in the direction of Jack, who no longer showed any pretense of being unaffected.

A couple of seconds later, the driveway was back. A white blur started in the lower right corner of the screen, and in the next instant the blur proved to be a vehicle. A large white Lexus SUV lumbered up the pictured drive.

Jack spoke for the first time. "Can you enlarge that?"

Sam reached towards the screen to zoom in close. There with fine clarity was a Georgia tag number. Unmistakable.

This time Jack did release a burst, as he swayed once more with the heaviness of the significance. He could barely speak, but he murmured a 'yes' when Sam took the zoom back out. The screen kept its sight squarely on the vehicle, and it was scarcely another moment before they saw more movement on the screen.

The vehicle's driver side door popped open. The figure spilling from the front seat was a woman. Sam worked the zoom immediately. The image showed a woman with long, dark-brown hair swivel from left to right to shove her truck door closed.

As the door closed, her head followed with the momentum that must have come from closing the door hard. Sam stilled the frame where the woman's face was tilted up and mostly facing them. Her expression looked determined and defiant.

It was Monica Henderson.

&

MONDAY, JULY 25, 2011

Monday morning at nine o'clock, Judge Claude came onto the bench. The courtroom was packed to hear the defense proceed. All eyes stayed on Judge Claude as she reviewed a couple of documents. When she spoke loudly, their eyes shifted.

"Is the Defense ready to proceed?"

Weinberg stood.

"We are, Your Honor."

261

"Call your first witness."

Weinberg paused. Many in the audience, and perhaps in the jury box as well, wondered if the name would be 'Jack Adams.' If so, they were surprised.

"Your Honor, the Defense calls Sam Matarazzo."

Audible gasps, rumblings and indistinct whispers sounded from the Courtroom.

"Very well."

The bailiff moved towards the entrance to bring in the witness, and McCleary stood from the prosecution's table.

"Your Honor, we object. There's no 'Sam Matarazzo' identified on the list of witnesses provided by the Defense in their discovery. They are not permitted by law to do this."

Weinberg, who was already standing, let a beat pass for effect. Then, he replied confidently. "Your Honor, we clearly stated in our list that we reserved the right to call any witnesses listed by the prosecution. The prosecution's discovery identified Mr. Matarazzo in detective reports that were provided to us. They can't now be surprised by this."

Judge Claude's face tightened into a scowl and she directed the attorneys from the bench.

"Okay. Let's see Counsel in chambers."

With a rap of the Judge's gavel, the Court was in recess. The attorneys crossed the courtroom over to the side door that a sheriff's deputy opened. They continued down the corridor leading to Judge Claude's chambers. During the brief walk, McCleary glared at Weinberg, and Weinberg simply smiled back at him.

Once in the Judge's outer office, the Judge's assistant led the men into the Judge's chambers. The darkly paneled room was spacious and lined with a wall of pictures and books. At the front end of the rectangular room, there was a long, solid conference table. Judge Claude gestured to the lawyers to take a seat.

"Mr. Weinberg, who is Mr. Matarazzo?"

Weinberg smiled politely before beginning.

"Good morning, Your Honor. The prosecution provided us investigative reports from their detectives. In two of those reports, Mr. Matarazzo was identified as a neighbor of Andrea Turner. Mr. Matarazzo actually lives across from the Turner house."

"And?'

Weinberg glimpsed sideways at McCleary. McCleary was riveted to hear whatever he could as to where this was going. Weinberg knew without a doubt that McCleary sensed there was a serious problem with his case.

"Well, we were able to speak with Mr. Matarazzo over the weekend. Seems he travels a good bit in the winter, but fortunately we managed to catch him at home."

Judge Claude shot a glance over to McCleary, who shifted anxiously and wordlessly in his chair. Judge Claude then looked back over to Weinberg.

"What do you expect from Matarazzo?"

"Your Honor, the prosecution was well aware of Matarazzo. I was surprised not to have any witness statements from the prosecution about him."

Judge Claude peered over to McCleary.

"What about it?"

"Judge, candidly, we don't have any. He wasn't around when we tried to talk to him."

Judge Claude didn't come out and verbalize her displeasure,

but a frown was enough to cause McCleary to look down and then back up.

Judge Claude directed her attention back to Weinberg.

"Alright, what do you have from this witness?"

"Judge, I'm reluctant to show my hand—"

Judge Claude interrupted Weinberg.

"Your hand won't be played if I don't permit the witness to testify. What's your proffer?'

"Matarazzo maintains a security camera over his garage. The camera surveys the area in front of the Turner house. It depicts a clear and unobstructed view of the Turner driveway."

Both Judge Claude and McCleary hung on Weinberg's words. Weinberg relished the moment, stealing a recollection of how McCleary had tried to extract a harsh plea deal from him previously. Once Weinberg studied McCleary's serious concern, Weinberg looked to his hands and rubbed them together, savoring the moment before continuing.

"We were able to view footage from the camera over the weekend. The footage from the night of the incident shows that a woman came to the house just before Adams got there. She got there, and then left abruptly, just before Adams arrived."

McCleary could be heard pushing breath out, and rocking forward in his chair.

"Judge, obviously we haven't seen this video."

Judge Claude looked to McCleary, and then refocused on Weinberg. Weinberg could detect there was almost a grin on the Judge's face. The Judge spoke firmly to both men.

"Okay, we will be in recess. Gentlemen, sit down and watch the video together. Mr. McCleary can consider his courses of action and let us know. We will reconvene in an hour."

Judge Claude rose to stand, obviously finished for now with the in-chambers conference. Weinberg was quick to follow. McCleary sat stunned a couple of seconds before he got to his feet.

જ્ઞ

WEDNESDAY, JULY 27, 2011

The white Lexus SUV had belonged to Monica Henderson. When Jack saw the video on the security monitor, he had physically recoiled at the sight of it. He had recognized it right away.

As relieved as he had been to see a vehicle captured on the scene that night, he had been just as shocked to see that it was Monica's. The meaning of her vehicle having been at Andrea's house at that time hit him hard: George's mistress had been Andrea.

At first, he had chastised himself for not somehow glimpsing the desperation by Monica. But he also knew that he was unaware of how she had reached her own conclusion about Andrea and her husband. Moreover, he had reached a point where he simply understood Monica's legal matter was ending. She had done as well as she could have rationally hoped. The legal part was coming to an end. Little did Jack realize that deep inside this wasn't enough for Monica.

The clanging of the metal jail doors still rang in Jack's ears as he saw her led into the bare room. A basic metal table with four chairs was centered in the room. Jack felt anxious being there with all that had gone on. Now, he was there as Monica's lawyer, having arranged to meet with her. He was intent on helping. He would help her obtain representation by a criminal lawyer. His area of practice was domestic relations, and Monica needed someone well versed in criminal law.

Monica came in hunched a bit forward. She still had a distracted look, which Jack realized had been showing for some time now.

She seemed at once sad and weak, clad in an orange jump-suit that hung on her like a cheap sack. Their introductions were awkward for Jack, as she seemed acutely aware of how she must have appeared to him. Nevertheless, she still gave that resoluteness that Jack also recognized. She was simply moving forward.

"How are you doing?" His concern came through in his tone.

"Oh, as well as could be expected, I guess." She smiled tightly. "Please don't worry about me. Thank you for coming, for your help."

"Absolutely. I want to help all I can. I can assist with your representation, you know. But, you actually need a criminal law specialist for this. This is beyond my practice area."

She nodded understandingly. "I figured so. If you'll come up with a couple of names you feel good about, then that will be fine."

He looked at her hard, and she knew his basic questions.

"I just think I wasn't able to handle everything, you know?" Her eyes searched his.

"I think so. I mean, I'm not sure I understand it all," Jack offered.

Monica's tone grew detached and cold. "It was like I lost control of things, really. I was on some kind of ... path. I was filled with pain really. 'Devastated' doesn't begin to describe it."

Jack squinted at her. He wanted to understand. "But you *went* there. She was shot pretty close in."

"It was like I was watching it happen. Jack, she had taken everything from me. Taken my life." Monica shook as if from a chill. "She caused this."

Jack turned his head back and forth slowly.

Monica looked at him with that night's memory seemingly about her. "She was very insistent. Like she was going to persuade me."

Monica flinched at her recollection of Andrea. "But she didn't know me. She didn't get how she destroyed my family, or what she had taken from me. From my children. All the way up to the end, she thought she was going to explain it to me, get me to understand. I had her posed, thinking I was going to take a couple of pictures with my phone to get at my ex. But I knew what I had to do. I didn't have any choice really. None." She closed and opened her eyes a couple of times, apparently thinking back on the intensity of those moments.

"She had followed along well until the end." Monica continued. "She was sitting posed for an angle at her temple. I had her hands still bound at that point. And you know what? She had the audacity to think that she was going to talk me out of what I was doing. Even then she had this idea that she was smarter than me." Her head dipped low and her voice dropped. "She was wrong."

Jack felt at once disappointed and taken aback. He had never perceived this capacity in Monica before, and the fact that he hadn't unnerved him.

"It struck me," Monica's voice trailed away some and her gaze went off to the side, "that she was looking to face me really. At the end, she turned her face towards me to talk more, and I took that to mean that she was facing me and what she had done. She looked at me just as I did it. That's why her head was at the angle it was. That's the only thing that really went wrong. But, you know? It seemed fitting that she was trying to face me."

Jack looked at her, and if he was uncertain before, then now he was convinced. Monica had lost her grip with what had happened. She couldn't have truly thought about what she did if she had been in her right mind. Part of her was gone, it seemed.

"I have to ask." Jack arched his eyebrows and looked for a tactful way to put his last questions, knowing they would forever nag him if he didn't.

"What's that?" Her voice sounded vacant.

"Well, what makes you so sure? I mean, you didn't actually catch them, did you?"

Monica drew a deep breath and her eyes got a distant look to them. "The day she pulled that stunt at your office. I saw her that day. Remember I was there?"

"Yeah, now that I think about it."

"I noticed she had this elaborate gesture she did. I saw what she was doing. It was something she did to entice men is all that it was. She would make a show of bringing her hands into her hair. Then, she would slowly run them through her hair. She'd stop for a second and stare at the guy. Well, she did that to you that day. And, as it turns out, that struck me as vaguely familiar. I had actually seen that little trick before, Jack."

"You had?"

"Yeah. I went back and looked at my copy of the surveillance video we had. The one at Peachtree-DeKalb when they were in his SUV. Sure enough, she did the exact same move with

George in the front seat that day. She put on the same little show. It was her."

"Jack," her voice grew insistent and she leaned closer to him, "I also followed him. I saw them."

Jack did a double take. "What?"

"Yeah. After George won the temporary hearing against me. I knew what he would do. *Exactly* what he would do. He took her to his plane and flew her to the BVI." She saw the incredulousness on Jack's face. "Listen, I saw how he looked at her. And how she looked at him. I know it. *I know it, Jack.*"

"What made you think he was going to do that with her?"

"It was what he would have done with me ... years ago."

"Monica, Monica," Jack's words shared a regret for her. He asked his last question. Something he didn't think fit.

"Um, why the text?"

"The text? To her mother?"

"No, the text to me. You really wanted me to find her?"

Monica paused just before answering. It was as if she wasn't sure whether to tell him.

"I didn't send that." Monica's eyes briefly shut, then opened. "I was there with her, and she had put it together that something awful was happening, but I hadn't tied her yet. She sent that to you. On her own."

Jack winced hard. It never occurred to him that she would try to contact him. Especially in that situation when she was in danger. He cringed in anguish, but there was nothing more to say. Any more discussion or argument with Monica was futile. One more thought struck him.

"So that's why you stayed in contact with me. After I was out of the firm and off your case."

"One of the reasons." She paused, but her even expression didn't change. "I never intended to bring you into that night. I didn't."

He felt sorrow on several levels and just shook his head.

He brought their meeting to a close. He reassured her that he would get her help. He asked about Dr. Misencik's counseling.

They both stood, saying goodbye.

"Thank you for being there for me, Jack."

He left in a daze, realizing he had misread her so much. He had not seen just how sick she had become.

14

PAMPAS ARGENTINEAN STEAKHOUSE FIT THE OCCASION. Dark wood circled the main dining room, and the white-clothed tables gave ample space for each party to have their own privacy. The lighting glowed with a golden glint. Smart, graceful servers glided about with discretion.

Jack savored a deep satisfaction. Jacob had picked this place, and as usual his decision-making hit its mark. Jack, Jacob, and Gene all soaked up the elegant atmosphere.

Jacob had referred to it as a 'victory dinner,' and that was fine by Jack. The trial had only finished in the last couple of days and he needed closure. This helped.

Drinks got the men started, and it wasn't a surprise that each of them took a different route. Gene ordered scotch, while Jacob tried a red wine, and Jack stuck with a cold Belgian beer. Mini empanadas followed, and the selection included beef, ham and cheese, and chicken. Each tasted tender and succulent.

The conversation started mildly enough, with an underlying energy that couldn't be denied. They all observed some genteel courtesy by starting carefully, when they each probably expected that analysis, at least to some extent, was forthcoming.

Their talk livened during the entrees, after a couple rounds of their drinks. Each man relished their chosen chop. Jack picked the house specialty, called "the Brick." The fourteen-ounce Ladrillo steak compared fairly with Gene's bone-in filet and Jacob's ribeye. À la carte sides of spicy roasted cipollini onions, sautéed wild mushrooms, and Lyonnaise potatoes topped off the main course.

Jack loved the indulgence of it all, and before he could get lost completely in the rich food and drink, he brought up his old concept of 'mutual promises.' He brought it up in the context of Andrea, and he again referred to it as a kind of principle. Jack had argued this same idea to Gloria Andrews when he had learned of Andrea's betrayal, and he had tried to discuss it with Gene when Gene had his heart-to-heart talk with him. The beer likely helped him resurrect it.

Jack first noticed Jacob brace, and then his eyes shot to Gene who sat a bit back in his seat and politely grinned. Jack figured Jacob worried that Gene might tear into this topic. At least, that was Jack's impression. Jacob helped himself to a long draw on his wine, and Jack thought this was a splendid idea, so he tossed a long gulp of his beer back.

Jack liked that Gene managed to keep a grin on as his voice pitched fully across the elegant table. They had to all know that Gene wouldn't be disrespectful in his take on Jack's theory, but yet they all sensed his intensity. Gene didn't disappoint.

"Listen," Gene scrutinized Jack, "I understand your point. I do. You held certain duties to Andrea. Confidence, protection, loyalty. You're a trial lawyer, and the Bar rules talk about 'the highest professional standards.'"

Jack listened and he realized he genuinely wanted to understand Gene's message about this. He forced himself not to worry about whether Gene understood Jack's point. That needed to wait. *Hear him out.*

Gene shrugged and kept going. "I also get how you feel that she owed something back to you. Some honesty, some loyalty. But hell, maybe I'm old school." He shook his head once sharply to the side. "You're the lawyer here. You're there protecting her and fighting for her. I mean, she should pay you. She should respect you. Sure. But you can't *depend* on her. She's not there to *help* you do your job. Fuck, half the time they're lying to us."

Jack couldn't hide a smirk and neither could Jacob. Gene fired forward, awash in expensive scotch and steeped with the best food.

"That's not what it's about anyway. Claim your satisfaction for yourself, protect yourself at all times, and remember that this is a privilege. But don't expect a lot back other than what you get out of it yourself."

Gene hit his drink again and didn't hold back.

"Let's not forget you're representing divorce clients. They can be the toughest. Look at Monica. She was a picture of the worst of them, Jack. She wasn't going to be happy, no matter what. Her life was all about her family, and she was losing that with her divorce. At least in her mind she was."

Gene leaned towards Jack. "You've just got to do your very best, and don't expect anything from a client. Damn sure don't rely on them for your satisfaction. Get that on your own. That's all you can do."

At first, a poignant silence hovered.

Gene's words rolled as easily as they soothed. "Hey, go recharge a few months. Come back and open shop with Jacob, here. I'll refer you some cases. I'm gonna stop this divorce work anyway."

Jacob piped in. "Indeed. You've learned from all this. Put it behind you. Just gotta keep moving forward."

And then, in a smooth, unrushed gesture, they all raised their drinks and saluted Gene's words. It didn't even feel like some agreed toast, but more of a mutual recognition of sorts. And at that moment, Jack understood what Gene said.

Gene looked old to him right then. But he spoke the truth.

❦

Leaving Pampas, Nick, their server waited at the door. Jack approached and Nick opened the door for Jack.

"Thank you, sir. Hope you enjoyed your time with us."

"Thank you."

Jack stepped into the night and at once there was a glow. A soft white tint surrounded him. He stepped lightly to where the valet awaited with his SUV. Had he felt any giddier he would have called a cab.

Before he climbed into the SUV, he couldn't resist gazing

up. There in the sky a thousand dots sparkled, giving the night its bright hue. No clouds at all. Just clear sky and stars.

Jack's breath caught at the enormity of it. The glorious view and his narrow survival. His vision clouded with moisture glazing his eyes.

I came too close to the end.

Over the next three days at the beach in Destin, he would no doubt replay his whole twisted saga. For now, he just thanked God for his freedom. There was a way out.

Upon his return from the beach, he would do research and writing to tide him over until he could practice again. Then, he would practice with Jacob. The plan calmed him.

He knew he had what it took to make it.

ACKNOWLEDGMENTS

This story has stirred around with me for years. Only after my wife, Emma, encouraged me, did I get serious about it. Her encouragement and support has meant everything.

My family has provided enthusiastic support, for which I am forever grateful. They include my mother, Geneva Nichols; my father-in-law and mother-in-law, Bob and Pat Patten; my brother and my sister-in-law, Danny and Pam Nichols; my sisters-in-law, Tara and Anna Patten; my uncle and aunt, Mike and Pamela Nichols; and the absolute best stepdaughter in the world, Madeleine Hitt.

I had the privilege and honor to work with the legendary editor, Alan Rinzler.

William Bernhardt provided invaluable insight and feedback that I will always appreciate.

Jared Kuritz and everyone at Strategies PR are the absolute best, and they have shown such tremendous support.

Gwyn Snider at GKS Creative did beautiful work on the cover and interior design, for which I am grateful.

Zeta Lordes provided the best of all beta reads and showed incredible patience.

Last but not least, I acknowledge you, the reader. Every time I sit down to write, I remember the many options you have available for your time and attention. Your time and attention is greatly appreciated, and I write with the ultimate goal of providing you entertainment and provocative thought that will stay with you.

ABOUT NICK NICHOLS

Nick Nichols was born on June 30, 1961, in Camp Lejeune, North Carolina. Educated at Wayne County High School and Georgia State University, he graduated in 1988, with a juris doctorate.

After clerking for a trial judge from 1988 until 1990, he started a trial practice that continues.

He lives in Johns Creek, Georgia, with his wife, Emma, and his stepdaughter, Madeleine.